Quarantine
Nick Holdstock

Swift

SWIFT PRESS

This paperback edition published by Swift Press 2023
First published in Great Britain by Swift Press 2022

1 3 5 7 9 10 8 6 4 2

Text design and typesetting by Tetragon, London
Printed and bound by CPI Group (UK) Ltd, Croydon, CR0 4YY

A CIP catalogue record for this book is available from the British Library

ISBN: 9781800751026
eISBN: 9781800751019

Quarantine

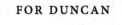
FOR DUNCAN

You who will emerge from the flood
In which we have gone under
Bring to mind
When you speak of our failings
Bring to mind also the dark times
That you have escaped.

BERTOLT BRECHT
'To Those Born After'

LUKAS

W E took down our mirrors at the start of winter. Not all of them, but over half, and more were sure to follow. In our camp fashions spread quickly. Three months before, we'd shaved our heads. We'd piled up clocks and watches.

No one planned these actions. They happened because someone had an idea that they hoped would make things better. They did it, and others saw, and if it made sense to them they copied it.

I don't know who took their mirrors down first because I slept late. I'd spent most of the night rereading *The Sorrows of Young Werther* and trying to think of something new to say about it. The sun was over the mountains by the time I took my coffee out onto the porch. I'd only taken a sip when I saw my reflection coming towards me. Automatically, I checked my face – I saw nothing wrong – then Jorge turned the mirror away.

'Looking good, Lukas,' he said, and laughed. If anyone else had been carrying the mirror I'd have asked what they were doing. But Jorge seemed like such an idiot that I didn't care. He was always doing things that made no sense. I'd recently discovered he'd been collecting wood for months, but in small quantities, whatever he could scavenge during hut maintenance, even legs from broken chairs. When asked why, he'd said, 'Just in case,' which was stupid because there was no need for fires. On the rare occasions the

3

generator ran out of oil – in bad weather we were sometimes cut off for weeks – the solar panels took care of our needs.

I was about to go back inside when Edie called out to me. 'Can you give me a hand?' she begged. She was struggling with two mirrors, the long one from her wardrobe door, the small one from the bathroom, and as soon as I saw them my heart felt like a fist opening and closing quickly. Yet there was also a strange calm. Of course we didn't need mirrors. They were just a crutch we used to hurt ourselves.

Edie sighed after I took the long mirror. 'Thanks,' she said, then kissed me. At first we only used our lips, but then our tongues took over. It wasn't long before I was ready to throw my mirror on the ground and pull her into my house. It was starting to slip from my hands when she said, 'Careful. We don't want seven years' bad luck.'

I laughed. 'That doesn't seem so bad.'

'True,' she said and put her mouth back on mine, then bit my lower lip hard. I pushed her away and she giggled.

'Did it hurt?'

I nodded.

'Is it bleeding?'

I showed her.

'Poor Lukas. I expect you want Mommy to kiss it better?' She puffed out her cheeks and then wobbled her mirror, which made my reflection shake. 'Why don't we finish our errand first? You don't mind, do you?'

'Of course not.' It was what I'd expected. Some days she'd come into my house and immediately take off her clothes. But even then she might put a stop to things before we got to sex. We'd be kissing and she'd suddenly 'remember' a driving lesson or golf appointment. Edie picked these impossible things to emphasise that I should take nothing for granted. Although this drove me

4

crazy she did it perfectly. She teased me just enough to keep me interested but not so much that I gave up.

'Shall we go?' she said.

'No, I don't think so.'

'Fine,' Edie said and hurried off, leaving me holding her mirror. She went round a corner, then peeked back and mouthed something that was probably obscene but I still didn't move; I had to score points where I could. She disappeared and didn't return, though I knew where she was going. The square was where we'd taken our clocks and watches. It might seem a stretch to say this was a tradition, given that our camp was only eight years old, but many of us took it seriously. Yet no one was criticised if they left their mirrors somewhere else, or preferred to keep them. There were still some clocks on walls, a few watches on wrists. Some of us could handle those reminders.

I wanted to wait before following Edie to the square, but it was too cold to be standing around, so I walked towards the north end of the camp. It was a clear morning and I could see all the way down the valley. The trees seemed so near. I stopped and imagined walking between them, the absolute hush, the sharp scent of pine. I wanted the anticipation that comes from moving through new territory. Surely everyone looks to the horizon and thinks *I want to be there.*

I stood there until I started shivering. When I turned my back on the valley I saw five people moving down the street ahead of me, all of them carrying mirrors. As the person in front turned right at the crossroads their mirror flashed when it caught the sun. This small, beautiful moment acquired significance as it was repeated. After three flashes they seemed meaningful.

It took less than a minute to catch up with them, but when I turned the corner two of them had disappeared. Either they had

5

changed their minds and decided to keep their mirrors or else the people had gone inside a house to tell someone what they were doing. That wasn't why I knocked on Min-seo's door: I just wanted to see her. While I enjoyed Edie's games, what I had with Min-seo was different, playful and yet serious.

While waiting I checked my reflection with a thoroughness that would once have seemed like vanity. All I saw was a pale, thirty-five-year-old face with bad teeth and what Tomasz used to call my 'joke beard'.

Min-seo smiled when she saw me, then said, 'Is this a present?' Before I could answer she took the mirror from me. She scratched at a stain. 'This is dirty,' she said, but without irritation; she merely wanted this to be noted.

I followed her in and smelt glue. A lot of people decorated their walls with colourful landscapes and patterns that could have graced a children's ward; Min-seo's mural showed a grey plain with dead trees and people whose heads were twice the usual size. She'd worked on it for nine months, and every time I thought it was finished she'd paint over the whole thing and do it again, only with different people. There must have been at least seven or eight layers by the time she announced she'd finished painting. 'But it's not done,' she'd said, and I knew better than to ask her to explain.

Once the paint was dry she began to cover it with feathers. She'd barely done half the wall when the feathers started dropping off. 'These feathers are too heavy,' she said and then swore in Korean, cursing either the feathers or gravity.

But either Min-seo had found better glue, or lighter feathers, because as soon as I entered I saw she'd finished the job. The wall was covered with different coloured feathers, ranging from light, almost yellowish ones to some that were jet black. At first glance their placement seemed random, but there were patterns: the lightest feathers formed broken contours that intruded on the darker parts, while in a few places tawny feathers made a circle.

'They look like wings,' I said.

Min-seo nodded and tried to smile, but her expression twisted. 'I think they are going to fall off again,' she said and began to cry.

I put my hand on her cheek, then kissed her forehead. I kept my lips there, feeling the warmth, smelling the rose oil in her hair. As I held her she sang to herself. I think the song was about a ship and a girl, but whether it was about a ship named after a girl or a girl waiting for a ship, I had no idea.

Min-seo wiped her eyes. She took my hand and led me towards the bathroom. We didn't need to speak. She sat on the toilet while I ran the bath; when it was full she took off her clothes. I don't know why I looked away, given that I was about to wash her. Perhaps it was because over the previous few weeks she'd seemed to be getting younger even as her hair turned grey and the wrinkles spread. She seemed more like a teenager than a woman of thirty-nine.

She got in the bath and immediately put her head beneath the water. Bubbles kept floating up, big ones, then little ones, then no more bubbles, but Min-seo stayed under, her eyes open, as if she didn't need to surface. I wondered if soon I'd knock on the door, receive no answer, then have to go in and find her. That was how most of us went once the end got close. Usually people did it quietly, without fuss, but occasionally they made it into a party. When Ella and Sharnaz had sent out joint invitations it wasn't a surprise: even though Ella was the sick one, there was no way Sharnaz was going to continue without her.

When Min-seo surfaced she had a dolphin smile. I washed her hair, then her neck. 'Like cleaning a corpse!' she said, and laughed. 'Don't miss any part, I want to be clean in heaven.' I soaped her arms, then her breasts, then she lifted one leg. 'Especially here.

7

And just one finger.' I did what she wanted until she lay back with a long sigh that seemed to empty her of breath. Then she stood and I dried her.

On the way to the bedroom she stopped and put her hand around my wrist. She brought my hand to the wall then used it to stroke the feathers. They were soft and deep. As the feathers parted I caught glimpses of an arm, a leg, a branch, faces swollen like balloons. I didn't understand why she'd gone to so much trouble to paint the mural if she was going to cover it up. The only thing I'd seen like it was in a book my ex-girlfriend Sasha had on outsider art. I guess that label applied to Min-seo, who hadn't painted before she came to the camp, just as Edie had only started to dance after she arrived. Others took up whittling, collecting bottles, the stratagems of chess. We had to do something.

~

It was late afternoon when I left Min-seo. As I was getting dressed she woke, said, 'I'm hungry,' then went back to sleep. My stomach was also complaining. The canteen was only three house rows away, but I was so ravenous I considered running. My body was tense, ready to go, but it seemed better to exercise self-control. It had become too easy to want something and then to do it without caring about the result.

As I walked briskly I recalled a third-year tutorial in which we had argued over whether you can really be in two minds. Everyone was glad to debate this proposition except a smart but lazy student from Lublin, who was silent for most of the discussion. Only after we'd exhausted our borrowed arguments did he raise his hand and laconically say, 'You can want two different things, but not at the same time. You switch between wanting these things, back and

8

forth, so fast you don't even realise.' He said this with a smirk, as if his idea was something we secretly believed but wouldn't admit. If that probably now-dead student had been jogging alongside me as I started to half-run towards the canteen, I'd have refuted him by saying that I was perfectly capable of wanting to eat a piece of toast while watching Edie unhook her bra. I could want to experience the tang of her sweat while enjoying hot butter. Even if I was, by his logic, only wanting one thing, two impulses were simultaneously present within that apparently singular desire. My mind didn't have to choose.

But this wouldn't have won the argument. I could picture the rich student quoting Goethe's epigram 'All Nine who often used to come to me, I mean the Muses: But I ignored them: my girl was in my arms.' I wouldn't have had an answer for that. While eating and sex might go together, lately I'd been unable to reconcile wanting to work on my thesis with the impulse to get drunk and high and spend long afternoons in bed with Edie or whoever. It was like being a student again, except that then I hadn't needed to choose: it's easy to be monkish when no one is willing to sleep with you.

As I reached the canteen there was a rich smell that made me think of the incredible goulash Tomasz and I had eaten in Zakopane on our last skiing trip. I used to dream about going back to that small restaurant, but even if I could, it almost certainly wouldn't be there. A lot of people had fled to the Tatras thinking they'd be safe, but by most accounts things had deteriorated in the countryside faster than in the cities. All that scenic beauty returned people to a natural state that was more Hobbes than Rousseau.

The menu outside the canteen had one of Brendan's little jokes. It was blank except for a rabbit's head that had been nailed to the board by its ears. When I entered, Brendan looked up from behind the counter, nodded, then went back to chopping. This didn't feel rude or unfriendly, and was about all I deserved. After I'd filled my bowl with stew I tried to break the ice. 'No Easter for those bunnies,' I said, though Easter was still very far away.

'I suppose not,' said Brendan. He paused long enough for me to turn away before adding, 'But no doubt the Lord will shine His face on them and bring their leporine souls into the glory of resurrection.'

I laughed, mostly out of relief. 'That would be nice. But is He doing that just for the rabbits?'

'I don't know. I guess we'll see. Here.' He handed me a plate of small dumplings then walked away. It was the longest conversation we'd had for six months, but I still felt awkward. Rather than stay in the empty canteen and eat on my own I was about to take my meal outside, but then I saw Fatoumata huddled in the corner. I went over to her table and pointed at an empty chair. She inclined her head to signal permission. Some people said she was unfriendly, but I thought it was more that she wasn't talkative. As for whether that was due to her poor English or awful back pain, I had no idea.

'How's the food?' I asked.

Fatoumata chewed and then swallowed. She pushed her plate away. She stood, picked up her coat, then said, 'Metal. All is metal.' She flicked the air with her hand as if trying to dispel something only she could see. As she passed me I smelt something pungent. After she'd gone I realised it was garlic. Either it was for her health, or she was trying to keep something away.

For the next few minutes I ate with my eyes closed, to concentrate on the flavours. With a little paprika it could have passed for that goulash Tomasz and I had eaten ten years before. My brother and I had sat at a rough wooden table at the back of a small restaurant whose floor was slippery with melted snow. We were so cold the food made its way through our bodies like fire. A pair of big, stupid grins took control of our faces.

When I heard someone come into the canteen I kept my eyes shut. I hoped whoever it was would respect my privacy.

'Good stew?' he said.

'Yes,' I said, and opened my eyes. A black beret was perched on Bob's head like a saucepan lid. The lump beneath it resembled a turnip. He was standing still, his mouth slightly open, about to repeat an offer I couldn't wait to refuse.

'I wondered if you'd had a chance to think about joining us next Sunday. I think it's going to be our best evening so far.'

'Mmm,' I said. The only thing worse than watching him stage *Hamlet* in thirty instalments would be taking part.

'You'd make a wonderful Laertes.'

'That's very kind of you, Bob. But I'm sure whoever takes the role will benefit from your direction.'

'Thank you,' he said, as if I'd meant it, but I doubted he believed me. Bob was pompous, not stupid. He fashioned a smile, then went and spoke to Brendan. I couldn't hear what Bob said, but given how quickly Brendan started shaking his head, I guessed he too was being offered a great theatrical opportunity. After this second refusal, Bob exited stage left.

After I'd finished eating I took my plate and Fatoumata's into the kitchen and washed them along with a stack of other dishes. In some ways this gesture was totally normal, but it had been a long time since I had volunteered to help in the kitchen.

Brendan thanked me for doing the dishes but didn't say anything else. I wasn't sure he wanted to talk about anything personal, so I picked a safe subject. I said I hadn't seen him at the chess tables for a while.

'Yeah, I've pretty much given that up.'

'Why?'

'I want to do different things. I'd rather have a conversation than sit opposite someone in silence for hours. I have four or five months left, and I want to make the most of them.'

This sounded a bit dramatic; none of us knew how long we had. He must have seen my scepticism, because then he added, 'I have a brain tumour. I got it just in time for Christmas. I suspect I'll be getting some other presents soon.'

I was shocked, because Brendan looked healthy. His hair was still dark, his face unwrinkled. I briefly hoped he was lying to gain sympathy, but I knew he wasn't. With me he was always truthful.

'I'm so sorry. I didn't know.'

'It's alright, Lukas. Would you believe me if I said it was a relief? Well, not entirely. But a little bit.'

I understood. We all hated the waiting, the clocks in our bodies, their hands turning too fast.

I took a step towards him and hugged him close. His beard was soft like fur as it moved against my cheek. It had been almost a year since we'd slept together. I'd told him I was too busy with Min-seo and Edie, but that wasn't the reason. It was to avoid the long looks he gave me afterwards. I've never trusted what people say to me after sex. The brain is too drowned in hormones; we're basically drunk. Though Brendan never told me he loved me, or suggested we not see anyone else, the looks he gave me as we lay together had put me on my guard.

We went into the storeroom. He moved some boxes, then spread a blanket on the floor. 'Are you in a hurry?' he asked, and his voice sounded tired, as if it had required a huge effort to climb up his throat.

'Don't worry,' I assured him. 'We don't need to rush.'

~

When I left the canteen it was dusk and something was burning. Not wood – the smell was too harsh, it was more like melting rubber. I was sure the fire wasn't inside the camp, where they were sensibly prohibited, since apart from the meeting house the buildings were mostly made of wood. By the time I reached the north fence I could see a straight plume of grey smoke rising from the valley floor near Zaqatala, assuming that's what the place was actually called. None of us could go down there, so we had to trust what we'd been told, which I did, because its location and size matched the map. That didn't stop Erik saying we'd been deliberately misinformed so that if we escaped we'd be disorientated, but for most of us that didn't apply. We'd chosen to be in the camp.

The smoke bent in the wind. Loud detonations and their echoes competed with each other. At first I thought it was firecrackers, then decided it was gunfire.

'The sounds of a party,' said Alain. I don't know how long he'd been standing behind me; I hadn't heard him approach because the ground was soft by that part of the fence. He had only been a guard for six weeks, which meant people were still curious about him. We'd spoken a few times, not for long, but enough to make me like him. He seemed able to do his job without being over-whelmed by the role.

'Do you think it's a wedding?' I asked.

'Could be. But I'm sure they're celebrating.'

'Celebrating what?'

'Oh.' He looked away, then lifted his right hand from his holster and turned it over so his palm was facing up, like he was trying to show me whatever he was reluctant to say.

'It's been five years since the last new case of Werner's.'

13

He looked so sheepish I laughed, which made him even more uncomfortable.

'Sorry, Lukas. I shouldn't have mentioned it.'

'It's fine. I'm glad you did. And that's a very good thing. None of us would say that doesn't deserve to be celebrated.'

I paused to wonder if this was true; I was confident that Erik would find a shitty underside even to such good news.

'And I can't say I'm surprised. It's obvious our numbers are going down fast. When I came here there were around four hundred of us. Now it's less than half that.'

Alain nodded while looking away. He still had the guilt of the healthy around the sick. I took pity on him by changing the subject.

'Have you been to the square today?'

'Yes, just now. So many mirrors. It was like an art project.'

'A bad one.'

'Maybe,' he said, smiling. 'But I've seen worse. In Marseilles I went to a gallery where there were melting blocks of blue ice hanging from the ceiling.'

'Sounds cool.'

'It could have been. But it was called "Eternity" and you had to put a blindfold on and be led in by a young child. On the way out they gave you a little box wrapped up with a ribbon and told you not to open it until you were very sad or very happy.'

'Let me guess. Inside was a mirror.'

'Worse. A stone.'

There was more gunfire, followed by actual fireworks, which we both admired. Tactfully, he asked what I'd done before the camps, and maybe he already knew: I was sure it was all in a file.

'I was a lecturer,' I said. 'Technically, I was still only a postgraduate, because I hadn't finished my thesis. But I had started teaching, and I think they would have offered me a real job if civilisation hadn't decided to take a sabbatical.'

He nodded, and looked uncomfortable. After all, he couldn't say, *I'm sure you'll get back to your career soon*. He asked if I was still working on my thesis, and I was impressed; he could easily have assumed my studies were over. That I'd given up.

'Yes,' I said, and felt a small flush of pride. 'But it's taking a long time. I've had to redo most of it and I don't have many books. Being without the internet doesn't help either.'

He nodded. 'I can imagine. But do you think this might have some positive effects? It might force you to think of something original.'

'Maybe. I don't know,' I said, though this had occurred to me. It was best to keep this small idea asleep. If it should wake, and start to grow, I'd end up with fantasies about standing at the podium to deliver a keynote lecture.

To change the subject, I asked Alain what his ambition was.

'I want to open a Mexican restaurant in Paris. After working here for six months I should have enough.'

'Paris is great,' I said, then told him I'd taken a summer trip there with my brother. Our coach broke down three times, the first time before we even left Warsaw. By the time we got to Paris, thirty-nine hours later, we'd quarrelled so much he stormed off immediately. I spent a few hours looking for him, then gave up and went and sat by the river. I'm embarrassed to say I started crying, because although I had wanted to visit Paris, what really mattered was going somewhere with Tomasz. When I saw him that evening he couldn't stop saying sorry, and even though a lot happened over the next two days – we took acid in Notre Dame; Tomasz slept with a Canadian girl – my happiest memory of that trip is still my brother holding out his hands as he apologised.

'But why Mexican?' I asked.

'I don't think I'd get sick of being around that food. I spent six months in Oaxaca and loved it. Did you ever go to Mexico?'

'No.'

And he didn't exactly hesitate before making a sound of acknowledgement; it wasn't a proper pause. In normal conversation the moment would have gone unremarked. If both of us hadn't been thinking of the typical response to what I'd just said – *You have to go* – and why he couldn't say that, there'd have been nothing awkward. But it didn't ruin our conversation. We spoke about classical music (he preferred Debussy to Ravel), then about Flaubert (I said I preferred *Three Tales* to *Madame Bovary*). We could have been on a slow train, or waiting in a queue, anywhere two strangers might pass the time with casual, friendly talk.

Alain's radio produced a crackle of static, then a woman's voice said his name. 'Excuse me,' he said and walked a few steps away. For a few moments he spoke quietly enough for me not to hear. When he returned he said, 'Sorry about that. I have to go to the south fence.'

'Everything alright?'

'Probably. Someone thinks they saw a light on the ridge and we want to make sure no one's out there. I don't think there is, as they'd have had to climb the mountain, but we should check.'

His casualness didn't stop me seeing burning torches, petrol bombs, a mob wearing face masks and gloves.

'I suppose some people might want to celebrate with a trip to the zoo to put down a few strays. It wouldn't be the first time.'

'Lukas, that's not going to happen.'

'You're probably right. They just need to be patient.'

He'd turned away to go, but then stopped.

'They'll find a cure,' he said. 'I really believe that. They have to.'

I nodded, because it was pointless to argue. It didn't matter what we believed.

REBECCA

THE night before the celebration Rajeev came round for dinner. Even though he was bringing his own food I wanted mine to be ready when he arrived so we could eat together. With most people this would have been tricky. You tell them eight but they think you don't mean it, they come at quarter past, even later, when you're getting angry with hunger. But Rajeev was always right on time.

This kind of punctuality required dedication. Rajeev's place wasn't far into Queens, and should have been a twenty- or thirty-minute drive, but over the last three months a ton of roads had been closed to prepare for the celebration. With the subway still shut, this made getting around a total nightmare; festivities that were supposed to encourage a return to normality were doing the opposite. To make sure of being on time Rajeev had to allow an hour for his journey. This was clearly overkill, but it was sweet that he didn't want to be even a little bit late. He was without doubt the most considerate guy I'd ever dated.

Inevitably, when traffic was light, Rajeev would end up outside my building half an hour early, yet he didn't ring my buzzer. He thought it would bother me, though I really wouldn't have minded. In his place I'd have sat somewhere to read the paper or phone my dad, neither of which were options for Rajeev. He had little interest in the news and no concept of reading for pleasure; his only surviving relative, a sister I'd never met, lived in a cabin in Alaska without internet or phone reception. All he did, even if it was raining or cold, was find a quiet place to sit. A bench, a wall, a stoop, anywhere he wouldn't be disturbed. Once sat he didn't read, look at his phone or listen to music. All he wanted to do was sit and pay complete attention to whatever was happening on the street, even if, by some New York miracle, that turned out to be nothing.

I've no doubt he was able to do this without his mind wandering. His ability to focus was one of the reasons he was such a gifted epidemiologist. It would be unfair, and reductive, to suggest that Rajeev's preternatural concentration stemmed from where he placed on the autistic spectrum (in my informed, albeit non-professional opinion, on the Asperger's border), and for most of our relationship this side of him had a geeky charm. I liked his awkwardness when I teased him about his Quest for Focus. 'I just want to be in the moment,' he'd say. 'You understand, don't you, Rebecca?' To which I'd laugh and reply, 'Yes, of course,' while wondering why he only used my name when he was uncomfortable.

The buzzer went at eight o'clock and I had to smile. As I took the pan from the heat he came in and said, 'Hey,' and I blew him an air kiss back. While he went into the bathroom to wash and then spray his hands, I got a plate out of the cupboard, a fork from the drawer, then spooned out some risotto.

'Smells good,' he said, then brought his bag over to the table. He sat at the far end and took out a container. I laughed when I saw its contents.

'Shrimp again?'

'Afraid so. Right now it's all I want.'

'Fair enough. But how long is this streak?'

'Eleven days.'

'Eleven days of shrimp. And will there be twelve?'

'Maybe.'

After dinner we sat on the couch and watched some old black and white musical from the 1930s. It was sexist, and sometimes racist, but Rajeev laughed a lot. After watching three big song and dance numbers I started thinking about all the people in the US who had been starving while this expensive stupidity was taking place. One of Matthew's favourite dinner party provocations was to ask someone if they'd seen the latest Hollywood blockbuster, then launch into a paean of its merits. If someone objected he'd say that the multiplex still served the same need as cinemas had during the Great Depression, that the entertainment offered by those palaces of light and wonder – he actually used those words – was exactly the distraction people needed during those terrible times. As soon as they seemed convinced, he'd laugh and say, 'But yeah, that film is crap.' I didn't mind him amusing himself: I knew he agreed with me about escapism being a form of denial. You can look away, laugh, fill your mind with music, but when the movie stops your problems are still there.

Our movie ended. Rajeev yawned. 'I'll get things ready,' he said, and I was grateful because I was pretty beat. The guys I'd dated before him hadn't been so understanding. Karl accused me of being afraid of intimacy, an odd thing to say to someone who'd been jerking him off twice a week for a month. Scott went even further. We'd been seeing each other for two months and things seemed to be going well. But then one night, when I was almost asleep, he said, 'Listen, I really like you, but I'm not into this glory hole stuff. I don't know if this is some kind of a fetish, but if not, then it's dumb. There's no need for us to use it now. I want to be in you.' He'd been lucky the screen was between us.

Rajeev clapped his hands to turn on the bedroom light. I lay on the couch, my eyes half-closed, listening to the hiss of the spray, the protest of latex stretching. 'Do you need a hand?' I asked faintly.

'Almost done. Just putting on the covers.'

Hearing shrink-wrap being unrolled always makes me think of Mom wrapping up leftovers, even when no one was likely to eat them. She was thrifty like that. But I pushed the thought away. I didn't want to get sad.

Rajeev was spraying the openings as I came into the bedroom. His head twitched toward me, but he didn't look around. He was concentrating.

Once he was done he went round the other side of the screen and took off his clothes. Apart from a little paunch, he had a good body for a thirty-seven-year-old who spent most of his day indoors. Perhaps it was all the shrimp.

He didn't say anything as he watched me undress. I stopped when I was down to my underwear, then held my bra strap and looked at him. He came closer. He pressed himself against the screen but didn't speak. Talking was a distraction.

I moved closer until I was right against the screen. As I took off my bra Rajeev reached for the gloves. He put one on his right hand, then his left. He rolled a condom on. I took off my panties, put on my gloves, and then we began. I put my gloved hand into one of the lower openings, then pushed it through until it filled the screen's thicker glove. When I took hold of Rajeev he sighed.

At this point both Karl and Scott had closed their eyes and waited to be jerked off. But because Rajeev was considerate, and not a prick, he pushed one hand through the screen and put it between my legs. As I pulled him off, he pushed his fingers inside me, and we got our rhythm just right.

Soon I was close to coming, and I think he was too. But Rajeev had been too thorough in his preparations. The inside of my glove felt so wet I thought it couldn't only be from the spray. Which meant the glove was torn. Which meant the moisture I felt was from Rajeev. I pulled my hand back sharply.

'What's wrong?' said Rajeev. 'Did I hurt you?'

'A little. But don't worry.'

I wished I'd told him the truth. He'd have understood. He wouldn't have laughed at me. But I was too embarrassed by my overreaction. Of course I trusted the gloves. There used to be all kinds of stories about intentional screen damage by jealous lovers and people settling scores, though these were ridiculous tales that happened to one in a million, if they happened at all.

For a long time we were silent as we lay on our different sides of the screen. We were facing each other but my eyes were closed.

When he spoke, his voice seemed to be coming from further away.

'Is it because of the celebration? I can understand if that's difficult. If you're thinking about Matthew.'

'No. It's just been a long day,' I said, which was true.

He didn't reply for a few moments, and when he did, he spoke almost in a whisper. 'Maybe you should come to the party tomorrow. You shouldn't be alone.'

A lot of other shouldn'ts came to mind. If four years hadn't been a big deal, then five shouldn't be celebrated either. In wedding terms, it was wood. All the radio stations who kept playing Bowie's 'Five Years' seemed to have missed that it was a song about the end of the world.

Rather than have that argument again I said, 'You know what I think about that.'

'I do. But being at the party doesn't mean you approve of the celebration. Our party is more about the Institute and our work.

I know you're proud of that. If you come it would mean a lot to everyone. It would mean a lot to me.'

He had me there. Although my colleagues and I didn't agree on some things, they were without doubt the most dedicated people I'd ever worked with. Their faces should have been on coins and banknotes, carved into mountains. They, more than anyone, had earned the right to celebrate.

'Fine. I'll come,' I said, then clapped my hands.

'Thank you,' he said in the dark.

⌁

When my alarm went off at seven Rajeev was already gone. I lay in bed another ten minutes, thinking of him driving home in his old Prius, the early light touching the East River, how it might feel to kiss him.

After showering I put on a black skirt and jacket, then immediately took them off. Everyone in the lab knew what I thought of the celebration: there was no need to be petty by dressing for a funeral.

I settled on a navy skirt and jacket with an eggshell blouse. It was dressy enough for the party but wouldn't stand out too much on the way to work. In an attempt to be open-minded, I was going to take the just reopened subway. Although I was nervous about going into a place with so many potential vectors of infection – every handle, button, door – I was also curious to see this 'completely safe way to travel'.

The new 14th Street station was like the bathroom of a rich old lady with an obsessive hygiene disorder. The air was moist with antibacterial spray; the wall tiles gleamed with a resin that apparently digested microorganisms. As a final prophylactic, the trains were sealed off from the platform by airlocks. On these a yellow hazard sign informed passengers that they would receive a dose of UV radiation that fell 'within acceptable levels'. In ten years, commuters with cancer would probably be suing the city, but for a while no one would complain about something as minor as the irradiation of their soft tissues.

It was all very impressive and yet, in a perverse way, I missed the medieval ambience of the old subway, even though I'd never liked it. Matthew used to say the shittiness of American public transport was class warfare by other means. I just thought it was weird to be travelling under the ground.

There was a distant roll of thunder. The air seemed moist with spray. I could smell ozone, bleach, then the train was roaring in at a threatening speed and volume. I was sure it hadn't been so loud before, but perhaps it was because I hadn't heard the noise for seven years. As a little girl I'd struggled to understand how big trains stayed on the little rails, and as the subway train curved in there was a childish instant when I worried that it might swerve onto the platform.

After the train stopped we entered the airlocks in single file. It took several claustrophobic seconds before the inner door opened. On the old subway, with hundreds of people trying to board, it would have taken ten minutes to load a single train. But there were only twelve of us on the platform. Even allowing for the city's reduced population, this was a tiny fraction of commuters. I guessed that despite the celebrations, all the hype, many were still cautious. Better to walk quickly down the street, in the open, scanning every approaching person for that upward tilt of the head that warns of a convulsion that expels forty thousand nasal droplets. On the street you could throw yourself to the ground, cover your head with a coat, duck behind a tree. On the subway there was no escaping a sneeze.

The new train cars were about the size of a school bus. I took a seat at one end, an old woman crept to the other, and a young guy went straight for the middle. Only when I noticed his breasts did I realise he was a young woman wearing a mask, no doubt an expensive one because it was convincing. The male face had glasses, a wide smile and a short brown beard. I wondered if she wore it only on difficult days, like his birthday or death day, or whether she was one of those who refused to take it off except to wash or eat.

Every surface in the train had the smooth, straight-from-the-factory sheen that makes me think of spaceships and the far, far future. Outside it was interstellar dark, the walls invisible. But we were hurtling down tunnels more than a century old, and no matter how much they had been bleached and blasted, I bet there were still rats.

The new train was a spaceship in at least one regard. We got from 14th to 242nd in fifteen minutes. The speed of this was disorientating; part of me was downtown. To give myself time to adjust, and to avoid starting work so early, I went into the park and called Dad. His phone rang for ages, but I was sure he was up. When he finally answered he said, 'Be quiet. I've told you.'

I laughed. 'It won't be much of a conversation if I do.'

'Not you, honey. It's Lesley. You know the phone makes her crazy.'

He raised his voice. 'It's Rebecca,' he said, the way he used to say it to Mom. Lesley barked in answer.

'How are you, Dad?'

'Oh, you know. Just rattling around. I don't suppose you're calling to wish me a happy fifth?' He laughed, then coughed in a phlegmy way that apparently wasn't of medical concern.

'Would you like me to?'

'God, no. It's all a big distraction. And a waste of money too. We're supposed to think everything's fine and back to normal, but what was so good about the way things were? It's still a world where everything's controlled by corporations and you have to pay for water. Of course it's good we have a vaccine. But let's not pretend there's anything to celebrate.'

'Dad, I'm hugging you.'

'Hugging you back.'

We paused and I thought of his long arms, his terrible cologne. He and Mom had been so close, but I still hoped he'd remarry. He needed someone.

'So Dad, are you staying home tonight?'

He laughed. 'Well, no. Do you remember Bobby Greene?'

It took a second. Then I saw his red face, his crooked nose, the faded orange hunting jacket he wore whatever the season. Mom had never liked him.

'Is he alive?'

'Oh no. He died in the big Philly fire. But his brother Johnny was working on a rig in Alaska the whole time, so he was fine. He's coming back into town tonight for the first time in ten years. Apparently he's been waiting until he thinks it's totally safe. First thing I'll do when I see Johnny is tell him what *you* think. He'll probably get the first plane north.'

'Dad, I don't *want* people to panic. That makes disease spread faster. I just think we aren't really safe until we have a cure.'

'Alright,' he said, and I imagined him holding his hands up in surrender. 'What about your plans? Hitting the town with your pals?'

Who did he think these 'pals' were? Dear friends from work or college that I never mentioned? After all I'd said, did he honestly think I went out to bars?

'Dad, if it was up to me I'd stay home. But I have a thing at work I can't get out of.'

'Is it a party? Have you got a date?'

'It's not like that. It'll be boring, just lots of rich people and speeches.'

He sighed. 'Becky, I know you don't want your old dad to keep playing the same tune, but because I'm your old dad I *have* to. I know you're brilliant at your work and I'm so proud of you, but—'

I forced a calming, nasal breath.

'I'm worried you're not letting anyone get close to you. It's been almost six years now.'

Six years and two months.

'Don't you think it's time to start seeing people again? You're gorgeous, you're wonderful, I don't believe guys aren't interested in you. Or women.'

At least that last part was new.

'It doesn't matter to me who they are, whether they're young, old, rich, poor – I only want you to be happy.'

'Dad, I *am* happy. I just don't have time for a personal life.'

This was one of those true lies. I really didn't have time. Even the attention I paid to Rajeev – which was nowhere near what he deserved – made me feel selfish.

Dad cleared his throat. 'You had time for Matthew, and that was during the worst of the epidemic. Are you telling me you have less free time than when we all thought we were going to die?'

This was so unfair I couldn't speak. And I think Dad knew he'd gone too far, because then he backtracked.

'Becky, I love you, you're my only child, and nothing matters more to me than your happiness. You should do what you think is most important. If that means just working, so be it.'

'I love you too, Dad. But I have to go now.'

'Alright. Call me next week?'

'I will.'

After I hung up I sat on a bench and smoked a cigarette so quickly I got lightheaded. Lying to Dad felt awful, but if he knew I was seeing someone he'd have too many questions. He'd be so happy for me he'd forget all my boundaries. His well-intentioned enthusiasm would make me feel like a monster for not wanting to share. He and Mom hadn't been too nosy about my personal life when I was in high school, but once I was far away, and they had nothing to go on, they wouldn't stop fishing. I didn't respond well; I was so determined to give them nothing that I ended up making Johns Hopkins sound like a single-sex college. Matthew and I had been dating for a year before I mentioned him.

I finished my cigarette, and it was my last one, so I left the park and walked quickly to the kiosk by the Institute. There was a line, so I had the chance to try out some of Rajeev's waiting-as-meditation. I failed almost immediately because the women in front of me was trying to destroy someone. Her phone was stuck to her mouth as she said, 'Your laugh. Your nose. The hairs in your ears. The way you swallow so loudly.'

She paused, though only for breath.

'And you think everything you say is interesting, but when I try and tell you something you look bored. You're stingy and you have no patience. You're ignorant. You're a slob.'

The list of failings continued; I guessed she was leaving it as a message rather than telling him or her directly. Although maybe the person deserved it, I found it unpleasant to hear such direct aggression. With an effort I was able to tune out the woman's voice long enough to think it was warm for October; that I'd left my bedroom light on; that next time Rajeev came round I'd spray the screen and gloves myself.

'You cockroach,' she said, then made a remarkable segue. 'Hello, Carlos. The usual, please.' And of course he was already reaching for it. He handed her the nasal spray as she swiped her card.

'Thank you. You have a good day,' she said. As she walked away she muttered, 'I will step on you.'

It was a pleasure to hear Carlos's friendly voice. 'Good morning, Dr Rebecca. Happy anniversary.'

'You too,' I said, because Carlos got a free pass. 'Are you doing anything special tonight?'

'I'll be here.'

'Do you have to be?'

He spread his palms as if the answer was written there. 'I want to. This is where I was during all that time. I should be here tonight. Here you go.' He handed me my cigarettes. 'On the house.'

When I asked why, he said, 'None of you should have to pay for anything today. Tell your colleagues to come see me.'

Although this wasn't necessary, it seemed wrong to deny him the pleasure of generosity. He was a remarkable person. His wife and son had died right at the start of the epidemic, before we even knew there was one. Within a few months the stores that hadn't closed completely were doing all their business online or through security hatches. By the end of the first year Carlos's was the only place left open in the area. The *New York Post* tried to lionise him as yet another heroic New Yorker standing up in the face of adversity. Carlos still had the article pinned up in the kiosk. It was very faded, except for where he'd written BULLSHIT in black marker across it. He didn't stay open out of civic pride or because it's what his family would have wanted. He just didn't give a fuck.

I lit up at the side of the Institute's main entrance and took another stab at the noble art of Waiting. In theory it made sense, and I liked what Rajeev had once said about trying to pay attention to all the things he usually ignored, but I was sceptical about learning anything new about a section of street I'd been seeing for the last seven years.

To my surprise, once I relaxed and let my eyes drift I did notice some new things: a sneaker dangled from a high branch; the security guards had bigger rifles; on an opposite doorway there was a piece of stencilled graffiti of six red crucifixes followed by a question mark. But I also thought: so what? It was still the same street. I didn't feel any different for noticing those things.

After checking the sidewalk and windows of the vacant building opposite for further revelations I had half a cigarette left. I wondered what else I was supposed to pay attention to; I couldn't notice something that didn't exist. Instead I focused on the burning sound as I inhaled, the tightness of smoke in my throat. I'd only been smoking on and off for six months, so it wasn't entirely automatic, and I didn't really think of myself as a smoker. Growing up I'd considered smoking a kind of mental disorder I'd never suffer from. Seeing my aunt and my mom coughing so badly should have inoculated me against it for life, but six months ago I'd bought a pack on a whim. My hands liked having a task.

The last thing I saw before I went into the Institute was a cyclist wearing a huge breathing mask that covered her whole face. Though I'm sure it was an advanced device, with both air and chemical filters, to me it resembled the frightening gas masks worn during World War Two. After that war ended there were probably people, both civilians and military, who still carried their masks around for a while, but I was sure almost no one had kept doing so for five years. Those lucky folks had seen pictures of bombed cities and foreign soldiers with their hands raised in surrender. They knew it was over.

LUKAS

S OMETHING about dusk that night made me think of Christmas. Without light pollution our sky shifted smoothly from deep blue to black. The first stars emerged quickly. Walking between the huts, looking at the yellow and orange squares of windows, the cold pushing through my clothing, made me want to hang coloured lights from the eaves, dust everything with snow. It was the time of year when Tomasz would appear with a tree whose provenance we had given up questioning.

Although we could have found ways to celebrate the season, most of us didn't bother. None of those rituals made sense any more. A few years ago Dr Nilsson got Bob to organise a carol concert, even found us a tree for the square, but as soon as the singing began the Gnostics started screaming and wouldn't stop. Later they burnt the tree.

Since no one else had mentioned the anniversary I assumed that our weekly gathering at Rustam's house was going to be the usual bacchanal. If your organs are likely to fail or become cancerous at short notice, there's no reason not to overdo things. What made these parties possible was the very generous alcohol allowance we received from the authorities. The wide range of different conditions among us meant there were plenty of drugs to go round. Through trial and error we managed to create a lot of states that were more interesting than simple drunkenness, and so far no one had died.

But although many of us acted like we were having a second youth, it was technically my first time around. At university I'd been too busy drowning in German Romanticism – and too shy – to have any fun. In Rosa Khutor, my first camp, there had been a strict no alcohol policy, but since I'd come to Zaqatala I'd given my liver an education. I'd woken up naked in strange places: several times on the roof of my hut, and six months before that tied to a section of fence. Sexual life was much simpler. If you wanted someone, you just asked. And while people might still say no, that didn't happen often. You didn't have to like them. Even if you weren't attracted to someone, it would be a new experience. Bob hadn't been terrible.

Min-seo's house was on the way to Rustam's, so I stopped to check on her. All the lights were on but when I knocked there was no answer. I opened the door quietly and went into the lounge. I called her name, and there was still no answer, so I went into the bedroom. I found her lying on the floor with all her clothes on, deep in what was probably a medicated sleep. There was a faint scent of vomit but I couldn't find the source.

I lifted Min-seo – by then she weighed about as much as a large child – and put her to bed. Although she made some little noises she didn't wake. I wasn't sure whether I should stay with her. After listening to her breathe regularly for a while, I decided it was safe to leave her. She wasn't due for dialysis till Monday. Her best option was to sleep.

As I approached Rustam's I heard someone inside playing the drums so badly he must have been turning in his grave. The drummer was smashing them, hitting without rhythm, as if they had to be punished. The neighbours weren't about to complain; Patrice had died two months before, Julia the previous week.

When I pushed the door it wouldn't open. My repeated efforts were greeted with jeers from inside. I tried to take this in good humour, having been on the other side of the door and mocking someone struggling to push a chair or table out the way. But soon it was annoying. I was about to give up and go back to Min-seo when someone whistled behind me.

'Need a hand, sport?' said Erik and put his shoulder to the door. I must have been angrier than I realised because I said, 'Fuck off, I can manage.'

'Suit yourself,' he said and stepped back with a smile. 'After you.'

'Sorry.' I gave the door a feeble push. 'I was just frustrated.'

Even with Erik's help it was difficult. As the door started to move Khunbish shouted, 'Watch his head!' and then started laughing.

'You bastards,' yelled Erik and shoved the door hard, and then we were inside. On the floor a man lay face down. He had white hair and a very red neck; for a second Erik and I were confused because we didn't know him. It's not that we didn't see strangers in the camp – there was a high turnover of guards – but they certainly didn't turn up at our parties.

Erik stared at Khunbish and Dejan until they stopped laughing.

'Who the fuck's this?'

'It's Kim,' said Dejan, and rolled the man over. It was true, except that Kim's hair had been black the day before. His face wasn't older, his skin was still smooth; it was as if a familiar picture had been sneakily reframed.

I was too shocked to speak. I'd seen people go grey in a week and decline fast, but never such an abrupt shift. Whatever awful disease we developed was supposed to give us a countdown of at least a few months. But if Kim's hair could change so quickly, anything was possible. A heart could fail in a week; cancer might last no longer than flu. I had to close my eyes to stop seeing Kim's white hair, just as when I dropped a glass I shut them, as if not seeing something meant it wouldn't happen.

When I looked again Erik was squatting next to Kim. He parted Kim's hair, as if looking for lice, then examined his collar. He chuckled. 'Bastard. Why would he do that?'

'What?'

'It's bleached. Perhaps he meant it as a joke. What did he tell you?'

Khunbish shrugged. 'Not much. Kim said he was sick of waiting for it to happen.'

Dejan whispered something to Khunbish, who looked delighted, then murmured something back.

Erik gave Dejan a shove. 'What perversion are you wankers cooking up now? More vegetables up the arse?'

'Nothing like that,' said Dejan. 'We are only thinking about a shearing of the sheep.'

'Is that what you call buggery in your country?'

'We call it many things. But today I only mean what the words say. Some removal of hair.'

'Go on then,' said Erik wearily. 'Be gentle with him. His head's going to hurt enough. Lukas, shall we leave them to it? I have a bottle hidden upstairs.'

As I followed Erik he said something over his shoulder, but then the drumming started again so loudly I couldn't hear. Once we were upstairs he banged on a door and the noise stopped.

'Thanks,' he said, and was immediately answered. 'You're most welcome,' said a woman trying to fake an English accent.

'Edie?' I said hopefully.

There was no answer, but the door opened slightly.

Erik clapped me on the back. 'Don't keep a lady waiting.'

I entered the room slowly with my hands in front of me. Sometimes Edie's idea of foreplay was a punch in the face. She thought if you triggered 'all kinds of pain-related stuff' in the body, and then made it quickly switch to pleasure, the end result would be a better orgasm. 'It's the rebound effect,' she would say with all seriousness, as if this was a well-documented phenomenon rather than something she said to justify hitting me.

But it wasn't Edie who'd been playing the drums. Valentina had arrived five months before, though we'd barely spoken. She had a small, boyish face, a look her bobbed hair accentuated. All anyone knew about her was that she used to be a hairdresser in Madrid and that she'd been in prison in Nur-Sultan when she was diagnosed. There was no way to know if this was true. It was pointless trying to query someone's biography, and I suspect most of us were in no position to do so. The only freedom we had in the camp was to be someone else.

I didn't go far into the room because Valentina was standing in the corner diagonally opposite, pressing her back into the wall, as if there was some chance she could pass through. Even though she'd opened the door, she obviously didn't want me in there. She looked terrified, and I didn't want to make things worse.

'Sorry,' I said and turned away, but she called me back.

'Wait. Don't be rude.' She beckoned to me. 'Come in. Sit down.'

There were no chairs, only the drum stool.

'Yes, there,' she said. I sat and she smiled her approval before going to close the door.

'Better,' she said, then leant against the wall. She slid her back down it until she was sitting next to me, and stared into my eyes without speaking. I didn't think she was flirting; Valentina had made it very clear to everyone that she was finished with sex. With her and several others it was more than just a loss of libido. They were the people who sat in their houses or drifted around without speaking to anyone. Edie called them clock-watchers.

As Valentina said my name slowly, and with great import, I realised she was high. Her forehead was bright with perspiration and there were dark patches under her arms.

'Lukas, do you know about birds?'

'A little. But not much about the ones round here.'

She looked devastated, then covered her face with her hands. As I reached out to console her she tore her hands away so quickly I was startled.

'Feel them,' she said and thrust her palms at me. 'If we turned off the lights they'd glow.'

'Let's do that,' I said. Valentina looked hurt.

'Why do you want to check? Don't you trust me?'

'I do, but I want to see for myself.'

She waved this away, then sighed. 'I wish there were cats here. Even wild ones. Just so I could see their faces.'

'Were there some in your previous camp?'

'Yes, but they were killed. There was poison. I managed to keep one under my bed for three weeks until a bitch told someone.'

Valentina yawned, then leant to her left. She started tipping over then stopped herself. I asked her what she'd taken.

'Pills.'

'What kind?'

'A blue one and a green one. Together that's a yellow.'

She whistled through her teeth before becoming fascinated by her toes. She wiggled them, made fists, then splayed her toes on the floorboards. I foresaw her doing this for the next few hours.

'I think I'd better go.'

'Why?'

'Erik's waiting for me.'

She looked forlorn. 'Didn't you like it?'

'What?'

'Our kiss.'

'We didn't kiss.'

'We did. I remember,' she said, as if that proved it.

'Oh really? What was it like?'

'It started very small. You had your mouth closed. You were afraid.'

'Sounds awful,' I said and stood up. She wasn't making any sense. But I hesitated. If she believed we'd already kissed, she'd be fine with us kissing again.

I sat down. She smelt strange, like vegetation, as if she'd been walking through tall grass. Beneath her ear there was a long thin scar that travelled down her neck. I put my lips on it, then moved my mouth downwards. She made no objection, so I continued this kissing. I had exposed her shoulder when she said, 'Lukas, how long have you been here?'

'Three years.'

'And before that?'

'Four years in Rosa Khutor.'

'So long!'

I started unbuttoning her shirt. 'Not really. Erik was diagnosed eight years ago, and Brendan's had it almost that long.'

'Brendan's dying now. And Erik will be soon.'

I stopped what I was doing. 'No one knows that. He might not. Some people had the disease for almost nine years.'

'But then they died. I've had it six years and I'm bored of it.'

She stood up. I think she'd already forgotten what I'd been doing.

She went to the window and rubbed away the condensation, then breathed on it until the window was fogged again. 'All better,'

36

she said with great satisfaction. 'And Kim! Did you see him? Wonderful!'

I asked Valentina what she had liked about it. Instead of answering she closed her eyes and shook a little, her mouth opening slightly and then closing. She was smiling in a beatific way. I don't know if she even noticed I was still there. I didn't care. I'd heard enough. I was going to get wasted.

I was almost at the door when she stopped me. 'You fucking wait,' she said, and put her hand around my wrist. Her pupils were so dilated they seemed about to vanish.

'Kim's not going to pretend any more. He's not taking his fucking mirror down. He wants to see his hair like that so he doesn't forget he's sick.'

I looked at her cleavage, her throat. We could have been kissing, grabbing each other, but instead we were wasting our time with this crap. With my free hand I took hold of her shoulder and shouted, 'You think any of us *forget* that we're dying?'

Her laugh was a slap that made me lose control. I shoved her backwards, and when she tripped it was like another glass was falling and could not be caught. My eyes closed for an instant, though that changed nothing. Her head struck the wall. She made an almost silent cry just before she hit the floor. She seemed unhurt and was breathing; I was shocked. It had all happened so fast. It was like something I'd watched rather than something I'd done.

I debated whether to go and get the doctor. Perhaps she should sleep it off. I stood up, then noticed her shirt was torn. I bent down to cover her up and when I got close I saw her nipple. It was very soft. I expected her to wake up but she didn't. Nonetheless, I hesitated before pulling her bra down far enough to let me cup her breast. I closed my eyes while I held it. I heard nothing smash.

REBECCA

A s soon as I entered the building I saw my boss in the security queue. When I had joined the Institute, in the second year of the pandemic, I was surprised to see Damian waiting to go through the same checks as the rest of us. Though there were plenty of reasons why he should – it set a good example; no one was above suspicion – it astonished me that he was willing to wait the five minutes it took to be scanned, searched and tested. If I'd had a quarter of his responsibilities, and was under that much pressure, I'd have made people get out my way. But after I'd gotten to know him it made sense. He had a very even temperament and stayed calm without seeming cold, at a time when a lot of people were cultivating a shell of detachment (which inevitably cracked). Damian seemed neither unfeeling nor uncaring, but he also never overreacted. I've no idea how he managed this – he was as much at risk as the rest of us.

I joined him in the queue and said good morning.

'Morning, Rebecca. Ready to celebrate?'

'Oh yeah. Absolutely. Can't wait.'

He laughed, but not unkindly. He liked my scepticism, though I was positive he didn't share it. That wasn't his role. He was supposed to look ahead, to reassure; mine was to risk crying wolf.

A lot of people would regard a few minutes of one-on-one time with the country's top scientist as too valuable to waste on small talk. But apparently you can't always talk about work. Before I met Matthew I was still inflicting cell biology on everyone I met because I couldn't imagine people not wanting to hear about what was happening inside them – the quiet war of the immune system, the seven or eight viruses in their bodies at any given time. At college, then grad school, this was fine: conversation was the background noise for drinking. The boys I dated were just as boring about their interests, so that made us even. With Matthew it was different, because he couldn't talk about his work without breaking confidentiality, and after a while it seemed unfair for me to keep gabbing on if he couldn't. With others I learned to talk about movies, celebrities, viral videos. When people asked about my research, I'd deflect their question and change the subject; Matthew used to joke that he'd infected me with his British reserve.

I was about to ask Damian about the catering for the upcoming party when he said, 'Rebecca, I've been thinking about your work a lot over the last few days, and I want to reiterate how valuable it is.'

I felt like I'd stopped breathing. 'Oh,' I managed. 'Thanks.'

He smiled at my pretend casualness. 'Just because the vaccine has worked incredibly well for the last five years, that doesn't mean we should be complacent. It's wrong to speak about intention when it comes to a virus, but I've always believed it's useful to remember that its behaviour, if I can use the word, is geared toward making more copies of itself. Whether this is "intentional" or not doesn't make much difference. The result is what counts.'

I nodded but couldn't speak; I was still stunned by his compliment.

'Whether I jump off a cliff or accidentally fall, either way I'm in the sea. Afterward the reason is irrelevant.'

This seemed a dubious analogy. Reasons are everything. Reasons are all you are left with after you hit the water. Reasons are why you swim, or don't. But although I didn't want to disagree, he was waiting for a reply, and as director of the International Institute for Infectious Diseases, he was probably used to receiving a response to anything he said. When I said nothing, it got awkward, and then it was his turn to step through the security gate.

Damian handed his slim leather briefcase to George for inspection, and then, because it was still a Friday, celebration or not, he went into a cubicle to be tested. After George checked my laptop he had his usual struggle flicking through my sheaf of papers with his gloved hands, during which we probably exchanged low-level pleasantries – it's amazing what you can do without paying attention – but all I can remember is the frantic circling of my thoughts about how to tell Damian that I knew exactly what he meant. In my silly panic I even worried he had only offered those encouraging words because he believed my work was certain to fail, the way that Mom in junior high used to tell me I was going to come first in every quiz or race. It didn't matter that I was a splashy swimmer, a slow runner, and only good at math; she told me I was sure to triumph. When I placed fourth, or ninth, it felt like coming last.

After I'd gone through security it was my turn to be tested. As I stepped into the cubicle I braced myself: Melanie seemed to view every new day as a cause for celebration.

'Rebecca, you look so nice,' she chirped as she rubbed a swab in my cheek. 'I think we all want to look our best today.'

Given her hand was in my mouth there wasn't much I could say. Her strain of forced happiness was still very much in vogue. Grown-ups were wearing orange or yellow, playing ukuleles and singing a cappella in any public setting. They were like children left alone in a house at night who turn on all the lights because they think it will protect them.

Melanie took the swab from my mouth then put it into a test tube of yellow liquid. She asked what I had planned for the celebration, and I told her I was going to the Institute party.

'That sounds wonderful, Rebecca. I wish I was coming, but I have other plans. My besties and I have a whole night organised. First, we're going for drinks at the Opal Lounge, do you know it, that's the bar in the penthouse of what used to be the Standard. The views are amazing. The place was fully booked six months ago but Sandra knows the duty manager's wife. They've been friends since kindergarten and she says she feels so fortunate to still have her in her life.'

'Uh-huh,' I said and looked at the test tube, which I thought had darkened slightly. But it was still yellow.

While Melanie mapped out the rest of her plans I nodded and wondered if I had misjudged her. Maybe to her a person waiting for their test results was like a child alone at night, her prattle like a cartoon or candy. I wasn't too worried about my result, but hearing about her dear, dear friend's housewarming in Charleston did stop me worrying about Damian. By the time I got in the elevator I was convinced that whatever slight offence I might have given didn't matter. He was reasonable. He wasn't petty. We would talk later.

My first task that morning was to check the tissue cultures. For the last year I'd been trying to infect vaccinated human cells with a modified version of the virus. Although I'd succeeded with mice and rats (albeit with lower infection rates) I couldn't infect human cells, and was running out of ideas. For experiment number twenty-five the temperature of the cells' environment had been raised slightly above normal body temperature, because there were other retroviruses more virulent in those conditions (and atypical Werner's was essentially a tropical disease). I didn't have high expectations for this, but I had to try.

I swiped into the lab then said hi to Chris, who looked up from his microscope long enough to give me a nod. Outside the lab he was great fun, but when working he was monosyllabic. Unsurprisingly, he and Rajeev got on well.

I put on my lab coat, then washed my hands with our weapons-grade sanitiser. Although I had a mild allergy to it, nothing else was as effective. I had to wait a few minutes for my fingers to stop trembling before I went to check on the tissue cultures. Dropping things in a lab is never good, especially not ours.

Once my hands settled down I went to the safety cabinet and turned on the ultraviolet light. In that watery glow I saw that something had finally happened. One of the ten Petri dishes was lightly speckled with bright dots that resembled city lights seen from a plane at night. Each dot was an infected cell. My new virus had beaten the vaccine.

A good scientist shouldn't hope for a particular outcome – every result tells you something – but when I saw those glowing dots I admit I felt relief. This was immediately followed by a drumbeat of horror. It's one thing to hypothesise that you're not safe, that there are wolves and monsters out there, and another to see a snout pressing at the window.

But it was only one dish. Perhaps the cells in it had not been properly vaccinated. There might have been contamination. It was not a result I wanted to trust.

I took a long time cleaning my hands, then went to my office. Once again my computer had gotten stuck on the screen saver. Usually I just restarted it, but that day I sat and watched the coloured image of the virus rotate. I was waiting, yet pretending not to wait, for a Eureka moment. Rajeev thought this a romantic notion that devalued the hard, unglamorous work on which every breakthrough was built. Although I agreed with him, I figured it didn't hurt to spend a few minutes every now and then letting my mind wander. Left to its own devices, it might come up with something.

Part of the virus looked like a red sunflower. There was a bit that resembled a blue tail, or perhaps a cresting wave. The whole thing could have been some luminescent devilfish from the bottom of the ocean, or the painting of a child. Someone who didn't know what it was might think it beautiful.

I stared at the screen a few more minutes. Then I hit reset. I wrote up the results of experiment twenty-five, then added my conjectures. Damian still required us to record everything we did, no matter how trivial. Some of my colleagues thought it unnecessary now that the danger had passed, but to me this was just good practice. There were still plenty of ways to die.

My plan for experiment twenty-six was a scientific no-brainer. The previous experiment had to be repeated. There was no other way to tell if those glowing dots were something to be scared of. I was impatient to find out, but the next experiment would take another week. After lunch I could prepare.

The Institute's cafeteria was the only place outside my home where I trusted the food. All the produce was screened; every week the catering staff got tested. When I entered I saw my colleagues having their usual Friday get-together. Chris was telling Rajeev and Gulmera something that required him to interlace his fingers for illustration. Rajeev was listening intently and nodding; Gulmera was fixating on a pot of chocolate mousse. I waved to them all, then went to the counter, where I faced an impossible choice. Option #1 was slow-cooked lamb with new potatoes brushed with rosemary butter. Option #2 was pan-fried halibut with baby carrots and wild rice. I asked the servers if they still had both options, hoping they'd say no so I wouldn't have to choose.

'Oh yes,' I was told by Wanda, whose pleasure at serving food never seemed feigned.

'Alright,' I said. 'I'll have option one. And that's to go.'

Wanda scooped up lamb, then potatoes. My stomach made an audible gurgle.

'Not long,' said Wanda. Even in the styrofoam the food looked amazing.

There wasn't time to eat with my colleagues, but I wanted to at least say hi. I walked past a free space by Rajeev and sat next to Gulmera. Our relationship wasn't really a secret, but at work we didn't like to draw attention to it.

Gulmera shifted toward Rajeev to make more room for me, which was kind of her but unnecessary: I don't take up much space.

'Thanks, but I'm not staying long.'

'Are you sure? What did you get?'

'The lamb.'

'Oh, I wish I'd got that. Chris made some disgusting sounds while he was eating it. I think he'd have preferred to eat in private.'

'She's exaggerating!'

'Not by much.'

Chris responded by taking a spoon and pretending to scoop some chocolate mousse. He brought the spoon to his lips then licked it sensuously. 'Remind you of anyone?' Rajeev laughed and pointed at Gulmera. She protested but laughed as well, and it was definitely funny. But the sight of Chris's tongue, its thick sheen of saliva, killed my appetite.

Although it was nice to be with them, I was nervous that someone would ask how my work was going, more out of politeness than interest – I was sure they all thought I was wasting my time. Usually this was no problem, since all I'd done for the last nine months was fail, but I felt awkward, almost embarrassed to have potentially broken their vaccine.

When I stood up to go Chris and Gulmera stopped laughing. They looked concerned, why I don't know: we rarely ate together.

'Are you going?' said Gulmera. 'Come on, sit with us. You have to eat.'

'I really have a lot to do.'

'Give yourself a break, today of all days,' said Chris.

'Sorry, it can't wait,' I said. I didn't like that they thought my work wasn't urgent.

Thankfully Rajeev jumped in.

'But we'll see you at six?'

'Of course.'

He smiled when he heard me confirm I was going to the party. I remembered the pleasure on his face as it approached the screen, as fervent and open as if there was no barrier between us. As I left the cafeteria I wished we were going to have a nice night at home, with shrimp and old movies and everything our hands could do for each other. Instead we'd have to mingle with strangers who had no idea there was nothing to celebrate.

LUKAS

I WAS relieved to find Erik in Rustam's bedroom. He was lying on the bed with an upended bottle in his mouth, his cheeks pushed out by fluid he was holding there. It was a childish game but he seemed to be enjoying himself. He raised his hand in greeting, then indicated for me to sit. He was a big man, so there wasn't much room on the bed; it was good to be close to someone.

Erik had to swallow his huge mouthful before he could speak. His throat bulged and I thought he might choke, but he managed. The first thing he said was, 'That sounded intense. I don't really know Valentina. Should I?'

Although I felt the need to confess what I'd done, I wasn't sure how he'd react.

'She's interesting.'

'That's not an answer. We're all *interesting*. You know what I mean. Was the pillow talk good? Did she tell you about being in prison?'

'No.'

'I'm sure that's bullshit. No one who tested positive in prison got out alive. Either the authorities killed them or they let the other prisoners do it.'

Erik had a conspiracy theory for everything. Sometimes it could be annoying, but I understood why he did. It was less frightening to think that terrible things had been planned.

He handed me the bottle. I thought it was vodka, but it tasted stronger and burnt my throat. I coughed. 'What's this?'

'Some local hooch. Since those savages can't burn or shoot us, they're trying with poison.'

I pretended amazement. 'So you finally agree we need protection? I have to drink to that,' I said and took another swig.

He raised his hand in protest. 'We only need protection *because* we're in here. We could walk down any street and nobody would know we were sick. It's not as if we've got a brand on our foreheads, although I'm sure it's been considered.'

'But you agreed to come here. We all did.'

'Only because we were scared and wanted to believe that crap about it being temporary. And not everyone agreed. Some people were definitely forced to.'

'Who did they force? No one here.'

He shrugged away the fact. 'In my previous camp there were two blokes from Sydney who'd refused to go into quarantine. They said they were grabbed and drugged by guys in protective suits. When they woke up they were in a stockade on Melville Island.'

'Why does no one else have a story like this? Why didn't I hear anything from the hundreds of people I knew in Rosa Khutor?'

'I don't know, Lukas. Why didn't you?'

'Oh, so it's *my* fault I didn't meet the human evidence that undoubtedly existed?'

He shrugged. 'We believe what we want to.' He reached for the bottle. 'So anyway. Valentina. What happened? You look upset.'

I told him everything. For all his flaws, Erik could keep a secret.

'I know I fucked up,' I said. 'I just lost it.'

'You did. And you should be more careful.' He sighed. 'Why don't you wait here while I check on her?'

47

Erik got up and went across the hall. He softly closed the door.

I quickly finished the local poison – the trick was not to think – then went downstairs to find something less toxic. Kim had been moved to an armchair but was still unconscious. Khunbish was cutting his hair with a pair of kitchen scissors. The floor was covered with clumps of white hair that made me think of Mizzi, the little fox terrier that had loved my mother and bitten the rest of us. After my mother died she had run off.

'Where's Dejan?' I asked.

'He went to get a razor. Did you see Valentina upstairs?'

I nodded.

'I don't know what's up with her. She's barely spoken to me since she arrived, and then tonight she turned up and made us do shots with her. Kim didn't last half an hour. My guess,' he said, as Dejan came in, 'is that she got some bad news at the clinic this morning. My appointment was after hers, and I had to wait twenty minutes. It doesn't take that long to say there's been no change.'

He looked at me expectantly. I liked Khunbish, but after knowing him for two years I still wasn't sure that the feeling was mutual. There was the same sense of minor sufferance I'd noticed among Tomasz's friends. I told him Valentina had passed out, and Khunbish was starting to answer when Dejan interrupted. 'Found it,' he said and held up a straight razor that looked so terrifyingly sharp I couldn't believe it had been permitted. It was especially worrying to see Dejan wielding it. In the last month he'd broken someone's nose, another person's arm, and smashed a lot of windows. Although at other times he was his usual jovial self, something had shifted in him. Often this happened in response to a diagnosis, but sometimes it was like an alarm went off in people that they couldn't stop. Everyone made allowances for Dejan because of what had happened to his family, but I don't think any of us, including the authorities, knew where this tolerance should end.

'OK,' said Dejan. 'Now we wash him.'

Khunbish brought over a bowl of water. He lathered up Kim's hair while Dejan perched on the arm of the chair.

'What would you like, sir?' he asked Kim. 'Something for fashion? Something for the ladies?'

He lifted the razor, checked his reflection, then blew on the blade. I thought of Valentina's hot breath on the window. I hoped she could forgive me. There's nothing worse than knowing someone hates you for a good reason.

'Hold still,' said Dejan, then grasped Kim's jaw. He brought the blade to Kim's temple and made a few tentative scrapes before stepping back. He looked pleased with the result. 'This is possible,' he said and continued with more confidence. In a few minutes he had shaved the right side of Kim's head.

'Nice work,' I told him.

He inclined his head to accept the compliment, then added, 'That was easy side. Left is more tricky.'

As if to prove the point, he drew blood. Although it was accidental, and only a nick, it was still unpleasant. Thankfully Kim remained unconscious as we held a towel to his head. Once the bleeding stopped Dejan resumed, but now he seemed less certain. The gap between scrapes got longer. When he brought the razor away there was mostly foam on its blade.

After a few minutes he stepped back. 'Maybe is enough,' he said, although he hadn't finished.

'You want me to carry on?' asked Khunbish.

Dejan looked affronted. 'No, it is fine. No problem. I finish.'

He moved round to the back of Kim's head. 'This is better,' he said. The first few cuts went well, then Dejan seemed to falter. He muttered in Croatian, then bit his lip.

'Too much,' he said and wiped away foam. Slowly, carefully, he finished the left side. I realised I was holding my breath. Neither Khunbish or I spoke. Dejan was reciting a monologue of self-encouragement. At least his hand looked steady.

Dejan was smiling as he started on the top of Kim's head. Maybe then he sped up, or his hand was tired. Perhaps there was something about the curvature of Kim's skull he did not expect. But suddenly there was a spurt of blood. Everybody panicked. Khunbish shouted and ran outside. Dejan tried to staunch the bleeding with his shirt and got covered in blood. He gave up and retreated to the corner, then turned his face to the wall.

As for me, I just stood there. I'd often imagined Tomasz lying on the ground with a missing face. On a Berlin street, or in Paris, or in the woods near our house. He must have died somewhere.

Erik ran down the stairs and into the kitchen. He opened drawers and cupboards, swearing as he searched. He then rushed over to Kim and emptied a packet of white power onto his head. 'What the fuck have you done?' he yelled in my face.

'It wasn't me. It was Dejan.'

'Where's Khunbish?'

'I think he's gone for help.'

'Help?' he said disgustedly. 'There's no help for this.' He pointed at Kim's bloody face. The powder had formed a thick paste that stopped the bleeding.

Erik put his finger lightly on the wound, then took it away. He licked the tip and smiled in a ghoulish way.

'Want some?'

'No. What is that?'

'Sugar. My ma used to put it on me and my brother's scrapes.'

'Did that work?'

'Of course. She wasn't daft.'

'I didn't say she was.'

He laughed. 'Actually, she was. But in the right way. Daft about us.'

Dejan called to us from the corner. 'Is he? How is he?'

'Relax. You didn't kill him. What happened? Did he say the wrong thing?'

'No, nothing. It was accident. Mistake.'

'Alright, I get it. You're drunk and things got out of control. What I don't understand, *Lukas*, is why you didn't stop these idiots. Using Kim as a doorstop is funny. Giving Dejan a razor is not.'

Dejan shrugged as if to say *that's just your opinion*. He wandered into the kitchen. He turned on a tap then started washing himself. Erik and I watched him splash his face. It was hard to believe he'd been a terrified wreck a few minutes ago. There seemed to be a switch in him that could be flicked on and off.

Erik shook his head. 'I don't blame Dejan. He's not in control of himself. But you, on the other hand... Until tonight I thought you were one of the sensible ones.'

'Look, I didn't think anything bad would happen. They got carried away and so did I.'

'I understand. I'm all for getting carried away. But I hoped that while I was up there sorting out your *situation*, you'd keep an eye on these hooligans.'

'You didn't ask me to.'

'Petulance? Really?'

He had a point, but I didn't get a chance to apologise because the door opened and Alain came in. He glanced around the room and muttered into his headset. Then the door opened again and Dr Nilsson rushed in. He went straight to Kim and took his pulse.

'How much has he drunk?'

'A lot,' said Erik.

Dr Nilsson sighed. 'It's like you're all teenagers again.'

'What do you expect? We're certainly not treated like adults.'

'Can we have this debate later? Although it's interesting I should probably make sure Kim doesn't go hypovolaemic. Alright with you?'

'Be my guest,' said Erik and smiled. Dr Nilsson was probably the only authority figure he had any time for. Many people said him being in the camp wasn't a great sacrifice, as it was just something required by his faith. But there were a lot of nicer places for him to do missionary work.

'Get his legs,' said Dr Nilsson. I took them and together we laid Kim on the sofa. He stirred but didn't open his eyes. We propped up his feet with all the cushions we could find, then the doctor put an IV into his arm. Without even needing to be asked Erik dragged a standing lamp over to Kim and ripped the shade from it. Dr Nilsson hung the bag of saline from its golden arm.

To get away from Kim's bloody face I went over to speak to Alain. He was looking grave as he talked into his headset, no doubt informing his superiors about our situation. When he'd finished his face relaxed.

'So you had a celebration as well.'

'The usual. Until it became a horror film.'

'It could have been worse.'

'True. How was the south fence?'

He paused. 'There was nothing.' He hesitated. I suppose he wasn't sure how much I should be told. He lowered his voice. 'We didn't find anyone. But there were broken branches and some old cigarette butts. I think some people are still curious about what's up here.'

'There's just a circus,' I said as Dr Nilsson cleaned Kim's face. Once he wiped the blood off, Kim started to look alive. When the doctor examined the wound he paused, leant forward then sniffed.

'Was this you?' he asked Erik.

'Afraid so.'

The doctor laughed. 'You're a useful idiot.'

He finished cleaning the wound then put on a dressing that seemed incredibly white. I stared at it, certain I was about to see a crimson spot appear, that this spot would bloom, the redness advancing until no white was left.

Dr Nilsson gathered his equipment, then came over to us. 'I think he's fine. But it's best we don't move him. Can one of you stay with him?'

'I will,' said Erik.

'Me too,' I said.

'Thank you. Now I'm going back to sleep. Dejan, come and see me tomorrow. We need to have a talk.' Dejan looked startled then nodded.

Erik cleared his throat. 'Doc, before you go, can you tell us how Anurag and Noor are doing? Will they be coming back?'

I wasn't surprised when Dr Nilsson shook his head. Noor's last seizure had broken her leg; in two weeks Anurag had gone from being wobbly to being unable to stand.

'Erik, I'll see you tomorrow afternoon,' said the doctor and then left.

'What's that about?'

'Oh, just my check-up. Any excuse to shove his finger up my arse. What about you and Alain? You seem pretty chummy. He probably has clean hands.'

'He's a nice guy.'

'Sure. He's a terrific Nazi.'

This didn't deserve a reply. I went and stood over Kim. I watched the rise and fall of his chest. The bandage was still white.

'He needs blanket,' said Dejan, and started to go upstairs.

'Wait,' I said. 'Look in Rustam's bedroom.' I didn't want him to disturb Valentina.

Erik put his hand on my shoulder. 'Lukas, you don't have to stay. I don't sleep much as it is.'

'I want to. I feel responsible.'

'Fair enough. And I'm glad. I don't think there's much to read here. Rustam wasn't exactly a bookworm.'

Dejan came back down and laid a blanket over Kim. He tucked it around him in a way that seemed tender. Dejan's three children had been burnt so badly he couldn't tell them apart.

'He is OK,' he said and let go of the blanket. Although this didn't sound like a question, both Erik and I agreed.

'Why don't you get some sleep, mate? We can manage.'

'OK,' he said, and looked relieved. He shook both our hands.

When he'd gone Erik and I went quiet. I was already regretting offering to stay; I could have been with Edie or Min-seo.

He yawned. 'What time do you think it is?'

I copied his yawn, then guessed it was around three.

'I'm going to get a watch again. And a fucking clock as well. I can't believe I got carried away with all that shit. As if it makes any bloody difference knowing the time. Anyway, what do you think? Either we keep drinking or switch to coffee. Your call.'

≈

Rustam's kettle was broken so I had to use a saucepan. While I did this Eric restored some order to the room. He made an

54

impressively small amount of noise as he gathered the cans and bottles and put them in a box. The main problem was the blood. It was mixed in with the hair, so there were sticky clumps all over the floor. Dejan had also left bloody fingerprints on the furnishings. In some places they looked good; there were four marks on a green cushion that Min-seo would have appreciated. It wasn't just the colour contrast – Dejan's fingerprints had an amazing double whorl that looped right, then left, making an S-shape. I imagined him putting his fingers on her walls, building a wet row of marks that would slowly darken.

'How's the coffee coming?' asked Erik.

'Slowly.' The water was steaming but reluctant to boil. I decided that Min-seo wouldn't like having the fingerprints all at the same time. She'd get Dejan to add them gradually, so the blood would be different colours depending on when it dried. She'd use them to mark an occasion: a good dream; an orgasm; a day with less pain.

Erik came over and looked at the saucepan. 'No wonder,' he said and put a plate on top of it. 'That should sort the bugger.'

I spooned coffee into mugs. A minute later the plate was rattling.

'Thanks,' said Erik when I handed him a mug. He took a sip.

'Hot and shit. But it'll work. I barely remember what proper coffee tastes like.'

We sipped our horrible coffee while watching Kim do nothing. I pointed at his small white Mohican.

'Do you think he'll keep that?'

'Probably. He was trying to make a statement, and it still does that.'

'Yeah, it does, though I don't think it's worth making. Even if he doesn't have to check his hair any more, there's still a thousand other things to worry about. Every time I go to the toilet I'm consulting an oracle.'

'I know it's stupid but at least Kim's trying. I'm in favour of anything that gives us a shake. Right now there's too many sleepwalkers.'

'What about the mirrors? Isn't that the same thing?'

'Yeah, that's a waste of time too. You don't see the Gnostics getting rid of stuff.'

'Are they role models now? I thought you hated them.'

'I think they have a ridiculous view of the world. But that doesn't make me a bigot. They may not give a fuck about anyone else, but at least they believe in *something*. They've organised themselves.'

'To do what? Swap bags of shit? Drink each other's blood?'

Erik put down his cup. He wasn't looking at me when he spoke.

'Do you think things can stay like this? Something has to change. When I came to the camp five years ago there were six hundred of us. Now there are fewer than two hundred. In another six months we might be down to a hundred.'

I wasn't sure what to say. He was probably right, though I didn't see what difference it made if we were fifty or five hundred. We only had one hope.

'They might still find a cure.'

'Yes, they might. If they're still looking.'

'Oh, fuck off. You really think they're not looking for a cure for a disease that's killed almost a billion people? That would be insane.'

He shrugged, then said calmly, 'I don't know, Lukas. Maybe their wonderful vaccine makes them feel safe. They've probably gone back to worrying about the normal things that kill them.'

I wanted to shout but had to make do with an angry whisper. 'So you're saying there's no hope? That we should just wait to fucking die?'

'No,' he said with maddening patience. 'What I'm saying is that we need to remind people they still have choices. They need to remember they're not helpless.'

I had no idea what he was talking about, nor did I want to know. I stood up, because if I didn't I was going to lose my temper.

'I need more coffee.'

'Me too,' he said, then passed his mug.

While the water heated I looked through the kitchen cupboards. There wasn't much except for plates and bowls and a lot of empty bottles. Under the sink I found a rusty tin box. Inside were three letters written in Kazakh. I couldn't work out who Rustam had been writing to – it was in Cyrillic – but each of the letters had been dated. The most recent one was from two weeks before his death.

I carried the box over to Erik, then went back to the kitchen and refilled our mugs. I put too much in Erik's so had to be especially careful as I brought it to him because my hands were shaking a little (which didn't worry me – they'd always done that). I was really pleased I hadn't spilled a drop.

'If we were getting married, this would be good luck,' I said. I was smiling at my own joke when I realised Erik was crying.

'Poor fucker. Rustam was so far gone at the end he was writing letters to his mum.'

'What's wrong with that?'

'She died ten years ago.'

I wondered if Rustam had known this. Perhaps he'd just wanted to talk to her. I'd certainly written a few letters it would have been pointless to send.

Erik wiped his eyes. 'Of course, even if she was alive she'd never have got them. This is what I mean. It's bad enough we have to stay here. But why are we cut off? Why in fuck's name can't we receive mail? There's no reason for that which makes any bloody sense. Oh, go on.' He looked at me angrily. 'Give me the official bullshit. Tell me it's for our *safety*. That otherwise our location wouldn't be a secret.'

I tried to reply but he hadn't finished.

'This place can't be a secret. People know the camps exist, and it's not hard to figure out roughly where they might be. You can bet everyone within a hundred miles knows *something* is going on up here, even if they think it's a military base.'

Although many of us respected Erik, he wasn't our leader. For all his talk about choices and freedom he didn't understand that some of us had already chosen what to do with our remaining time. Some of us wanted to write books and cover our walls with feathers and fuck in every possible way. Some of us wanted to get high and develop a rating scale for sunsets. We'd made our decisions, and he had to respect them, just as we heathens had to respect the wishes of those among us who wanted to defile their bodies to punish God.

Outside it was still dark, but dawn had to be close. I sat and watched Kim breathe while Erik read the letters. I wondered whether I should check on Valentina and decided it was best not to disturb her. I'd wait a few days before talking to her about what had happened.

I got up to make more coffee; Erik asked for a shot of rum in his.

'That might mask the taste. I should have thought of it from the start.'

'Good idea,' I said. I filled the saucepan and put a glass plate over it. When the bubbles began to rise they looked like frog-spawn, and though at first they ascended tentatively, soon they rose in one great burst. The bubbles broke and then more rose, and they broke as well. I should have turned off the heat, but I was mesmerised. The action kept repeating, staying the same while it changed. Soon I was able to close my eyes and see the water in detail. The bubbles made a wonderful hiss. I knew Erik would get impatient, and even if he didn't, the pan would boil dry. But the way the bubbles kept coming, over and over, made me think the process would never stop.

When I opened my eyes only half the water was left. I filled our cups and poured rum into both. I brought Erik his cup, and he nodded his thanks, then went over to Kim and put a hand on his forehead.

'How is he?'

'Hot. But there's no fever.'

'Good. What will we tell him when he wakes up?'

'The truth. We'll tell him he got so pissed he passed out and then they played a prank on him. Is there something wrong with that?'

'Nothing. I'm just worried Kim might try and get revenge.'

'Well, he could. That's a risk. But I don't see there's any other way to explain why his hair has been shaved. And we certainly shouldn't *lie* to him. There's too much of that shit going on already.'

Sensing that Erik was about to launch into another rant, I tried to change the subject.

'Yeah,' I said, then paused, as if thinking. 'Erik, you know what I was doing ten years ago today?'

'No,' he said without interest. Erik was one of the few people who didn't like to talk about their lives before they got sick. To him it was escapism.

'I was planning a trip here. Well, not here exactly, but to this region.'

'Why? It wasn't a fun place even before they started setting fire to anyone who sneezed.'

'I wanted to visit a tomb that had been found in the hills.'

'A mass grave? Oh wait, they don't bother to bury people. They just burn them.'

'No, it was nothing like that. It was an ancient burial place.'

Erik worried his lip. 'For who?'

'The Scythians. They were nomadic warriors who were here around two thousand years ago.'

'I know who they were. And more like two and a half. There are tombs all over this region. They've been finding them since the nineteenth century,' he said dismissively. But then he sipped his coffee, looked away, and said, 'So what was special about this tomb?'

I suppressed my smile.

'It was a king's burial chamber that had been in the permafrost, so it was really well preserved. It wouldn't have been found if it hadn't been for climate change.'

'Well hooray for that. What did they find? The usual horses and gold? Cannabis? Rudenko found plenty of that in the 1940s.'

'Yes, but the horses were so well preserved it was apparent they'd been buried in a circle. And the king's body was intact enough for them to see his tattoos.'

'Of what? Reindeer? Horses?'

'Yes, and also a panther. And a lot of creatures with the heads of an eagle and the body of a lion.'

Erik nodded. 'That makes sense. Griffins were believed to be very powerful. They were chosen to guard treasure.'

He scratched his beard with the satisfaction of someone solving an itch. There were a lot of words to describe Erik – passionate, garrulous, overbearing, dogmatic – but professorial wasn't usually one of them. I often felt he did his best to be the opposite of how he'd been before he got infected. He wanted his life to have a clear Before and After, and he wasn't alone in this. A lot of people claimed they'd become a different person since their diagnosis, and maybe that was true for them; as for me, I felt the same.

Erik had been quiet for a few minutes. His chin was on his chest. He looked exhausted, more like seventy than fifty. I wondered if he could confine his thoughts to dead horses and kings without remembering his time as a professor, the faces of colleagues, awards he'd won, the comfort of being accompanied by books.

'Lukas, what do you think about heaven?'

The question caught me off guard. Although I wouldn't have told him, he didn't wait for my answer.

'Do you think it will be anything like life? That's usually how people imagine it. They take the best things about life, the most special occasions, and then have them go on forever. For the Scythians, the happiest time was when they wore golden crowns and owned all the best horses and had massive feasts. If you could believe the afterlife was just more of that you wouldn't be scared of death. You might even look forward to it.'

He turned away from me, apparently not needing my reply, like I was a student whose only role was to receive his teachings. This didn't bother me. There was no need for him to know that sometimes, when I felt sad and needed comfort, I imagined being in a better place.

He coughed, then continued, 'This was how everyone used to live. In the Middle Ages people thought of their time on earth as preparation for eternity. It probably seemed like a good bargain. A short, virtuous life in exchange for eternal bliss.'

He stood up but didn't move from the spot. It was clearly just to aid his delivery.

'Of course, it was a gamble. They didn't get to do the things they wanted. They didn't get to have much *fun*. Not much fucking. Not much drinking. Getting their knees all bloody from kneeling in prayer. A big step back from the Scythians, who got to gallop about and steal.'

It was dawn. Kim seemed stable. As soon as Erik finished his lecture, I was going to leave. I'd go home, get in bed and shut my eyes, imagine myself sat at my old desk with papers to grade and all my books behind me.

'So maybe the Scythians were smarter than us. They got to live fully without burdening themselves with guilt. They weren't afraid of the end.'

'That's good,' I said, and the interruption made Erik frown. He took a few steps away, as if the lecture was over, but then he turned to face me.

'What about you, Lukas? Do you believe in an afterlife?'

'No.'

'Are you sure?'

'Yes.'

This wasn't a lie; I knew I'd never sit at that desk again.

'Alright then. Whatever you say. Let me rephrase the question. Do you believe in God?'

'No.'

I stood up.

'Do you believe in any kind of all-powerful force?'

'No.'

'Do you believe in a soul? In reincarnation?'

'No,' I repeated. 'I told you already.'

'That's right, you did. But let me ask you one more question.'

'I'm tired,' I said and opened the door.

'It's a very simple question. Yes or No. Do you think you're going to live forever?'

He was still waiting for an answer as I went outside. A light rain was falling, little more than a mist, but it felt good on my face. The only person I saw on my way home was Fatoumata. She was kneeling at a crossroads, her hands raised over her head, her gaze aimed at the sky. I don't know if she saw me. If she did, she gave no sign.

REBECCA

I N the lab I sprayed my hands then put on gloves. After twenty-five iterations the preparation required so little thought my body seemed to be following a script. The cell cultures were sitting in the main fridge like a TV dinner. I checked the incubator was set to thirty-eight degrees, then unlocked the smaller fridge containing viral samples. Adding the virus was like dropping a small tear onto each of the dishes.

After I'd finished I still had two hours before the party, so I took a pile of journals from the stack on the floor. Even though it would have been much easier to read on-screen, I clung to the habit of print out of nostalgia for my undergrad years, when an afternoon with a stack of journals made me feel involved in science as an ongoing process being carried out by people like me.

The first three journals had nothing of interest. In the fourth there was an intriguing paper on a possible vaccine for HIV-2 but the authors were hopelessly in thrall to the drug company funding the research. In the most promising paper, from a recent issue of *Virology*, a team in Oslo suggested that people's susceptibility to atypical Werner's might depend on their genetic profile, with some being either immune or less vulnerable. They based this hypothesis primarily on the fact that 'only nine per cent of the world's population had become infected and died'.

When I read this, I gasped at the *only*. The Norwegians also made the excellent point that there are plenty of diseases – especially the spongiform encephalopathies – where there can be a long gap between infection and the first symptoms, a gap that often depends on one's genetic background. If you're lucky, it takes an extra ten years before you become symptomatic. And if you hit the jackpot, you're only a carrier.

The authors raised interesting questions, but the overwhelming majority of people definitely had no resistance to Werner's or they wouldn't have died within a year of being infected. And as the Norwegians admitted, their idea would be very hard to test. I was starting to pull at the threads of their theory when there was a gentle knock on my door. Rajeev was wearing the nice blue wool jacket I'd bought for him on the off chance we ever went to a restaurant together.

'You're keen, aren't you?' I said.

He looked confused. 'Am I? It's five to six.'

I didn't believe him. It felt like I'd only been sat there a half-hour. Although it was good to see him it seemed premature. I certainly wasn't ready to mingle with the super-rich.

But I didn't sigh or pull a face. I put on my jacket, smiled, and then he was smiling too.

'Darling, shall we?' he said, and offered me his arm, and it wasn't his usual voice. In the time it took me to realise he was pretending to be some aristocrat from a black and white movie his smile had faded.

'Sorry,' he said. 'I didn't think.'

'Why are you sorry?'

'About doing a British accent.'

'Is that what that was?' I said, and laughed. He'd sounded nothing like Matthew.

As we waited for the elevator Rajeev took my hand. He did this without saying anything, or even looking down. I wanted to take mine away, because someone might see, and his hand was slightly moist. But after freaking out the night before, I didn't want to overreact. I let him keep hold of my hand as we entered the elevator. He asked if I'd had a good day.

'Not bad. You?'

He sighed. 'It was OK. But I didn't do much. Mostly I was thinking about my mom and dad and brothers.'

The doors closed. He didn't press a button.

'I was thinking of the last time we were all together. We'd flown into Chicago for Mom's seventieth. Dad insisted on paying for me and my brothers' hotels and for every meal. He wouldn't even let us get the tip. At first it was annoying, then we were laughing about it. I kept saying, "We're grown-ups with jobs! When does this end?" Dad didn't think it was funny. He said, "It never ends. Not while I am your father."'

'That's a nice story,' I said and pushed the button for the top floor. I was still uncomfortable being in confined spaces with others. It made no difference that Rajeev, like myself, had been tested that morning – the habit of fear remained. For a moment I was so angry with myself for being stupid that I wanted to kiss him fully, properly, our tongues in each other's wet mouth. Over the last nine months he'd been as patient as anyone could expect. He hadn't made a joke of my caution. He hadn't made me justify myself. He'd been amazing.

As the elevator slowed I realised there was something I could do to show him how I felt, something long overdue. I squeezed his hand, because I was happy to hold it, and I was going to hold it all night. I wanted everyone to see that Rajeev and I were together.

But as the doors opened he released my hand. He'd thought my squeeze meant *that's enough*. And he was obviously hurt, because he quickly stepped out of the elevator without waiting for me. While he didn't exactly storm off, he was already three or four steps ahead of me before I recovered.

It didn't help that I was intimidated by the noise and presence of more than two hundred people in gowns and tuxedos. Our sparsely furnished conference centre had been given a serious makeover. The walls had been covered by orange fabric that hung from wooden frames, giving the room the look of a huge, posh yurt equipped with a string quartet. An impressive transformation, but I wasn't convinced; like the subway, it was a trick.

As I followed Rajeev to our table I let my eyes glide over the faces. There were a few famous people, some actors, a singer; the rest were just the anonymous rich. I looked longest at the back of the head of a man whose hair was so black it must have been dyed. *Black* didn't do it justice – it was dark, but not like night, more the absolute kind you get in a cave. I had to see his face to know if it was natural, but his head stayed still, probably because he was listening closely to a Chinese woman with thick glasses that didn't mask her prettiness. All I could do was imagine different faces for him, wondering which would fit.

Next to him Gulmera was wearing a long, backless white dress she must have brought to work. She was a brilliant geneticist who had somehow found time to raise two teenage daughters, for which I admired her, but despite working together for a long time we weren't especially close. Our only real heart-to-heart had taken place just over six years ago, during those awful months when I'd lived in the basement of the Institute. After what had happened in our apartment there was no way I could stay there, and I had nowhere else to go. No one wanted guests and the few remaining hotels were far too expensive. After drinking most of a bottle of wine Gulmera had confided that she hadn't been in love with her husband – he cheated, he drank – and would have left him if he'd survived. With what she told me, and what I said to her about Matthew, there was a real foundation for friendship. But maybe that exchange of confidences had made us scared to go further, both because of what we'd hear and what we might say. Since then we'd rarely talked about anything except work. Each time I'd invited her to my place she'd said she was busy; when she'd asked me out for a drink six months ago I'd reminded her that I didn't think it was safe.

At the party I realised Gulmera had other reasons for not pursuing our friendship. As I headed toward her she still hadn't noticed me. She was staring in the opposite direction, apparently captivated by the big screen that showed the view outside. Damian had had these installed to make the Institute feel less like a maximum security fortress. The resolution was so good that most of the time I forgot they weren't actual windows. Only when they showed something impossible – the ones in Damian's office had a view of the Pacific – did I remember that behind them there was a thick wall.

As I got closer it became obvious that Gulmera wasn't looking at the darkening sky or the lights winking on in the buildings. It was Rajeev who had captured her attention. Perhaps she'd been gazing at him like that for months, years, without me realising. It was weird, yet not a problem; I was sure he loved me.

She kept watching him for the ten seconds it took me to reach her. When I said her name she turned and her smile was so full and self-assured that for a second I doubted whether she'd really been perving on my boyfriend.

'Rebecca! I'm so glad you made it. Are you having fun?'

'Not yet. It's kind of overwhelming.'

'I know what you need,' she said and stopped a server, took two glasses off his tray, then handed one to me.

'Cheers!' she said and touched her glass against mine. And I don't think she meant this in a mean way. She just hadn't given any thought to the fact that these were outside caterers who had maybe not been tested. It was only embarrassment that made me lift the glass to my mouth, which was interesting; I was willing to do something that might kill me to avoid looking dumb.

The champagne was cold and bitter. The liquid burned through my chest; I imagined the alcohol, and maybe something else, pushing into my bloodstream. But I didn't panic. I kept it together while Gulmera commented on the other party guests, pointing out who was hot or not, who was well or terribly dressed. When she said, 'So where's Rajeev?' I couldn't figure out what she was trying to imply with this lie. Perhaps she thought there was some mileage in drawing attention to the fact that we weren't together.

'Oh, he's somewhere,' I said casually, then we both pretended to look around the room. I let Gulmera find him first.

'There he is, with Chris.' She sounded triumphant, as if finders meant keepers. 'Shall we join him?'

'You go ahead. I forgot something in my office.'

My anxiety about what I'd drunk must have frothed into visibility because she said, 'Are you alright?' But I was already moving toward the open elevator. When I bumped a woman who spilled her drink, I apologised but didn't stop.

A group of women dying of laughter blocked my way. Maybe for them it was just another Friday night, another fundraiser. Had Werner's become another Disease of the Month?

By the time I'd got round the group the elevator doors were starting to close. Without thinking I stuck my hand between them as they shut. My hand was trapped –it wasn't painful, only a squeeze, yet there was enough pressure for me to imagine the hand being ripped off. That would break up the party.

In the elevator I lost control. My heart was racing, I was sweating. The disease was about to enter my cells. The entry would be gradual, somewhat tentative; it would seem a delicate act. It made no difference to think, to *know*, that I was being dumb, because there was virtually no risk. That cognitive intervention was useless against the buzzing in my ears, the light-headedness. It was a curiously non-specific sensation that could be mistaken for many other things. Tiredness, anxiety, low blood sugar, maybe even joy.

The elevator stopped. I started trying to get out before its doors even opened. As soon as a gap appeared I shoved myself through, scraping my shoulder badly, not that this mattered: I was as good as dead.

As I ran down the dark corridors the lights flickered on ahead of me, as if they knew where I meant to go. But even smart lighting isn't that clever. A sudden right and I was in darkness, running, seeing nothing.

At the lab the lights caught up. I swiped my entry card. It didn't work. I tried again more slowly but the door still didn't open. I cried and said all kinds of things to a God I don't believe in. I begged. I made promises. I told God to fuck Himself.

I slumped to the floor and stared helplessly at the small red light of the entry system. After I'd been sitting there a while the smart lights went off. I decided to stay there till morning, wondering who'd find me. Usually Chris came in first, often incredibly early. Even if I arrived at seven, there was no need to key in the out of hours code, because he'd done that already.

The lights came on when I stood again. I put in the code, swiped my card and the little light went green. Once inside I went straight to my office, where the virus was caught on the screen.

My hands were shaking as I unlocked the desk drawer. I brought out a testing kit and put it on the desk. I grasped my wrist to steady it, then unscrewed the tube. After putting it down carefully, I opened my mouth and scraped cells from my cheek.

Once I had put the swab in the yellow liquid I felt strangely calm. Doing those simple actions had brought on that trance-like state that comes from laboratory work. It's boring, but also absorbing. Everything else goes away. There's just what you see and what your hands are doing, except that it doesn't even feel as if it's *you* that's responsible. You're there and you're not.

While I waited I stared at the screen. If I didn't look at the tube, it could be any colour.

~

It was yellow. Of course it was. I cried until my eyes stung. It felt like they were bleeding. In that state the last thing I wanted was to go back to a roomful of complacent people. But I'd promised Rajeev I'd be at the party. I couldn't leave.

I put the vial in my desk drawer, then left the laboratory. In the bathroom I washed my face and tried to avoid my reflection. I suspected there'd be a crazy woman in the mirror.

By the time I got back to the party it was after half-eight. Some of the guests were already drunk, and while there was a lot of laughter, the mood close to raucous, a few people were crying. I suspected there'd be a whole lot more of that by the end of the night.

As I made my way to Rajeev's table a bell rang, as if we were at the theatre. When he saw me he immediately stood up, which was a bit dramatic, but also touching, because it was good to know I'd been missed. He started to come toward me and I signalled him to stay where he was. As I reached him the lights dimmed then brightened again, and a deep male voice asked us to take our seats.

'Are you OK? Where have you been?'

'I'm fine. I just had to take care of something.'

'Couldn't it wait?'

'No, it was personal.'

In my mind this was meant to hint at a menstrual issue. I don't know if he picked up on this, but he took a typically male moment before replying.

'I understand,' he said, and there was no follow-up question.

I said hi to the other people at our table; they said hi back and returned to their conversations. I wondered if they had any idea that they were sharing a table with the man who had pushed through the smoke of bad and incomplete data to figure out that an oppressed ethnic group in western China had an infection rate two-thirds lower than anyone else, exactly the sort of data that's handy when trying to make a vaccine to save humanity. No sudden inspiration had made Rajeev consider the Uyghurs. He was just being thorough.

'Sorry I kept you waiting,' I said. 'Did you talk to anyone?'

'Gulmera was here for a while then Chris dragged her off to meet someone. It was fine. Mostly I was checking the crowd for my brothers or my parents. I know they can't be here, but I still have to look.'

He took a long drink. I put my hand on his, then called to a server. The liquid in the flutes was golden and glowing, the bubbles racing each other. Watching them rise in long strings, I had a sharp presentiment that I was on the verge of perceiving some crucial analogy between what I was seeing and the morphology of the virus. I stared at them intently. Nothing was revealed. But what Gulmera had forced me to do, I now did deliberately. I took a glass and raised it.

'I'm sorry I've been so difficult. I'm really glad to be here with you.'

My glass touched his. I raised mine, swallowed. The champagne Gulmera had made me drink had been acidic; this was light and sweet, what my dad would call the good stuff. As I took a second, larger mouthful I realised Rajeev still hadn't drunk. He was staring at me with a confused happiness. He had not forgotten my rules.

'Cheers,' he said, and there was a lot in that word. Relief and joy; a fleck of wonder; a note of disbelief. He took a grateful gulp; I heard the liquid push down his throat. As I drained my glass he said, 'I wish we could leave right now.'

And if he'd left, I'd have followed. We'd have received some shitty looks, but we wouldn't have gotten in trouble.

Rajeev beckoned to a server, who topped up our glasses. 'Could you leave the bottle, please?' he asked.

The server hesitated, perhaps noted that the bottle was half-empty. 'Of course,' he said smoothly.

After he'd gone I said, 'Are you trying to get me drunk?'

'I think you're already halfway.'

'Bullshit. You'll be on the floor before me.'

But he was right; I was pretty tipsy, having eaten so little at lunch. As the lights dimmed a wooziness spread through me. For a few moments both the room and myself seemed to be fading out of existence. Then the applause began. People were cheering Damian as if he was a political candidate or movie star, someone who'd have acknowledged the crowd's reaction with a smile and a wave, a pause for the cameras, a modest admission that they deserved such a welcome. Damian's only sign of acknowledgement was a short nod to the audience when he reached the podium. That was enough to still the room.

'Five years ago, a thirty-three-year-old woman in Boston called Ericka Standish woke up after a night of heavy drinking to find she had blurry vision. She didn't worry much. She put in eye drops and spent the rest of the day in bed. Next morning her vision was worse. By the time she came into the ER of St Elizabeth's there was a faint black area in the centre of her visual field. She was diagnosed with macular degeneration, a disease unusual in the young but certainly not unknown. She had, of course, been tested for atypical Werner's many times and each time had been clear. And at that point we were sure the worst was over. Ninety-seven per cent of the population had been vaccinated. Infection rates had plummeted. Many hospitals had already stopped mandatory testing.'

He paused, and I don't think it was for effect. It was more like a thought had interrupted his prepared remarks.

'So it was by no means a certainty that they would test Ericka for Werner's, especially as on that same day there had been an explosion at a junior high school. Fifteen children had died, another ten were critical, and there were over sixty children with burns and other serious injuries. In the midst of all that chaos and grief it would have been entirely understandable if her doctor had opted to skip testing her in order to devote those five minutes of attention to a child in pain. Ericka might have left the hospital and gone home. Or she might have gone to a bar. Later that night she might have kissed a man or woman who hadn't been vaccinated. And so we might not be here tonight.

'I don't mean that we wouldn't have beaten the disease: like I said, we were almost there. What I'm saying is that we might be having this wonderful celebration a month from now, or six months from now, if that exhausted doctor at St Elizabeth's hadn't tested Ericka. It would probably be little comfort to her to know that she was the last case, or that her name, unlike most of the victims, will always be remembered.'

This time his pause was intentional. He bowed his head, and so did his audience. For the next minute I watched people turn inward, travelling back in time to the beach, bedroom or dinner table where their loved one had seemed most like themselves, though for some there was probably no single setting in which they found their deceased, just a frozen image, a burst of speech, perhaps the person saying their name or a phrase they often used. I saw Rajeev, who may have been remembering his family gathered in Chicago. I saw Gulmera, who was probably not thinking of her husband. I saw Chris, George from security, our lab technician Elaine. I watched them all.

When Damian continued his voice was quieter, as if there was a sleeper in the room.

'I think most of us would agree that we were lucky Ericka was tested. If she hadn't been, more lives would certainly have been lost.'

One of our fellow diners put his face in his hands.

'And although it's common, and normal, for people to say they feel lucky to have survived, some days I don't feel lucky at all. My wife died. My sister too. Most of my close friends are gone. It can be hard to think about anything connected with the epidemic that seems like good fortune – whether it's Ericka Standish being tested, that Werner's can't survive in low temperatures, or that China was able to control its borders so well. If you put that up against a billion dead, the destruction of knowledge, culture and community, the loss of basic trust, it seems obscene to have any notion there was anything good or fortunate about what happened. There were no small mercies.'

I was pleasantly surprised. Given the occasion, he could easily have banged the drum of total faith in the future.

'Yet there are other days, such as today, when I'm able to see things differently. It took incredible dedication, and the expertise of the global scientific community, to find a vaccine. We should never forget the incredible sacrifices people made, some of whom gave their lives. But to say we succeeded entirely through skill and persistence is wishful thinking. In hindsight our success may seem inevitable, but without many coincidences, and some lucky guesses, we wouldn't be here.'

According to my watch, he had only three minutes before the fireworks began. Not much time to segue to the happy message his audience had dressed up (and paid) to hear.

'You may say this is how science always is: hard work, inspiration, a little serendipity. However, if you'd asked me ten years ago what the odds were of us finding a vaccine in so short a time, and under such pressure, you wouldn't have liked the answer. So when your hangover clears tomorrow, and you meet for coffee or brunch, remember that you, we, all of us, are truly lucky to be alive. Maybe that's a platitude, but it's never been more true. It's something I hope we can all celebrate.'

His timing wasn't perfect. For a few dead seconds the screens stayed dark. Then golden balloons were dropping on us and the sky went patriotic. The fireworks made it feel like New Year's Eve, except no one was hugging and kissing (even with the vaccine, it was too soon for that). The fact that everyone else was nonetheless cheering, whooping and yelling made me think they hadn't been listening.

I heard toasts to Damian, the country, the Institute, a few to God and Jesus. I raised my glass to Rajeev and said very sincerely, 'To drinking.'

And for the next few hours that's what we did. I have a clear memory of the first hour, but after that things get hazy. When

I was still vaguely lucid Damian broke away from his entourage to come talk to us. He told us we all deserved to be up on that stage, and even though he was a little drunk, I'm sure he meant it. Right before he went back to his people he said, 'Rebecca, we didn't finish our conversation this morning. Let's continue Monday.' Stupidly, all I did was nod, although fireworks were going off in my chest.

At some point Rajeev and I joined Chris and Gulmera. Chris didn't drink, so he was fine, but she could barely stand. She was mostly trash-talking the other guests, laughing at hairstyles, mocking dresses. Then she leaned toward me and whispered, 'You're amazing. You're so strong. After what you went through, most people wouldn't have gotten up.'

I was in no state to tell if this was a simple compliment or a backhanded one; it felt a bit like my mom congratulating me for making the eighth-best Pompeii diorama.

By one o'clock most of the guests had left. Chris said, 'This has been wonderful, but now I need to go and dance for five hours.'

He air-kissed mine and Gulmera's cheeks, then high-fived Rajeev.

'I think we'll go as well,' said Rajeev. 'Let me just use the bathroom.'

'Me too,' said Gulmera, and I was left on my own. I didn't mind; it gave me time to replay what Damian had said. I imagined the two of us in his office, me making a great point, him nodding vigorously. To stop myself being nervous I'd be looking in his direction but not directly at him; part of my gaze would be on the Pacific's waves that kept lifting without ever arriving.

I was too absorbed in this fantasy – and also too drunk – to focus on what was going on around me. The people moving past were just vertical lines. Some made sounds, but I kept them as irrelevant as a line of fence posts. I also wanted some of the lines to be carrying drinks, so every now and then I focused.

One of the lines was the Chinese woman with glasses, who'd gone from immaculate prettiness to sexy dishevelment. Her hair was a mess, her lipstick badly reapplied. The sleeve of her blouse looked damp, as if some substance had gotten on there that had to be quickly removed. She and the black-haired man must have been fucking in the bathroom or a stairwell. I liked that they'd been celebrating properly.

Rajeev came back first. 'Can we go?' I asked.

He sighed. 'We really should wait for Gulmera.'

'She could be ages.'

He nodded but didn't say anything else. And so we waited. My eyes kept closing, and as soon as they did I started to feel unsteady. I had to open them every few seconds, and on the third or fourth time I saw the dark-haired man at the edge of my vision, again with his back to me as if he was trying to hide, ashamed to show his face. To respect that I closed my eyes and saw once again the swell of the Pacific.

'Sorry,' Gulmera said. 'I passed out in there.'

Rajeev laughed. 'It's definitely time to go. Rebecca, are you coming or do you want to sleep here?'

'Are there beds?' I opened my eyes. The man was gone.

'Let's go,' I said, and headed toward the elevator. I didn't wait to see if they were following; I wanted to leave as soon as possible, to see no one else. I pressed the button, then pressed it again to make sure. Footsteps on the stairs behind me made me look round. 'Wait up,' said Rajeev, but behind him there was a tall man with sharp features and thin lips shadowed by a moustache. Thick, very black hair hung over his forehead. He smiled at me and I smiled back and if Rajeev hadn't been there I'd have asked the man if he minded turning around. I wanted to know if it was his head I'd been staring at earlier. He was possibly someone else.

LUKAS

W HEN Tomasz and I were growing up our father told us many stories whose moral was the same. Whether it was the tale of how he and my mother first met on the tram they took each morning, or the story of how his father nearly died in a flood, he'd usually end with a sigh, a scratch of the head, then say, 'Boys, everything is timing. That's why things happen.'

My father didn't elaborate on this, perhaps because his education ended at fourteen – he left school to work in a munitions factory – but more likely because for him this was a self-evident truth. Even during his final weeks in hospital he sought proof of his theory. He'd point to one of the other patients then proceed to relate the man's life history. As he told us about the car crash that had led one man to meet his wife, or the storm that had made two future business partners take shelter together, my father seemed to forget his pain. I never heard him say he believed in fate, or any kind of controlling power, though I wonder whether he derived comfort, or at least satisfaction, from the idea that apparently random conjunctions were meaningful within the context of a life. But it was a significance that could only exist in hindsight, once it was too late.

Inevitably, I've spent a lot of time thinking about how I got infected. It took a lot of contingencies, three of which seem crucial.

If I hadn't messed things up with Sasha I wouldn't have been in that bar on my own. If Ivanka hadn't found out that Pyotor was cheating on her, she wouldn't have been there either. And if Pyotor had been fucking someone who wasn't infected, then Ivanka would have been fine. To which you can add as many other variables as you can stand to think about: the absence of people she would have fancied more; the two for one special on vodka; my new haircut, which even Tomasz said looked decent; the fact that she had turned off her phone so did not see the begging messages from Pyotor. Even with all these things, she might simply have flirted and then gone home. And though I did consider the risks – there were already cases in Warsaw – I wasn't strong enough to say no. A single night with her would be a victory against the rules of attraction.

We had gone back to her place and had what I'd like to say was very passionate sex but was far less exciting. She said Pyotor's name a lot. I kept thinking about Sasha.

When I woke up Ivanka was buttoning her blouse.

'Come back to bed,' I purred.

She didn't stop what she was doing. 'Why?' she said, then passed me my clothes.

Obviously I can't be certain I got the disease from Ivanka. But until then I'd only slept with Sasha, and she was clear when we were all forced to get tested a month later. I suppose someone might have dripped their blood into my coffee, sneaked semen into my soup, but given that Ivanka tested positive at the same time as me it had to be her.

She was equally sure that I was to blame. While I spent the rest of the day after getting my diagnosis lying on the lounge floor, crying, she took more decisive action. She dispatched her two murderous brothers to get revenge. Since they were teenagers they had been involved in the kinds of criminal activities that made even someone with porous moral boundaries like Tomasz shake his head. They mostly dealt drugs, but also had overlapping sidelines in prostitution, webcam shows and blackmail. They kicked in our front door and then threw me down the cellar stairs. They probably would have tortured me – I saw them eyeing the power tools – if I hadn't flicked blood at them and asked if they wanted what their sister had. That stopped them, albeit not for long: apparently they came back two hours later wearing face masks and gloves. By then I was boarding the fast train to Kiev. As we left the station Tomasz sprinted onto the platform. He was running so fast, like it was his train too, and he was shouting something I couldn't hear. Although I could have opened the window, his expression told me not to.

For a long time I thought that getting infected was just bad luck. Sasha and I had been happily together for five years, and while I knew I shouldn't have been watching her cousin sunbathe topless, as I'd sat in the bar I'd been certain I could find the right words to fix things between us. That had worked with all my other mistakes – why should this be different? And as I walked through the camp in the dawn, considering my more recent mistakes, my apology to Valentina was already starting to form.

At home I undressed and considered masturbating, but I was too tired. For the few minutes before I fell asleep I was back at my desk, reaching for *Elective Affinities*, while the still awake part of me wondered if I'd ever see a copy again.

It was dark when I woke. I was cold. Outside someone was whistling a familiar tune I couldn't name. I tried to sit up to rearrange the blankets but didn't get far because my wrists had been handcuffed to the head of the bed. My ankles were also fastened. There was only one thing to do. I lay back and began to count out loud. I'd got up to forty-seven when I heard a giggle. Edie was under the bed.

'I guess I'm on top,' I said.

'That's right.'

I waited for her to speak again; she was in control.

She hummed to herself. Then she said, 'How did you sleep?'

'Very well, thanks.'

'I know you did. You didn't hear me come in.'

'Have you been here long?'

'Just a few hours.'

'Why didn't you wake me?'

'Oh, I don't know.' Her fingers drummed on the mattress. 'I probably wanted you to be well rested.'

I heard her shift position.

'Comfortable?'

'Not really. You have a very hard floor.'

'The bed is much softer.'

'Is that an invitation?'

'If you'd like it to be.'

'Fine.' Edie rolled out from beneath the bed. She was wearing one of my thick coats; underneath she was naked.

'I'm freezing,' she said and picked up the blankets. She lay down and covered us both. 'Let's warm me up,' she said and snuggled closer. She rested her head on my shoulder. As her breathing slowed I closed my eyes; perhaps we would sleep. I was drifting off when she whispered, 'So where were you all night?'

'At Rustam's. With Erik and Dejan. Things got out of hand.'

'How?'

'You know those guys. They always go too far. When I arrived they were using Kim as a doorstop.'

'Who else was there?'

'Just Khunbish.'

'So no one else was there?'

'Oh, Valentina was there too, but she wasn't part of the whole fiasco. Did you hear about it?'

'Maybe. Why don't you tell me?'

I told her, then said, 'I know I should have stopped them.'

Edie made a non-committal noise. She slid her hand down my chest, then let it rest on my belly.

'This is nice,' I said. She didn't reply. Her breathing was slow and even. 'I'm sorry I wasn't here,' I said. 'I'd been hoping to see you all day.'

She snuggled her nose into my neck. 'Why did you want to see me?' she murmured. 'Did you want to fuck?'

'Of course.'

'How sweet,' she said then kissed my neck. Outside people were running.

'Do you know what that's about?' I asked, but without much curiosity.

'No,' she said and moved her hand onto my penis. Someone banged on my door.

'Maybe you should see what they want,' I said, except I knew there was no chance of that. We were doing something new that I suspected she must have been preparing for a long time. She could only have got the handcuffs from a guard, which raised all sorts of questions. Even with their vaccine, they didn't like to touch us.

'They can wait. I don't want to be interrupted.'

Her hand began to move. She brought her lips to my ear. With each movement of her tongue her hand stroked up and down. This wasn't going to be quick. She'd probably make me beg.

'Lukas, why did you lie?'

'About what?'

'About Valentina.'

'What do you mean?'

'You didn't say she was there when I asked you.'

Obviously she wanted to add 'fake-quarrel' to the prisoner fantasy.

'Yes I did. I just didn't mention her the first time you asked.'

'You mean you lied.'

'I wouldn't call that a lie.'

'Most people would.'

When I replied, I tried to sound irritated, despite the fact that I was enjoying myself. 'What is this really about? Do you have something against Valentina?'

'Not at all. I just think there's something you're not telling me.'

I laughed. 'Are you jealous? It's a bit late for that. We're both fucking at least two or three other people.'

'Way more,' she said, and her grip tightened. 'But now I'm curious. *Did* you fuck her?'

'No, although I wanted to. At first I thought she wanted to as well, but then she changed her mind. She was incredibly high.'

Someone outside shouted my name.

'That sounds important. If you're not going to untie me, will you at least see what they want?'

'I know what they want.'

I opened my mouth to speak but she put her hand over it. She reached down, picked up one of my socks from the floor, then stuffed it in my mouth.

'They want to know why you raped her.'

Edie was kidding. Even though she wasn't smiling or laughing, she could still have been joking – someone who will hit you in the face for fun clearly has a strange sense of humour.

Someone banged on the door again.

'I'm amazed they haven't tried to come in. If I was looking for a rapist, I wouldn't have such good manners.'

I was still sure she was pretending until she said, 'It happened to me when I was fourteen. One of my dad's friends. He and my dad were drinking and then Dad got a call and had to leave for an hour. I knew this guy well, he'd been at all my birthdays. He was Uncle Max.'

I tried to push the sock from my mouth but it was too far in. Whatever my eyes were saying, it wasn't enough.

Edie got up from the bed. She left the room and a minute later I heard the toilet flush. When she returned she was wearing one of my sweaters and a pair of jeans.

'I thought my bladder was going to burst,' she said. 'Also, your toilet is filthy.'

She shook her head, then sat down next to me.

'Uncle Max was good-looking in a rough-around-the-edges way. Although he had a house, he sometimes slept in his car. In the mornings I'd see him, still unconscious, his head on the steering wheel. I used to think about kissing him. I practised on the mirror, sometimes on the back of my hand.'

She brought her hand to her mouth, perhaps to demonstrate, perhaps to relive the experience.

'Afterwards, Max said I'd wanted to. And I did like him kissing me. Apart from his scratchy beard, he was a good kisser. In my mind we'd never gone further than that, so when he started touching my tits it felt wrong. I told him to stop, but he didn't, and when I shouted he hit me. Not very hard, but it was a shock, and then I was scared he'd hit me again.'

She stood up, then sat down again. She spoke with her hand on her throat.

'You know what surprises me? I didn't think you liked getting rough. Every time I asked you to be dominant, to pretend to force me, you always got shy. If you like to fuck that way for real, why couldn't you pretend?'

Her voice cracked. Although she didn't cry, she was close to it. She bit her lip, then looked up at the ceiling.

'It's stupid that I'm shocked. I don't know you, and you don't know me. All we've done is play games.'

Edie lifted the blanket and looked at my body in a detached way. She could have been a coroner lifting the sheet off a corpse.

She dropped the blanket, then slapped me across the face. 'That felt good,' she said. 'Let's do it again.'

I managed to twist my head to the side, so all she got was my ear, but her fingernail scratched me. She put her finger on the spot, then showed me the blood and laughed.

'You bleed so easily. If I were you, I'd be really worried. You know how it is. What seems like a small problem turns into other things. You go see Dr Nilsson about a rash on your stomach and two weeks later you have cancer. After they find you guilty they'll put you in some little room without windows. Given how long you've been infected, you'll probably die in there.'

That removed any trace of doubt that Edie was being serious. We didn't joke about each other getting sick. Even if you disliked or hated someone, you weren't glad when they got ill: no one liked the reminder. I didn't know what Valentina had said, but the longer I seemed to be hiding, the worse it would appear. Through the sock I tried to say, 'You have to let me go, I didn't do it, please believe me.'

I kept talking, hoping to make her curious enough to remove the gag. All Edie did was smile. When I stopped, she yawned.

'I suspect you'll make out that she wanted you to. It's a cliché, but it might convince some of the men. And Valentina is definitely a tease. She floats around and pouts and has that whole ethereal vibe. She drives me crazy too. There's probably no one in the camp who doesn't want to fuck her. No one has, though, for the simple reason that she doesn't want to. Even the biggest assholes have respected that. It's one of those Important Boundaries you're always going on about.'

Calmly, she hit me in the chest. It wasn't painful, I wasn't winded, yet that was when I really started to be frightened of what she might do. There were knives in the kitchen. She could strangle me. Put out my eyes. Chop off various things.

The next time she raised her arm I flinched, although she was only scratching her cheek. She laughed, then shook her head, as if she was answering a question.

'And of course you didn't think how this would affect other people. I feel totally sick, like I've been poisoned, but I'll be OK. The person I'm most worried about is Min-seo. She depends on you. What's she going to do when you're not around?'

Edie stood, then went to my bedside table. She opened it and took out the pack of cigarettes she kept there.

'Don't go anywhere,' she said and left the room. I guessed she was going to light her cigarette from the cooker, though the kitchen might give her ideas. As well as the knives, there was a hammer, a skewer. I'd broken a glass a few days ago and the shards were on the table.

When Edie returned her cigarette was half-smoked. I couldn't see a knife in her hand, but it could be concealed.

She flicked ash on the floor, took a long drag, then blew out the smoke. She didn't look at me as she spoke.

'How hard did Valentina fight? Is that what made it exciting? Even if you could talk, you probably wouldn't tell me the truth.

You don't have the guts. You're always wearing a mask, even when we're fucking.'

Edie took out another cigarette, then lit it with the tip of the one she was smoking. 'What really makes no sense about this, and makes me even more sad, is that you've been so dumb. One of the reasons I liked you is that you're smart. Not as smart as you think you are, but still someone who can say clever and interesting things most of the time. And of course you have a nice cock. Let's not forget about that,' she said, and lifted the sheet.

'But you must also be stupid. Only someone really dumb would think they could get away with rape in a place like this. You'd have had to kill her. If you were actually smart, you'd have made it look like a suicide.'

She dropped the sheet on the floor. She spoke without looking at me.

'Max was dumb in a different way. My dad would have shot him if he'd found out. And if I'd gone to the police they'd definitely have been able to get him for something, what with me being only a minor. Oh, I suppose he might have guessed rightly that I'd be too traumatised and ashamed to say anything to anyone. But he wasn't smart. He had no plan. He just did it and then was lucky.'

After that she went quiet. She sat and smoked and stared at the wall as if I wasn't there. Even if I'd been able to speak, I'm not sure what I could have said.

Her cigarette was almost finished when fists hammered my door. Then I heard glass breaking and Erik shouting my name.

'I suppose this was bound to happen,' said Edie. 'Oh well.' She stood up, took a deep drag on her cigarette, then put it out on my penis.

If you've never been burnt in a sensitive place you can't imagine how it feels. Although talking about how it feels is already a mistake, as this suggests that the pain is separate from you, a visiting sensation. But there isn't you and it: there's only the pain.

Dirk was first into the room. He stopped when he saw me naked and chained to the bed.

'What is this?'

Edie shrugged.

'What have you done to him?' He bent over me. 'Oh. I see. That's appropriate, but premature. We need to have the trial.'

'Bullshit we do. You've seen the state of Valentina. You think she wasn't raped?'

Dirk held up his hand in objection. 'I agree. She was. But was it this man? This we don't know yet.'

I'd never liked Dirk. In his former life in Bremen he'd almost certainly been in charge of giving out dog permits or fishing licences. He must have had a clipboard. Even in a glorified leper colony he had the air of a petty official who still lived with his mother. Whenever he didn't agree with someone, he wouldn't enter into a debate, he'd simply fold his arms and tell them they were wrong. Yet his pedantic approach to life might be all that would stop me being lynched.

'Edie, how long were you going to keep him here? We've been searching for hours.'

'And you only just thought to look inside now?'

'We considered it. But it seemed too obvious a place to hide.'

Erik laughed as he came in. 'Alright, we're idiots. But we found him in the end.'

Dirk scratched his chin and nodded. He threw a blanket over me, then stood aside to let more people enter the room. Brendan came in first, followed by Enzo and Mikhail. Having six people standing at the foot of my bed made me feel very strange; the only thing missing was a priest.

Erik put a hand on Edie's shoulder. 'How about you unlock him? Or have you done something dramatic with the key?'

'I wish I'd thought of that. Now where did I put it?' She put a hand in her pockets, then looked on the bedside table. But this was all theatre. 'Maybe it's under here,' she said, and whipped off the blanket.

'What's that?' said Enzo. 'Does he have a disease?'

Mikhail leant over and lifted my injured penis with his cold fingers. All I could do was make a muffled shout of protest. Mikhail moved my penis from side to side with the curiosity of a naturalist who has found an unusual growth. 'No, it is a burn,' he concluded.

Erik sighed. 'Edie, you've really been having fun, haven't you? Remind me not to piss you off. Now please unlock him.'

Edie swore and reached beneath the mattress. She brought out the key, unlocked my hands, then stepped quickly back. The first thing I did was take the sock out of my mouth. Then I covered myself with the blanket and said, 'I didn't do it. I don't know what Valentina told you, but you have to believe me, I'd never do that. I spoke to her, and then we kissed, and that's all that happened.'

'Bravo,' said Edie. 'Spoken like a rapist.'

'Erik, tell them. You went in after me.'

He looked away. 'I dunno, mate. When I went in, she was out cold and her clothes were all messed up.'

Dirk frowned. 'So why didn't you say anything?'

'I probably should have. But I just thought things had got intense.'

'Bastard,' said Edie. 'Next you'll say that most women like it rough.'

Mikhail turned to Erik. 'What do we do now?'

'I guess we should take Lukas to the meeting house. It'll take a while for everyone to gather. Brendan, why don't you stay with Lukas? Come to the meeting house in half an hour.'

'Wait,' I said. Things were moving too fast. I didn't want to have a trial, and certainly not without having more time to prepare. The last one had been a farce.

'We can work this out. If you'll just let me talk to Valentina, things will be—'

Edie cut me off. 'So you can try and convince her she was confused? Or that she led you on? Forget it. You won't be allowed near her.'

'Come on, Edie,' said Erik. 'Help me round up the flock.'

'Gladly,' she said, then spat at me. I understood why Edie was taking the accusation so personally – but nothing had been proved. Our history should have counted for something.

'You'd better get dressed,' said Brendan. He didn't look at me as he spoke.

'Brendan, I don't know what's happened, or why Valentina thinks I raped her, but I swear I didn't. You know me. Have I ever done anything like this?'

Reluctantly, his eyes met mine. 'No. And I don't want to believe you did. Although it looks bad. Something happened to the poor woman.'

'What did she say?'

'I don't know exactly, I haven't seen her myself. Apparently you pushed her against the wall and she hit her head and lost consciousness. The next thing she knew, you were on top of her and had your hand over her mouth.'

'That's not true,' I said, then hesitated. Only the second part was a lie.

'I'll give you some privacy,' said Brendan and went out of the room. I picked up a pair of trousers and a shirt, then realised they were both dirty. Wearing clean clothes wasn't going to get me out of trouble, but I still wanted to make a good impression. In court Tomasz always wore an expensive dark blue suit. He once said, 'I have to be the best-dressed man in that room. I want to look so good people will think I couldn't be guilty of anything.' I don't know if it helped – the evidence against him was usually overwhelming – though perhaps it softened the verdict (which was never all that heavy, given all he did was steal and sell dope). I wondered what he'd do in my situation. If he couldn't talk his way out of something, he'd usually run. When I told him things would catch up with him in the end he laughed then said, 'Not always.'

The first time I'd seen him truly worried was after he got caught stealing a truck full of cigarettes. It was right after my night with Ivanka, and I was feeling so good that his arrest didn't worry me much. My older brother seemed invulnerable. But when I entered the visitors' room I found him slumped forward and weeping like a boy who feared the wrath of his father.

'What is it?' I said. 'Are you hurt?'

'Agata says she's thinking of leaving me. She says she will if I'm convicted.'

'Oh.'

I wanted to say that she didn't mean it, but she didn't seem like someone who made empty threats. Agata was a geriatric nurse who had been part of the team that took care of our father. She was from a small village, went to church at least twice a week, and quoted scripture to people with a straight face. They were completely ill-suited and for the first few months I was sure Tomasz would get bored of her. And yet she had something none of his other girlfriends had had: I'd never seen him happier. She could be very affectionate. After two apricot brandies she liked to rest her head on his shoulder and nuzzle his neck. I preferred to believe the rumours that as a teenager she had been so wild that at night her parents locked her in her room. Though Tomasz was uncharacteristically tight-lipped about their sex life, he did once drunkenly let slip that he sometimes found it difficult to cope with her demands. 'If I don't come she's insulted,' he said.

All I could do to comfort him that day in the police station was to assure him that once he was granted bail he'd be able to change her mind.

'She loves you. God knows why, but she does. She's not going to break up with you simply because you're a petty thief who trusts a total stoner to be his lookout.'

He wiped his eyes. 'You're right,' he said. 'I guess all those books haven't made you completely stupid.'

We laughed and hugged and then I told him about my impossible night with Ivanka. When I'd finished he said, 'I've never been more proud of you. She's your first real 10.'

Next day Tomasz was denied bail by a judge who called him a 'career criminal' and a 'public menace'. He was to be held on remand until his trial, which wouldn't be for at least two months. Agata's response was to break up with him immediately rather than wait for the trial. Tomasz was so distraught he not only refused to listen to my very reasonable arguments – that she was just lashing out and would almost certainly wait for him – but then attacked me back. He said a lot of nasty things, the main gist of which was that I didn't know shit about real feelings and that the main reason I liked books was because they couldn't disagree with me. This was so hurtful I wanted to stand up and leave, but then he went pale and started apologising. He leant forward and whispered that he was going to try to escape.

That wasn't an option for me. Only one person had tried to escape from the camp, a Greek man who was an experienced rock climber. Costas had tunnelled under the fences and made it down the first ridge, then got stuck on a ledge. When the guards found him, a day later, they lowered a rope to him. He grabbed it, and as they were pulling him up, he let go. Either he'd been too exhausted to hold on or he'd preferred to fall.

At the bottom of the wardrobe I found a clean white shirt and a pair of black trousers. What I really wanted was a tie, though it was ridiculous to worry about being underdressed for our primitive version of 'justice'. I'd have felt much happier if the authorities were involved, but they stayed away from everything except murder. As I gingerly put on underpants, then trousers, I realised that if the authorities weren't involved there would be no physical evidence. It would be my word against Valentina's.

'I'm ready,' I called to Brendan. 'How do I look?'

'Like a prince,' he said and tried to smile. He didn't want me to see how worried he was. There were limits to what our 'court' could do to me, but for people who didn't have much time left, the prospect of any period of detention was awful. The last person who'd been found guilty had been Charong. There hadn't been much evidence against him; the only witness was Louisa, who said she had seen him going into Marta's house on the night in question, something Marta could neither confirm nor deny as she was in a coma. When Charong was found guilty of attacking her, it was mostly on the basis of Louisa's testimony, despite her well-known views about the 'wildness' of Asian men. Charong was sentenced to solitary confinement for six months. He hanged himself after three weeks. A few months later, as she was dying, Louisa confessed that she wasn't completely sure she had seen Charong. 'I can't say for certain,' she said. 'But I definitely saw someone.'

If that was enough to put someone in a cell for what might well be the last few months of their life, then I was in a lot of trouble. I imagined myself trapped in a small room with no windows. How painfully time would pass. My heartbeat would be an awful ticking sound.

'Are you alright?' Brendan asked. 'You're shaking.'

'I'm cold,' I said, but I wasn't.

'Let's wait a moment,' he said. As soon as he opened his arms I moved towards him. He smelt of grease and onions.

'Do we have time?' I asked.

'Who knows?' he said, then undid his trousers.

REBECCA

O UTSIDE it was dark and quiet. Carlos's kiosk was closed. Apart from a faint odour of smoke from the fireworks it could've been a weeknight.

'Let's go to yours,' I said to Rajeev and he nodded. Going downtown, toward the Park, would take us into the madness. It also meant we wouldn't have to share a taxi with Gulmera, who lived in Lenox Hill.

But we weren't quite rid of her. Rajeev said we should stay with her until she found a cab, and of course he was right. This meant we had to walk with her to the end of the next block as no traffic was allowed near our building. Six years ago a disgruntled food hygiene inspector had driven a truck through our front entrance, then tried to shoot his way down to the laboratories where we were keeping a secret cure that was reserved for Jews. (The man wasn't even infected.) The incident hadn't bothered me much. Compared to the virus, it didn't seem real.

Thankfully we had no trouble finding a cab. Gulmera hugged us both then got in. She started saying something but I shut the door.

'Alright,' I said. 'Shall we go home and fuck?'

Rajeev pretended to think about it. 'What makes you think I'm that easy?' he said, then offered me his arm. 'Let's walk to Van Cortlandt, it'll be easier to get a cab.'

For the first couple of blocks we didn't see any people, and then a bunch of glowing numbers appeared. They were fives, though they looked like the S of the Superman logo, and they were fluorescent. At first it was eerie because the rest of the people's clothes and faces were dark; after they got close I saw it was only four college-age guys and two girls. They weren't doing anything threatening but it was a strange night and there were more of them. When the guy in front raised his arm Rajeev and I flinched.

'Relax! We just want to high-five you folks,' he said.

'We're high-fiving everyone!' said one of the girls.

'Because it's the fifth.'

Rajeev recovered quickly. 'No problem,' he said. He raised his arm and the guy slapped his palm.

'Good job,' said the guy and Rajeev laughed and then the others high-fived him too. And I understood. By putting their skin on others' skin they were showing they weren't afraid.

We walked on. There were more fireworks. We went beneath the tracks and when we emerged we saw fires in the park. The bonfires were large, at least ten feet high, the air around them smudged. We had to go and look.

Inside, people were grouped around coolers and candles, perched on campstools and inflatable cushions, nodding to a composite soundtrack from various cellphones. Mostly they were young but I saw a few clusters of the elderly, one of them sat around a table covered by a white cloth on which the carcass of a turkey gaped. There were strollers, there were baby carriages. A teenage boy had a pair of greyhounds with the number five painted on their backs.

Though we tried to make careful progress toward the bonfires, we had to apologise several times for stepping on couples lying on the grass. So many people were standing round the fires that we couldn't see much until we were very close. No one complained about us making our way toward the front. Whatever was happening, people wanted to share it.

There were three fires, two that were ten feet high, and a smaller one the height of a person. I couldn't see any cops or firefighters, so I guessed this was all unofficial. It must have taken a lot of planning, and they'd have needed trucks for so much wood and the metal frames that enclosed the fires. The base of the frames was a large metal circle from which struts rose then converged to form a shape that looked like a volcano with a long tube stuck on top. I guessed they had been specially made.

Rajeev and I watched the flames in silence. The mood was subdued, more reflective than celebratory. But all those strangers standing close together was itself a statement. And there was nothing fake about this trust. When someone coughed or sneezed, only a few of them flinched. I wondered how they'd react if I told them about experiment twenty-six. With disbelief, annoyance, perhaps anger. They wouldn't have understood why it was necessary.

It was calming to stare at the flames. I was beginning to relax when people started whooping. The shouts and cheers had an edge that made me think of long poles and flaming torches, though not a noose. We'd moved on from there. The infected had been made to drink gasoline.

'What's happening?' I asked a man with a shaved head and a lightning bolt tattooed on his neck.

'They're bringing out another,' he said, then took out his phone.

'Another what?'

His face shuffled between surprise and disbelief before settling on amusement. 'You'll see,' he said, then lifted his phone as the crowd on the other side of the fires parted to allow a convoy of wheelbarrows stacked with logs. I thought they were going to replenish the existing fires but instead they made a new pile. When it became clear no more wood was coming, a slow handclap began. Its tempo quickened. I still had no idea what to expect. Acrobats, dancers, perhaps contortionists.

The entertainment, when it appeared, was an anticlimax. A line of ten people brought a long tent-like creature hoisted up on poles. The head had a big red crown; there was a long blue tail. To me it looked like a lazy version of a Chinese dragon; everyone else went wild. As the clapping got faster, the shouts louder, the scene felt primitive, like an old ritual, although it couldn't have been more contemporary. All the people carrying the creature were wearing the same mask. On it there was a good-looking young man's face I didn't recognise.

The creature was brought to the new pile of wood then lowered onto it with all the care of a hen positioning herself over a nest. The metal frame of the thing – its skeleton – resembled the metal structures of the other fires. The crowd had already enjoyed watching this creature burn three times, yet clearly that wasn't enough.

The masked people spent a few minutes stuffing wood inside the creature while the crowd kept cheering. It occurred to me that the man on the masks might have been famous and that this was all some sort of tribute, but when I asked the tattooed man next to me he said he didn't know him either. And then Rajeev said, 'Oh. It's the virus.'

'What is?'

He pointed to the creature. 'I think that red bit on top is supposed to be the viral capsule.'

I couldn't see it. The whole thing was so cartoonish it could have been a sporting mascot. I had to look again at the long blue tail to realise he was right.

'Burn the fucker,' yelled a woman next to me, and the crowd took up the call.

'Maybe we should get out of here,' I said to Rajeev.

'Why?'

'Because this is bad,' I said, and felt annoyed at having to justify the obvious. But leaving was impossible. The crowd was too thick. I couldn't understand why they were so excited about watching a lousy model get burned. If after five years they still needed this for catharsis, perhaps they didn't really believe they were safe.

One of the masked figures raised an arm and the crowd went silent. The space above our heads filled with bright rectangles.

'We are all Chad Williams,' he said in a deep voice, and the crowd repeated this back to him. It was creepy and cultish and incredibly pretentious. If you're truly grieving, the loss a constant source of hurt, the last thing you want to do is make a performance out of your sorrow. You can barely say their name.

The fire was lit with a surprising lack of theatre. Gasoline chugged onto the wood and a burning stick was inserted. When the flames roared, the crowd made a sighing sound of relief. A few people started to drift away, though I suspected most of them were going to stay until there was ash.

'Come on,' I said to Rajeev, and he didn't argue. We had to push through the first few layers of the crowd, who were oblivious to us. At that moment only one thing existed for them.

After that we still had to pick our way through the people on the grass, which was even more difficult than earlier because a lot of them had passed out. Some were in pretty bad shape; when I stood on a woman's hand she didn't even stir. She was by no means in the worst condition – a few people were naked. One couple had blacked out while fucking. At least he'd been wearing a condom.

'I wonder how they'll feel tomorrow,' said Rajeev.

'Terrible. But they'll tell their friends it was the best night of their lives.'

'I've never understood it. If you're really trying to celebrate something, why drink so much it puts a stop to the evening? It's like they want to avoid the thing they're supposed to be happy about.'

He was right. If they truly believed this was a wonderful, special night worth celebrating, why hadn't they tried to stay up? Instead of being awake to greet the rising sun, that symbol of hope and new beginnings, etc., they were passed out with their junk on display.

We got delayed at the gates by a scrum of people jockeying for position around a large tent. When we got closer I saw a sign that said FREE V TATTOOS. Next to the tent a girl with green hair was proudly showing off her roman numeral despite being in obvious pain. I heard her tell another girl, 'And I'll keep updating it. Next year I'm going to add an I, then another I the year after, and another the year after that.'

'Yeah, but what about after that?' said her friend, and the green-haired girl looked confused.

As we stood on the corner, waiting for a cab, I was so exhausted I wanted to lie on the ground. Even though it was 3 a.m. I felt that the sun should be rising. It was time for the darkness to end.

I passed out as soon as we got in the cab. The next thing I remember we were bumping onto the Throgs Neck Bridge. I lifted my head from Rajeev's shoulder to peer out the window but there was only black water and black sky.

We came off the bridge into Bay Terrace, where all was quiet. The party was in Auburndale. In doorways, on stoops, people were drinking from open containers. On several stages there were DJs, drummers, people on stilts. Dancers were on car roofs. The costumes had no particular theme. You might have thought it a neighbourhood Mardi Gras had it not been for the fluorescent fives, the fives composed of candles, flowers, LEDs, flags of former countries. I saw a lot of masks. Yet there was no sign of the fear and anger I'd seen in the park. They were just celebrating.

The only trouble we saw was in Fresh Meadows. We had to slow down because the road was partially blocked by ambulances, squad cars and fire trucks, most of them spread along the south edge of Kissena Park. Bodies lay on the ground and on stretchers. Although I couldn't see any fires, even with the windows shut I smelled smoke.

We drove slowly past a vacant lot in which a group of young women were dancing in the red light of a strobe that made each dancer into a jerking comic strip. Maybe they were trying to portray ghosts, or souls, but all I did was see and not see them; they were both there and not.

Rajeev's apartment smelled of pine air freshener, faded incense, leftover shrimp foo yung. The previous tenant had painted the windows shut and nailed them as well, because as far as she was concerned sick people were capable of anything (though not, apparently, breaking a window). While this broke every safety code, the rent was unbelievably cheap.

I went and fell onto his couch. It was wonderful to stretch out. Closing my eyes made me see the dancers from the vacant lot, their arms and legs jerking.

'Do you want anything?' Rajeev called from the kitchen. 'Water?'

'Please,' I said. Suddenly I was dizzy. I thought I'd sobered up but I felt sick. I must have looked bad because when Rajeev came in he said, 'What's wrong?'

'I don't know. Maybe I'm coming down with something.'

I wondered if I should test myself again. I'd had the tests at work for three years; their shelf life wasn't forever.

He put his hand on my forehead. 'You don't have a fever. Are you in pain?'

'No. I just don't feel right.'

'Maybe you're dehydrated.' He handed me the bottle and I drank half of it.

'Better?'

I nodded and lay down on my front. I shut my eyes again. It felt good to see nothing but know someone was there. I moved over, then said, 'Come and sit by me.'

I felt his weight on the couch, heard it softly creak.

'Maybe I'm just tense. There's an iron bar in my neck.'

He asked if I wanted him to rub it. I nodded and then his hands moved my hair aside. He stroked the skin, then applied pressure. It wasn't hard enough, but I didn't say anything: I hate talking during massage, it defeats the point. I'd been to a lot of masseurs who wanted to act like therapists, even after I'd asked them to remain silent. I wanted hands, not a voice.

Rajeev moved his to my shoulders. This was good, and yet I knew it could be better. Thankfully that blouse had easy buttons so I was able to undo them with my eyes shut. Once the last button was free he slid my blouse off my shoulders. It felt so much better having him touch my skin, especially once he started working my shoulders harder. After a few minutes I reached behind and undid my bra. I didn't mean this as a sexual gesture but as soon as I'd taken it off I wanted his hands on my breasts. It's remarkable how you can forget being totally exhausted or starving hungry as soon as there's the chance to have sex. Obviously this makes good evolutionary sense, though it sometimes made me uncomfortable. When I wanted to fuck was it me, Rebecca, who wanted to, or was it just a physiological drive? How could I decide whether or not to give in?

Rajeev's touch became lighter, more like a caress. His hands travelled up and down my back. He shifted position so he was kneeling over me. I raised myself slightly, allowing his hands to reach round, and as he caressed my nipples he pressed himself against my ass. I almost said something – we'd agreed that grinding could easily lead to unsafe sex. Having to pause to put on a condom was nothing compared to the five minutes it took to prepare a screen. No wonder so many smart, careful people, who understood the risks, ended up infected.

With Rajeev that had never been a worry. Everything he did was considered; there was nothing instinctive about him. I'd never expected him to get carried away. There had even been a few occasions when he was the one who stopped me making a mistake.

So when he pulled down my trousers I was speechless. Having ungloved fingers touching me felt amazing. At least I had my panties on, which meant we were still safe, but this was as far as we could go. Yet I was dreading hearing him speak; he'd need permission before going further, and there was no way I could agree. We'd have to stop and prepare the fucking screen.

If Rajeev wasn't acting like himself, then neither was I. All the booze, coupled with the hormones, had me totally confused. I could say it wasn't me who pulled down my panties and said, 'Go on.' But for one night I must have wanted to stop being careful. Life during the outbreak had been exhausting and awful but at least everyone was trying to be safe. Attempting to be careful while everyone else was acting like they were immortal had been so much harder. I knew I was judged every time I said I couldn't meet for drinks or brunch (or have unprotected sex). Sometimes I could almost see them doing the little sums of pop psychology, adding *trauma* to *grief* so as to arrive at *screwed-up*. It was interesting (i.e. fucking annoying) that so many people who weren't virologists or immunologists did not stop to consider that I might conceivably have rational reasons for not wanting to eat avocado toast in a room full of strangers.

Some of these people would no doubt have considered me a vanilla fuck. I've only ever really liked missionary. Being on all fours feels strange and impersonal because it means I can't see the other person, and for me that's always been important. Fucking is all about who you're doing it with. And yet that's how Rajeev and I had penetrative sex for the first time. It felt amazing. I couldn't think about anything except what he was doing. At no point did I turn around, or speak, and he didn't say anything either. We were just two people letting go. His rhythm was so steady I thought we'd never have to stop.

My orgasm was horribly premature. Rajeev must have been waiting for me, because shortly afterward he pulled out and I heard him gasp. Some of his cum touched my leg but I didn't care. I lay down, then he lay on top of me, propping himself on his arms. I felt calm and my mind was clear. I loved the warmth and weight of his body.

We lay like that for a long time. A faint light was oozing into the room when he whispered, 'That was incredible.'

'Yes,' I said. 'It was perfect.'

LUKAS

As I got dressed I wondered what to say in my defence. In my post-coital calm I realised I had to come clean and tell them everything, and not just for moral reasons: I'm a terrible liar. And while I didn't *want* to be locked up, it wasn't unfair. You have to pay for something.

'Are you ready?' said Brendan.

'I think so,' I said, then hesitated. I wondered if I'd see my rooms again.

On the way to the meeting house people stopped talking when they saw us. Most of them stared but a few said hello – at least some were keeping an open mind.

We were early, so we walked slowly around the building. The windows of the meeting house were coloured holes in the dark. They seemed to hang in the air without support.

'It's a grand building, isn't it? Do you know the story of it?'

'I think so. Wasn't it built by the Swedes?'

'That's right. And they had to fight for it. Most people wanted it to be a church, especially the Yanks and the Russians, who were putting up most of the money. The Swedes had to hold their feet to the fire to make it a place for all faiths.'

'They probably wouldn't be happy with how that's turned out.'

He laughed. 'No, they wouldn't. Now there's only the Gnostics, who I'm sure don't have any interest in all this pretty stained glass.'

'Isn't that better? Can you imagine being stuck here with a bunch of evangelicals?'

'I suppose so. Although they wouldn't last long. Erik would strangle someone who told him he could be saved. I was brought up Catholic, so I have my own issues with the bastards, but Erik's even worse.'

'I know. Last night he gave me a really hard time about the idea of heaven, like I was the one who'd invented it. He was furious.'

'He hates the faithful alright.'

'Why?'

'Not sure. It's hard to tell with Erik. But I don't think he hates the Gnostics. I saw him having a few words with them when we were looking for you. He was probably just fucking with them.'

I'd have asked more about this if Brendan hadn't taken my hand. I was a little surprised, but it felt right. He knew how to forgive.

We didn't speak until we were almost back at the entrance. Brendan dropped my hand then said, 'Do you want to go around again?'

'No. Let's get this over with.'

The room was almost full. For an absurd moment I hoped it was all a nasty trick to bring me to a surprise party. I wanted cheers, applause, an ambush of balloons. Instead people seemed like they were trying to get as far away from me as possible. I knew this was because during the judgment they'd have to stand near the edge of the room, but as I walked to the middle I felt I was already being shunned.

Tomasz was a great believer in making eye contact with the jury; he thought it helped make a connection. As we waited for the last few people to arrive I rotated slowly, so I could see them all. I was glad to see Kim looking better, although his head was still bandaged. He was staring at me in a way I didn't like.

Thankfully there were a few friendly faces – Dejan and Khunbish nodded to me – but the person I most wanted to see was Min-seo. I needed her to speak in my defence. I was about to ask if anyone had seen her when Stephan took a step forward and began ringing a bell. The doors closed. People went quiet. In his white shirt and black jacket Stephan looked like an elderly butler calling guests to supper. Even though the room was silent Stephan kept ringing the bell. Its heavy, ponderous clang seemed too loud to come from such a little object. Stephan rang the bell for almost a minute, then placed it on the floor. He cleared his throat. His first question was always the same.

'Lukas, are you innocent?'

Knowing Stephan's question in advance didn't make it easier to answer. 'Yes and no' was the truthful reply.

'I didn't do it,' I said. 'This is a terrible thing, and I understand why Valentina has accused me, but I didn't rape her. I hope that together we can find out who's responsible.'

When Lucia stepped forward and spoke her voice was too loud. She was losing her hearing.

'If you didn't rape Valentina, why has she accused you?'

'Something happened between us,' I said, then realised this was too vague. 'The two of us were upstairs in Rustam's house and we had a short conversation. We kissed, but things didn't go any further because we had an argument. I lost my temper and pushed her and then she hit her head against the wall.'

'You fucking shit,' said Kim. Some others began shouting, and Stephan had to hold up his hand for quiet. Once they stopped he turned to me and said, 'Continue.'

'They're right,' I said. 'I can't defend it. I just lost control. Afterwards I made sure Valentina was alright, then I left her. I went to speak to Erik, and after that we went downstairs. I didn't see her again that night.'

Georges frowned as he stepped forward.

'So, Lukas, I'd like you to please tell us, in as much detail as possible, exactly what you and Valentina argued about. I think that will help us make sense of this awful event, because that's what we need, to make sense of it, and of course it's what we're all doing every day, trying to make sense of an awful event that has happened to each and every one of us, an event that is still happening and will keep happening for the rest of our lives.'

Several people sighed; one actually groaned. But there was no malice in these complaints. Georges was our beloved, boring uncle. We'd miss him after he was gone.

I told him we'd had a very strange conversation because she was really high. I said we'd talked about how long some of us had been sick, and about Kim dyeing his hair white, and that we'd ended up arguing about that.

'And maybe whatever Valentina took has affected her memory of what happened. Maybe she's confused.'

Clara threw herself forwards.

'How can she be confused about having a dick pushed inside her? Do you think she *imagined* being raped?'

'No, and I didn't say that.'

'You fucking did.'

'No. If she says she was raped, she was. But she's mistaken that it was me.'

The next three people asked more or less the same thing. Then it was Senk's turn. She took such a small, jerky step forward she had to take another to be level with the other people who'd asked questions. Her body had the tension of someone trying to suppress their shaking. Only her voice was steady.

'If you didn't rape her, who did?'

'I don't know. Apart from myself, the only person who saw her was Erik, but he was in there a very short time. After that we both had to stay downstairs to keep an eye on Kim. No one could have gone upstairs without us seeing them.'

Senk whispered something to Aleksandr. Her brother nodded. He took a long step forward and asked if I was accusing Erik.

'No. And as far as I know, he's not into women.'

'That's true,' said Lucia.

'Believe me, we've tried,' said Clara.

'And thanks for trying!' yelled Erik.

People were smiling at this as Jorge came forward.

'Why are we still having these stupid judgments? They don't discover anything. We're only doing this because it makes us feel important. When we stand in this circle we think we're big dogs. All we do is bark and bark. We're chasing a silly red ball.'

He folded his arms and looked pleased. No one bothered to reply. Many of the questions that followed Jorge's statement seemed to prove him right. Most went over the same ground as the previous ones, which was pointless, as I'd already said everything I knew. The rest were only questions in a rhetorical sense – really they were pronouncements on the intellectual and emotional differences between men and women, the effects of altitude on our minds, and a long complaint about the corruption that meant there was never any decent jam or honey in the camp store. In different circumstances I'd have found this enjoyable, though it wasn't going to help me. The judgments were supposed to enshrine the presumption of innocence, but in practice there was a strong bias towards guilty verdicts. Out of the twelve I'd attended, in only one had the person been acquitted (few doubted that Jorge had had to break both of Patrice's arms in self-defence). It wasn't hard to understand why in that situation people who ordinarily seemed easy-going became quick to condemn. Finally we had control over something. It felt like being free. And for some reason exercising mercy didn't feel as good.

Maybe that's why Agata had broken up with my brother after he was denied bail. She hated him being in that situation, but he was also the only person she could punish. I could tell this decision bothered her. Before Tomasz got arrested her attitude towards me had veered from suspicious to mildly contemptuous (she was incredulous that I, a scholar, hadn't read St Augustine). After she broke up with Tomasz she started ringing me just to complain about him. She attacked his character, his morals, his lack of education, his dishonesty, feeding his flaws through our conversation like the beads of a rosary.

Inevitably, I had to endure these harangues in person. She invited me round one evening to drink cherry brandy that tasted like cough medicine as she talked and talked, both of us staring at the TV, which was on mute. Her favourite channel mainly showed documentaries and films about Russian, Nazi or Soviet crimes against the heroic, martyred Polish people, and perhaps against the background of those old atrocities the growing crisis seemed tame. I got drunk as fast as I could. It was the only way I could listen to her saying so much terrible stuff about Tomasz, especially the things which were true.

When she kissed me I was so shocked I didn't immediately react. Her lips were soft and tasted of sour cherries, but I pushed her away. I stood up, then she did too, and I was turning to leave when she pulled off her jumper and T-shirt in a single fluid motion. That stopped me for an instant, during which I stared at her surprisingly elaborate red bra and flat stomach. She took off her trousers.

Ten minutes later I lay on the floor with burning knees. There was a growing, post-orgasmic shock as I realised what we had done. She wouldn't look at me. Neither of us spoke.

REBECCA

Next day Rajeev and I took a drive to nowhere in particular. We had empty roads; a clear sky; leaves about to fall.

As soon as I'd woken I knew what I wanted to do. I'd only slept four hours but felt completely fresh, not at all hungover (I was certainly still drunk). Before I woke Rajeev I spent a few minutes appreciating that we were in the same bed. I lay with my hand on his arm and listened to him breathe. For the first time there was nothing between us.

When I did try and wake him he refused to open his eyes. I had to put my tongue in his ear to make him come to life.

'Who are you? Where's Rebecca?'

'She's gone. You've been fucking her evil twin.'

'You are evil. Why are you awake? It's not even nine.'

'Because we're going to get up and take a quick shower and then go for a drive up the coast.'

'Are we?'

'Yep. We sure are.' I had all the swagger of a still-drunk woman who had just had proper sex with her boyfriend for the first time.

On the street it was a regular Saturday in Rajeev's neighbourhood. Children in woolly hats and gloves were being shepherded into SUVs. Some of the people in line for the German bakery were swaying slightly to the samba music blaring from a food truck.

Rajeev was parked at the end of the block. He unlocked the car, then hesitated.

'What shall we do about food? Do you want to swing by your place?'

'No need. Let's grab something on the way.'

'Great,' he said and sighed. The poor guy must have been overwhelmed. He was going to have to man up and accept that he was now dating a normal woman.

We got in, then drove a few blocks. 'Mexican?' he said and I nodded. When he asked what I wanted I had no idea what to say. It had been at least eight years since I'd eaten Mexican food, because I never made it at home. 'Anything,' I said. 'As long it has chorizo.'

'No problem.' He pulled over on the next block and went into a place that had so YUMMY! painted in huge letters on its window. At first I watched Rajeev inside, but after he'd ordered there wasn't much to see. I rolled down my window and as I did someone in an upstairs apartment dropped the needle on a record. I heard the crackle of contact, the hiss as the disc spun, and in those pre-music seconds I expected classic rock, the swell of an orchestra, one of Dad's jazz tunes. Instead there was the deep drone of a single instrument that set up a vibration in my stomach, lungs and throat that made them feel as if they were being turned inside out. I saw everyone on the street stop and look up at the apartment in surprise or anger or curiosity but only for an instant; then my vision was blocked by a flood of tears. The music lasted less than a minute, yet by the time it cut off I felt thoroughly emptied. For the last six years I'd been stuck in a trench I'd dug. Every day I walked back and forth and made the trench a little deeper. If you'd asked me right before the celebration how I thought the rest of my life would be, I'd have said working in the laboratory, eating on my own, being fucked through plastic. And yet somehow, in a single evening, I'd managed to climb out.

I liked this romantic notion, but it couldn't have been so sudden. My recovery must have been building for years, just like a disease doesn't start in one day. You can go for a long time without any signs that you, your cells, are being altered. Only when you faint, find blood in your urine, feel something hard beneath the skin, is this change revealed.

I'd dried my eyes by the time Rajeev came back. He was holding three large brown bags, plus two coffees in a cardboard tray.

'What's all this?'

'I wasn't sure what to get you, so I got one of everything. I hope that's OK.'

Right then he seemed like the sweetest man alive. How many other guys would have put up with my restrictions for so long? I hadn't gotten out of the trench on my own.

I leaned over and kissed him. For the next few minutes our tongues explored what was still unfamiliar territory. The only reason I stopped was because the smell from the bags was making a greater demand. I pulled out two burritos, handed one to Rajeev, then unwrapped the other and said, 'Race you.' I pushed most of it into my mouth in a greasy rush of meat and beans. I'd finished mine before Rajeev had taken more than a few bites. He kept chewing slowly as he handed me a quesadilla and said, 'I think you win.'

He swallowed, wiped his fingers, then started the car. There was traffic on the way to the Throgs Bridge, but once we were flying over the East River we were unstoppable. Sunlight jumped from every surface. All that space, above and below, gave me a sense of expansion. I was in the car with the cold wind whipping my hair and I was in the far distance, travelling over the water, pursuing the horizon. I wanted the bridge to stretch for miles, or better yet, never end. Having to slow and rejoin land made me sad. We went from being a flying ship to just another vehicle on the interstate. When I was a kid I'd hated long drives, the monotonous road, the constant threat of other cars, knowing that despite our superficial differences we were all heading in the same direction.

Thankfully Rajeev hadn't forgotten it was supposed to be a scenic drive. After Pelham Bay we took an exit and then flew over a small bridge so fast the water beneath flashed several times. Although it wasn't cold enough for the river to be frozen it had a metallic sheen. I imagined us following the coastline for days as if we were explorers.

In Westchester most of the clapboard cottages were marked with a red X. I couldn't see the number sprayed beneath, but since the buildings hadn't been burned, they were almost certainly zeros.

Seeing the river from the car made me want to get closer. Not that I was intending to swim; I'd rather die than go in the East River in winter. But only when you're right next to a big body of water can you appreciate its size and power, the way it pushes the land. I guess we want to get near wild animals for the same reason. There are boundaries you can't cross, and yet if you get close enough, you can forget they exist.

So when we saw a sign for Five Islands Park I told Rajeev to turn off. We parked then got out and followed a gravelled path that took us to a small bridge onto Harrison Island. We stood staring at the water while the wind numbed our faces; my hand was warm in his.

'It's so good to be out of the cage,' he said.

'Which one?'

'All of them. The city. The Institute. My apartment.'

'You're right about the last one. You really should move. You might enjoy having windows that open.'

'Maybe I will. What about if I moved to Chelsea? Would that be too close?'

I wasn't sure if this was his shy way of asking if he could move in with me. I must have paused long enough for him to misunderstand.

'It's fine if it's not OK,' he said. 'It was just an idea.'

I put my hand on his cheek. 'It wouldn't be too close. In fact, I'd really like that.'

'OK,' he said, then looked away. He was embarrassed by how glad he felt.

We walked back over the bridge, then wandered among the trees. Rajeev was delighted to find a bullet lodged in a trunk.

'It must have been there six or seven years,' he said proudly.

That was the only sign of the fighting. The burned buildings were gone. Life in Five Islands was back to its old level of hyper-exclusivity. The marinas were once again a pageant of long white boats named after mistresses. Private security guards regarded us with threatening, bored expressions. Everything was 'For Members'. We tried three different restaurants before we found one that would let me use their restroom.

Afterward we roamed like happy trespassers. The mansions were so over the top I pitied the architects. But some kind of evacuation order must have gone out because the residential areas were deserted. It was as if the inhabitants didn't realise the all-clear had sounded. We'd been walking for at least twenty minutes when a young guy with a buzz cut jogged past, then a few moments later we heard him coming back. 'Hey you guys,' he called. 'Wait a second.'

We stopped and turned.

'If you're looking for the booth, you're going the wrong way. It's over there,' he said and pointed behind us.

'Thanks,' I said.

'You're welcome. Hope there's not too much of a queue.'

He smiled and then loped off. In his tight shorts his buttocks were two fists.

Rajeev yawned, then said, 'What do you think he meant?'

'No idea. But he seemed nice. Let's investigate.'

Following his directions brought us to more mansions. There was nothing resembling a booth, no hut, kiosk or stall.

'I think that guy was fucking with us,' I said, and Rajeev nodded. He looked tired, and I felt the same. My hangover was gaining ground.

We were considering going back to the car when we saw someone who stuck out even more than us. She was young, looked either Japanese or Korean, and was dressed in a way that made me feel old. She wore a sparkly red waistcoat over a huge pink shirt. Her yellow trousers ended in a pair of green Dr Martens. A baseball cap turned backward held most of her hair except for two long strands that hung down the side of her face, one of them black, the other silvery white. In her right hand a gold phone was warbling out what sounded like distorted birdsong. She was headed straight for the mansion on the end of the row, a large two-storey house whose pillars made it resemble a wedding cake. It wasn't inconceivable that she lived there: people had bought property wherever seemed safe.

She went toward the gate, then turned right and walked along the security fence. She was heading straight for a wall, but just before she met it she vanished through a small gap I hadn't noticed. We waited briefly, then followed. Ahead of us her silhouette was like a key in a lock. Foolishly, I wondered if we were being lured into an ambush. She and some other colourful character could be waiting to attack us.

Without meaning to, I slowed so suddenly Rajeev walked into me.

'What is it?'

'Nothing. Sorry.'

'Do you want to go back?'

'No, it's fine.'

We emerged onto a small headland and saw the woman standing a short distance away. She had her back to us and had stopped ten feet from the edge of the cliff. Near the edge there was a phone booth in which a man stood, also with his back to us. He had very black hair, like the man at the party, but I was sure it wasn't him. We moved a little closer. The slow, Midwestern drawl I heard wasn't the right voice.

While I was preoccupied with the idle question of how that man *should* sound – Californian? French? – Rajeev addressed the more relevant issue.

'Why is that phone booth still here? And how can it be working?'

'Oh, it doesn't,' said the woman. 'At least not in the normal way.' She had a soft voice that might have been Canadian. I'd thought she was in her early twenties but now saw she was more my age.

'Right,' I said. 'But why hasn't it been taken away?'

By the end of the second year, they, like the ATMs, had been long gone.

She paused, then said, 'Originally it must have been from some-where else. Who'd put a phone booth here?'

'I really don't understand,' muttered Rajeev.

I lowered my voice. 'It's simple. He's using a phone that doesn't work. And she's waiting to go next.'

We moved closer so we could hear. The man hadn't paused since we'd arrived. His imaginary audience was obviously an excellent listener.

119

'And then I went to meet Linda at the park. We had such a good walk. She's doing very well. She loves her new job.'

He recapped what he'd done the previous day in agonising detail. I tuned out and stared at the unfocused line of the Long Island shore. One of Matthew's colleagues had a beach house we'd borrowed the last summer before the epidemic. There the days had passed in a blur of reading and swimming and staring at a sky that seemed both empty and full. We were the only two people in a land of do as you please. At the end of our stay it was a shock when I realised we had to resume our adult duties. 'Do we have to?' I said, and Matthew mimicked me in a whiny voice until I threw a shoe at him. But I was happy to go back. Our life was great. After four years together I thought I knew him well enough to manage any problems. The usual causes of strife did not seem threatening. Our sex was far from routine. We were able to say, without shame, what we really wanted. We weren't clingy or cold. We didn't spend too much time together and yet neither of us felt neglected. We understood each other's work enough to have a very nice mutual admiration society. We fought enough to respect each other. We knew the shape and limit of each other's neuroses, when to criticise and when to indulge. He let me worry that my head of department at Johns Hopkins was only promoting my work to deflect allegations of sexism but stopped me tweeting about it. As for me, I accepted that he was a mild hypochondriac who was in perfect health. I was happy to take his pulse and temperature whenever he had a cold.

'I'll go tomorrow,' said the man. 'That mustard you love is on special.'

He recited the shopping list. And then his voice got shaky. 'When I'm there I'll be thinking about you,' he said. He didn't speak after that. He stood holding the phone while he looked over the water, as if he was listening.

Eventually he put the phone down. He picked up a canister and sprayed the receiver, then the numbers. At least this weirdo observed basic hygiene.

As he came toward us I saw he was far older than I had thought, in his sixties at least. His hair was dyed brown, not black.

'Sorry I took so long,' he said to the possibly Canadian woman. 'There's always a lot to say.'

'I know,' she said, already moving toward the booth. She picked up the receiver and dialled a number, which was a nice touch of verisimilitude. Then she waited, perhaps while it rang. When she began speaking she was too quiet for us to hear.

I nudged Rajeev. 'Seen enough?'

'Yes, but can we wait? I want to go next.'

I smirked, then realised he was serious.

'You want to stand there and talk to yourself?'

'That's not what they're doing. They're talking to someone they've lost.'

'You can't talk to someone who isn't there. You can only *pretend* to.'

'What's the difference? Look at her. Is that someone pretending?'

The woman's eyes were closed and she was breathing in gasps. Her free hand clutched her hair.

'Thinking something's real doesn't mean it is. I'm sure this is a powerful experience for her. But it's still a delusion.'

Rajeev didn't reply, although I was sure he had something to say. He had this infuriating habit of starting an argument then refusing to engage once it got going.

The woman started speaking more quickly.

'Maybe her money's about to run out,' I said and Rajeev didn't laugh. I considered saying that if he wanted to wait, I'd see him back at the car. But if I did I'd be painting myself into a corner. When he came to the car I'd have to give him a frosty welcome, and on the way home he'd get the silent treatment. It would be a petty end to a good day.

So I didn't say anything even though I was thirsty and chilly and a small spike of hangover pain was scraping the inside of my head. Clouds were starting to assemble. Meanwhile the woman wept.

After she finished she wiped her eyes, then sprayed the phone. As she approached us I averted my eyes; I was embarrassed for her. I thought she'd be similarly awkward, but she stopped and spoke to us.

'Is it your first time here?'

'Yes,' said Rajeev. 'Do you come here often?'

'Every week. I really like talking to my brother. I guess he'll always be a teenager. Anyway, I don't want to make you wait any longer.'

She waved at us, then left.

'I won't be long,' said Rajeev. 'I don't even know why I'm doing it.' He smiled, and I didn't believe him. I watched him walk to the phone booth, hesitate, then pick up the receiver. He held it to his ear and dialled. I wondered who he was calling, whether it was his parents or brothers or if he'd gather the entire family. When he said, 'Hi Mom,' I walked away.

At the edge of the cliff I sat on a low fence that might have saved a young child or pet but which an adult could step over. I glanced back and saw Rajeev talking. Although I didn't approve, I wanted to think it was harmless. He was a functional adult who usually managed his grief; he wasn't going to be unhinged by this bit of make-believe.

I could tell my mind was trying to think about work, the cells that by now might be infected or not, so to clear it I stared at the sky. Most of the clouds were over Long Island. I watched two sailboats heading for the marina and pretended they were having a race (and maybe they were). The one with red sails was in front until near the marina when it stopped and was overtaken. I was cold, my head hurt, and I was dehydrated. But I knew these symptoms.

Rajeev kept talking. He had his back to me and was repeatedly gesturing in the air with his free hand as if he was angry about something. I was glad I couldn't see his face. Certain expressions, once seen, haunt a face for a long time. Later, when the person is smiling, happy, all you see is last week's fear.

To distract myself I took out my phone; the battery had died. I looked for something else to stare at but there were no more boats on the water. No planes troubled the sky. I looked down at the waves breaking on the rocks below and the sound of their crashing got louder. There was something odd about the noise; it wasn't in sync with the waves. Obviously this was impossible, an acoustic trick of the landscape, and I found it fascinating. If I paid close enough attention, if I did not let myself get distracted, surely I could marry what I saw and heard. I leaned forward to concentrate; with each wave I got closer. I'd almost brought the two together when Rajeev shouted my name. I turned and saw him running toward me.

'What is it?'

'You were really close to the edge.'

'No, I was fine. You didn't need to yell. Have you finished your call?'

'Yeah. It was really good. There was stuff I needed to say.' He hesitated. 'Are you sure you don't want to try?'

'Totally. But thanks.'

LUKAS

D IRK brought the trial back to the main issue.

'Valentina says she couldn't see the man because it was dark. She doesn't know when this was. If it was immediately after she lost consciousness, we can assume it was Lukas. If it was later, it could have been someone else. Lukas had an opportunity to rape her, which doesn't mean he did. So my question is for Erik.'

This caused an upset – questions were supposed to be aimed at me – but Stephan allowed it. I wasn't sure that his willingness to bend the rules was going to work in my favour. He, like so many of us, had tried to woo Valentina.

'Erik, you told me that Lukas left Rustam's house before dawn. When did you leave?'

There was only a slight accusation in the question, but I welcomed it. Muddying the waters would help.

Erik wasn't fazed. He'd spent his professional life being politely cross-examined.

'Not much later. Kim had just woken up, so I went to find Dr Nilsson. I wasn't gone long, maybe fifteen minutes. If some sicko had come in, he'd have had to move very fast. He'd have had to go straight upstairs, find Valentina, and then do it. Although I'm not saying that's impossible, it doesn't seem likely.'

My first thought was that Erik was trying to remove suspicion from himself. Then it occurred to me that perhaps he believed I was guilty. Maybe I'd been wrong to assume he was going to be on my side.

The next question also wasn't for me. Enzo asked Kim if he'd been awake when Erik left, and since Stephan had allowed Dirk's question, he couldn't refuse this one.

Kim hesitated before saying, 'No. I must have passed out again.'

Mikhail was in such a hurry to speak he forgot to step forward.

'Kim, could someone have come in while Erik was away?'

With obvious reluctance, Kim said, 'I suppose so. But they'd have had to be very quiet.'

While this didn't exonerate me, it seemed like grounds for reasonable doubt. My prospects were also helped by Brendan's question. He stepped forward and asked Kim if he had any way to prove he hadn't gone upstairs to Valentina after Erik left. This made Kim furious, because he couldn't. Though this was to my benefit, it was a slightly unfair question, given that Kim had been in no condition to do anything. Under different circumstances I'd have felt sorry for him.

Kim was still seething as Xiao Mei came forward. She asked Erik what condition Kim had been in when he left.

'Not good. He was still woozy. I doubt Kim could have got up the stairs, let alone done the rest.'

Although Erik was just being truthful, this thoroughness wasn't helping me. In a real court I could have said *Objection. Speculation.*

This line of enquiry continued. The next three people asked me more about what had happened to Kim. The fourth speculated that the loss of blood might have made him do things he didn't remember. Kim tried to interrupt several times, and in the end

Stephan had to warn him. That made Kim shut up. He didn't want to lose his vote.

Khunbish was next. He smiled as he stepped forward. His question caught me off guard.

'Lukas, can you describe what condition you left Valentina in?'

I didn't see the point of this; we'd already been over that.

'She was fine. After she hit her head there wasn't any cut or mark. When Erik entered he'd have seen her lying on the floor.'

Dejan stepped forward. 'Hello Lukas,' he said, then looked away from me. 'Erik, did you see what he says? Is it same?'

'Yeah, I saw all that,' he said. And I wasn't the only one who thought he'd finished speaking; Mohinder was already stepping forward when Erik continued.

'Valentina was lying on her back and her clothes were a mess. Her blouse was torn and her bra was off. Her skirt was pushed up around her waist.'

This was wrong. Her skirt hadn't been like that. Erik was mistaken.

Mohinder asked me why Valentina had looked so dishevelled if all I'd done was push her. He wanted to know why I hadn't mentioned the state of her clothing.

I said I'd undone her blouse while we were kissing, and that it must have got torn when she fell, and although I'd more or less said this already, it made a lot of people angry.

I'd been so preoccupied with defending myself that I'd forgotten to worry about Edie. At some point she'd come in quietly, concealed herself, and now was suddenly next to Mina. Joining the circle after the bell had rung was against the rules, but when she stepped forward Stephan said nothing.

'As you all know,' she said. 'I have been fucking this man. I came here nine months ago, and on my third day in the camp I fucked him for the first time. I haven't fucked him every day since then, but I've certainly fucked him most days. He's been good company, a decent fuck, and I thought I knew him. Most of you probably think he's normal, maybe a bit boring, and I can see why. He doesn't get into fights or arguments and is nice to most people.

'But if you fuck someone a lot you eventually get to see what they're really like when they're not in control. Stuff they say, stuff they do. They can't hide all the time.'

I relaxed after she said this. Talking about our sex life wasn't going to embarrass me: in our camp you could pick almost anyone and name their specialities.

As usual I had underestimated Edie. She rubbed her wrists – she had mild arthritis – then said, 'Sometimes the person doesn't even realise they've revealed themselves. For the first few weeks Lukas and I fucked in a way that was good albeit pretty vanilla. After that he started being more forceful, mainly stuff like holding my wrists or pulling my hair. I liked this, it made the sex better. Then one day when we were in his house he suddenly pulled down my trousers then pushed me against the wall. I didn't mind, but soon it was the only way he wanted to do it.'

This was a huge exaggeration; that had happened two or three times. *She* was the one who was always trying to get me to choke her.

'Obviously, him trying to dominate me doesn't mean he's a rapist. Except that over the last few weeks there have been some odd moments, which now make me think he wanted to.

'He put his hand over my mouth a lot. And he liked to press my face into the pillow. Sometimes he tore my clothes. It's pretty obvious what kind of fantasies he has.'

Almost none of this was true. It was a fine performance. She could easily have overdone it. Instead she'd given them enough to make a story of their own. Although I could have replied, offered my side of things, I couldn't think of anything to say to this person I really didn't know.

Edie's contribution would probably have been enough to earn me a guilty verdict, but she wasn't taking any chances. She whispered to Mina, who then stepped forward, glanced around the circle and said, 'Remember when Lukas got drunk and had to be tied to the perimeter fence. Lukas, why was that?'

This was a strange question, but easy to answer.

'I've no idea. Like you said, I was completely drunk. I don't remember much about that night. I was with Erik and Rustam, and at some point Rustam tried to teach me to play the drums. I've always assumed me being tied to the fence was their idea of a joke.'

Tanya hobbled forward, then rested on her crutches. 'Erik, is that true? Was it a joke?'

Erik coughed. 'Sort of. We were definitely drunk and acting stupid. Rustam was in a pretty wild state. He was making a list of things to do before he died. He wanted to watch the sunrise from the highest ridge and to walk along the river down in the valley. You know, a normal bucket list, though of course not permitted to *prisoners*.'

He paused and looked around meaningfully. He was always recruiting.

'Anyway, when it was Lukas's turn he said he really wanted to have a threesome with Ella and Sharnaz but they kept turning him down. Rustam then gave him this whole *carpe diem* routine and told him to go to their house immediately. All of you who knew Rustam will believe me when I say he wasn't telling Lukas to *force* them to do anything, just that he shouldn't give up hope.

'Lukas didn't take it that way. He started talking about going to their house and breaking down the door. He said he had nothing to lose and no one was going to stop him. In hindsight, I don't suppose he'd have done anything bad, but Rustam and I thought it was our job to keep him from doing that, and not only for his sake. We didn't want him bothering those poor women.

'We tried to hold Lukas back until he got violent. Then we figured it was best to tie him to the fence until he sobered up.'

I didn't remember any of that. While it was true that I used to have a terrible crush on Ella and Sharnaz, the rest was bullshit. I'd always taken no for an answer.

Things were looking bad for me. Of the remaining thirty questions, ten were going to come from the Gnostics, who were certain to find me guilty. They believed that everyone who was infected was guilty of something terrible – if not in the past, then at some future point. This was a brilliant doctrinal leap: even the most virtuous couldn't be sure they'd never do anything bad.

As she stepped forward Fatoumata stared at me, or to be more accurate, through me. Whatever her eyes were focusing on was much further away. At the previous judgment all she'd done was slowly raise her arms over her head, then bring them quickly down. This had unnerved Charong, who yelled at her to stop; he thought she was putting a curse on him. Knowing her, it could easily have been a blessing.

I didn't mind Fatoumata wasting time: the longer things took, the better: nothing makes more sense than postponing the inevitable. I could also see my accusers getting annoyed. Edie lost patience.

'Fatoumata, this is too important for us to wait while you go into a trance. If you don't want to say something, just nod and we'll continue.'

When Fatoumata didn't respond, Edie appealed to Stephan. He shrugged. 'She gets her five minutes like everyone else.'

This was apparently a rule he believed in enforcing. And so we waited. I enjoyed watching Edie fume. Although she was still going to win, at least I'd scored a point.

'Time's up,' said Stephan but Fatoumata didn't react. She kept staring into what might as well have been infinity.

As Bob lurched forward he looked me in the eye and said, 'Lukas, you make me sick. The only thing that makes life in this place possible is that we have respect for each other. That doesn't mean we have to be friends or even like one another. I've always tried to act decently towards you, even when you've been at your most condescending. I haven't held it against you that you think you're better than the rest of us because you've read more books. And the reason is simple. Even here, in the middle of nowhere, we're still civilised. We have norms and values, we have boundaries. That, Jorge, is why we have these judgments. If something happens that violates these rules we gather together to listen to evidence and testimony and everyone gets to have their say, even if that means saying nothing. What we don't do is grab the suspect and beat them, even when, especially when, the crime is as awful as this one.'

I had to endure his sanctimony for another three minutes, but at least it taught me something about Bob. The tone of his remarks veered from a breathy, faux inspirational voice – he referred to 'the better angels of our nature' – to a strident one in which he informed his listeners that it was their duty to give me the sternest punishment possible. Yet the real message of all this grandiloquence was Bob's deep and sincere affection for the camp. And this was more than him making the best of a bad situation. He actually liked being there.

He would have gone on longer if Stephan hadn't held up his hand. Bob smiled, said, 'Of course,' then relaxed into a swell of applause only he could hear. I was tempted to say nothing in reply. At that moment, my innocence, such as it was, didn't seem important. Six months in solitary confinement was probably what I deserved.

Tomasz used to joke that the only useful thing you could learn at university was how clever girls liked to fuck. But one transferable skill you learn from all those hours sitting on uncomfortable chairs is how to spot someone's weak point. If you listen to anyone for long enough, eventually they hand you a knife. So it was perhaps more from a desire to hurt Bob than to save myself that I said, 'Thanks, Bob. It's always good to hear your thoughts. I was particularly interested in what you had to say about being civilised. It's true we have norms and values here in the camp, a certain way of doing things. The same thing could be said of practically any group of humans. In eastern New Guinea there are tribes who honour their dead by eating them. You probably wouldn't call them civilised, and neither would I, but by your definition they are.'

'No,' said Bob, then shut his mouth; he wasn't supposed to interrupt.

'My point is that just because a group of people think something's normal, that doesn't mean it's "good". And by "good" I mean something that's generally beneficial. If you think these trials have anything to do with justice or the rule of law or any other feature of "civilisation", then you're even more stupid than you seem. And you seem *very* stupid.'

Several people laughed. But name-calling wasn't enough; I wanted to go further.

'A load of people spouting opinions is not a trial. If this were a real court there'd be physical evidence, DNA testing and sperm samples. And what kind of court would allow the same people to act as lawyers, witnesses *and* the jury? No one here is impartial.

Everyone knows me and Valentina. You like me or don't like me. I've slept with many of you.'

'And you were shit,' yelled Clara, but this truth didn't bother me.

'These judgments are like everything else here – they're supposed to make us feel better about being left to die in a bunch of cabins in the middle of fucking nowhere.'

'That's true,' yelled Erik.

'Have you ever noticed how cheerful Bob is all the time? His life before he came here must have been really bad. He must have had no friends. I know he says he was a drama teacher, though I think it's much more likely he was the manager of a mobile phone shop. No, the *assistant* manager. His boss was probably a nineteen-year-old girl he had fantasies about. Compared to that being here must be a holiday.'

People laughed. Bob was scarlet. His nails were hurting his palms.

'But Bob isn't a joke. Quite the opposite. He's a serious problem. If we were in a real prison or had any prospect of getting out of here, his plays and concerts would be just a way of killing time. But although we want distraction, maybe it isn't good for us. We've all been infected for at least five years, some of us for seven or eight. We don't have much time left. Should we really be spending this precious time singing songs and dressing up? Do we want to spend the rest of our lives playing let's pretend?'

I didn't mean this – I'd genuinely enjoyed some of Bob's productions – but I hoped it would strike a nerve.

'If the authorities wanted to keep us passive and distracted, they couldn't do better than all these shows and performances and free alcohol. Maybe Bob is working for them. Maybe he's not even sick.'

This last part was so paranoid it was pure Erik. When I looked at him he was grinning. But no one else was laughing or smiling at this ridiculous notion. Most looked thoughtful or confused; a few were glaring at Bob. I felt a small sting of regret, which I quickly swatted. Bob had picked the fight.

Of course, Bob had his supporters. The next three people didn't even mention the rape. They contrasted his community spirit with my selfishness, his humility with my arrogance. And they definitely had a point. I had nothing to say in reply. I couldn't say what I added to the camp. Although I tried (and failed) to do no harm, apart from my relationship with Min-seo I probably made no positive contribution. Even after three years my being there felt temporary.

I also didn't have much to say to the Gnostics when it was their turn. There was nothing personal about their attacks; they said more or less the same thing at every judgment. Each of them assured me that this judgment was not even a whisper compared to the great shout of the verdict that was waiting for us all. Rabbiya said I should pray to be found guilty because being put into isolation would prevent me sinning further. Hassan reminded me that God loves those who turn to Him in repentance and He loves those who keep themselves pure. *A bit late for that*, I thought.

The rest of the Gnostics were so deliriously high they didn't make much sense. There was the usual stuff about our flesh being only shit and clay, then a fun tirade from the one Brendan and I called Rasputin about the inevitability of darkness birthing darkness, and who could blame an ape for acting according to its nature? That almost sounded like a defence of what I'd done, until 'Rasputin' said that in the true light that never wavers, anything born of darkness will burn as long as time persists. That did not sound good. But by then I was tired of the stupid trial. With the verdict no longer in question, my only worry was whether I'd be allowed my books and papers in my cell. If I could work, the isolation might not be so bad.

When Erik swaggered forward to ask his question I wasn't worried about what he'd say. He couldn't do any more damage.

'Khunbish, how was Valentina acting when she arrived at Rustam's house?'

'She was laughing a lot and wanted us to drink with her.'

'Was she high?'

Stephan cleared his throat. 'Erik, you know the rules. You've had your question and he's answered it.'

Esther stepped forward.

'Wait,' said Erik. 'I need a proper answer. This one-question rule has never made sense to me. Does anyone really care if I say something else?'

He glared around the circle. Nobody objected. Stephan stared at Erik and something appeared to pass between them. Erik continued.

'Khunbish, was she high?'

'Yes, although I don't know what she'd taken.'

'So she was already high, and then she drank a lot. Plus she was in a bloody awful state because she'd just found out she has Alzheimer's. I know this is going to upset some of you, but isn't it possible she's mistaken about what happened?'

'We've heard this misogynistic bullshit already,' yelled Edie.

'Shut up. I'm not finished. I know it sounds like sexist crap to question whether it was rape or not. And usually it would be. The problem is that we can't know anything for certain. That's not Valentina's fault, and although Lukas is a scumbag, it isn't his fault either. The people who run this camp are the ones responsible. They didn't even send Dr Nilsson to examine her. Frankly, I'm amazed they even pretend to care when a murder happens. They probably have to stop themselves from giving the killer a medal.'

While this was one of Erik's usual rants, his audience looked rapt. They could tell he was working up to something.

'Anyway, my point is that no one, not even Valentina, can identify Lukas as the person who raped her. What we're left with is a crime that may not have happened, that no one witnessed, and which if it did take place could have been done by anyone. Lukas might have raped her. It's possible. But that seems like a weak reason for deciding he's guilty.'

Erik folded his arms. While I was pleased, if slightly baffled, by his sudden show of support, I didn't think it would do any good. A crime had been committed; someone had to pay.

The rest of the questions went over the same ground. The penultimate one belonged to Yasmin. She stepped forward and asked, 'Why should we believe you?'

I don't think she meant this as an attack. Yasmin was a thoughtful, reserved person who spent most of her time carving faces from wood. She'd asked that question in an almost philosophical spirit. And really, it was the only question that mattered. In the absence of evidence or eyewitnesses, my credibility was the crucial issue. It was an excellent question that I had no idea how to answer.

'Why should you believe me? I can think of all kinds of answers, like that I'm a good person, that I don't lie, that I don't hurt people much.'

I didn't know what else to say, only that I had to keep talking. The right words might come out.

'If you think I'm a rapist it won't make any difference if I say I'm not. Let me ask you this. Can any of you think of something awful I've done during my three years in this camp? Have I hit anyone? Have I stolen anything? I know I've behaved badly sometimes' – I glanced at Brendan – 'and yes, I admit to being a condescending shit at times. That's probably a good enough reason to dislike me, maybe even hate me. But I've done nothing to suggest I'm dangerous.'

Edie snorted, then whispered to Mina, who nodded.

'I'm not saying I'm a good person. I tried to have sex with Valentina even though she was so high she probably had no idea what she was doing. And I was obviously out of control when it came to Ella and Sharnaz. Edie made up a lot of what she said, but maybe she's right about there being things I want to do yet can't admit to. But wanting isn't the same as doing.'

As soon as I finished speaking Edie and Mina started a slow handclap. About twenty people joined in. It took Stephan a few moments to quiet the room.

Kobby had the final question. 'Lukas, you have made many good points. There's a lot to think about. What I'd like to know is where you see yourself, and the rest of us, in terms of morality in a Nietzschean sense, given that your description of us corresponds to his concept of slave morality. I'm also reminded of his notion that instincts which don't express themselves end up turning inward. Are we soulful beings, or are we just cowards?'

My normal approach to this kind of convoluted, academic question would have been to methodically pick apart its assumptions and then say something about the ones that interested me. My tutors had made it clear to me that it was naïve, almost gauche, to try and offer a definitive answer to a philosophical question. I'd also learned another way to respond to this kind of verbiage, a method that could only be rarely deployed — once a term, maybe once a year — and even then you couldn't be sure how the person would react. However, in the present situation, with nothing left to lose, it seemed fine to try it.

'Oh, fuck off,' I said.

A lot of people laughed. Even Stephan had a smile as he rang the bell for silence. Once the room was quiet he said, 'You'll now have five minutes to think about your verdict. You can talk to other people, but please don't move around too much. Try to stay in a circle.'

And so the great debate began. People pointed at me, they swore, hands were waved in the air. Dirk marked off his arguments on his fingers as he spoke to Enzo. Lucia and Kobby, who agreed about everything, played paper-scissors-stone.

Those five minutes passed slowly. I was both the centre of attention and yet also ignored. A few times I closed my eyes and tried to be elsewhere, but the room was far too noisy.

The bell rang. The room went quiet. Stephan turned to Kobby. 'Innocent or guilty?'

I wasn't looking at Kobby's face: that wouldn't tell me anything. I stared at his feet, waiting to see them lift as he took a step backwards. They stayed still, and so when he spoke, I already knew his answer.

'Innocent,' he said.

I moved my gaze to Yasmin's feet. They also didn't move. Only as she said, 'Guilty,' did she start to step back. The next five people did the same. I imagined the trend continuing all the way round the circle, the people stepping back, one after another, like falling dominoes.

Three more people said, 'Guilty,' before Nadeem said, 'Innocent.' The next four people stepped back.

By the time Stephan got round to Erik the score was something like twenty-one to four against. I was glad to see Erik stand his ground, but there seemed no chance of making up such a huge deficit. In some ways it was a relief.

Not even Stephan was able to hide his astonishment when each of the Gnostics didn't move. I wanted to yell *But why?* at them. They probably wouldn't have explained. Although they were crazy, they understood the power of mystery.

Bob began to step backwards before Stephan finished asking the question.

When Fatoumata was asked she neither spoke nor moved. She just stared at Stephan. After thirty seconds he had to speak for her. 'Innocent,' he said. The rules were clear about that. For all its farcical elements, the judgment at least attempted to enshrine the presumption of innocence. If you wanted to condemn someone you had to declare it out loud.

Dejan, Khunbish, Mikhail and four others declared me innocent. I felt strange, both pleased and confused, the same way I had at school when I passed a test I hadn't studied for.

Kim said, 'Guilty,' very slowly.

Jorge, like Fatoumata, ignored Stephan's question. He laughed when Stephan said, 'Innocent'.

Both Enzo and Dirk were on my side, as were Brendan, Aleksandr and Senk. I didn't know what the score was. But it had to be close.

Four more thought me innocent. When it was Georges's turn to answer he puffed out his cheeks, opened his mouth, then shut it. He scratched his jaw. His teeth worried his lip. He was obviously having a great debate with himself. That was fine with me. Another few seconds and Stephan would have to speak for him.

'Guilty,' he blurted, then stepped back so fast he staggered.

Lucia didn't need time to think. 'He's guilty,' she said.

That only left Stephan, who always voted with the majority. People were turning to each other and asking what the score was.

'It's a tie,' said Stephan with annoyance. I'd never seen this happen before. It had never even been close.

'I have my own opinion about what the outcome of this judgment should be. But Josef, whom some of you may remember, was very clear about what should happen in this situation. When he handed this position on to me he mentioned it explicitly. He said that one of the main functions of the moderator is to be optimistic about people. And so in the event of a tie' – he glared at me – 'this is what my verdict must reflect.'

For a moment no one spoke; I felt no urge to celebrate my victory. Then Edie shouted, 'Bullshit.' She and Mina started towards me. 'He's innocent,' yelled Stephan, but that wasn't going to stop them.

'Wait,' I yelled, then someone shoved me from behind. I stumbled towards Edie, and as she lifted her arm I saw a knife I'd used to cut an apple only yesterday.

I managed to stop myself falling; it would have been better if I had. The knife slashed my right shoulder.

'I'm going to put this in you,' she said and raised her hand to stab me. Erik grabbed her wrist. He twisted it, and she cried out and dropped the blade. As Mina went to pick it up Dejan pushed her away. My shoulder was bleeding badly; everyone seemed to be rushing at me. Some may have wanted to defend me, and some of them to hurt me, but I think many of them just wanted to fight. There were many scores to settle, grudges to repay. It was probably a good thing for us, and no one (except me) would have been badly injured if the guards hadn't got involved. When they charged in it felt like an intrusion. Alain probably thought he was rescuing me, and I suppose he had no choice.

At first the guards acted with restraint. They pushed people aside and only struck a few with their batons: I wasn't sorry to see Bob getting cracked on the head. Even so, their presence inflamed the situation. Using their batons was bad enough, but as soon as one of them tasered Edie they became a common enemy. As she writhed on the floor Erik hit the guard in the chest, then Dejan elbowed him in the face. I don't think I'd ever seen Dejan look so happy. Though he didn't get to enjoy this triumph. When he got tasered from behind his body shook with spasms that made him look like a puppet having its strings jerked.

More guards rushed into the room, all in riot gear. I thought that in the chaos I'd been forgotten until I was punched in the back of the neck. As soon as I turned round Kim hit me in the face and I fell. Before he could kick me Khunbish got him in a headlock. I was thinking how strange Kim looked, with his red face and white hair, when there was a loud popping sound.

'They're gassing us,' yelled Erik, sounding more excited than scared. He'd picked up a chair and was thrusting it at a guard. Then my eyes were burning and I couldn't breathe. I heard someone say, 'We'll get you out of here,' then I was pulled to the edge of the room. 'Lukas, you'll be OK,' said the guard, and I realised it was Alain. He looked concerned, then his face contorted; when he staggered I saw Dejan holding Edie's knife. I told him to stop, but it was too late. Dejan stabbed Alain again.

I'm sure Dejan would have killed him if a deafening sound hadn't made everyone freeze. Edie had a gun. She'd fired at me and missed. The guards told her to put the gun down; I didn't wait to see if she did. I ran towards the door and then was in the cold. My shoulder hurt; my eyes were on fire. As I ran I heard more shots.

I went straight to Min-seo's house. I knocked on the door and didn't wait for an answer. In the hallway I called out her name but heard no reply. All the lights were off. I wanted to go straight into the bedroom, curl up around her, pretend I was elsewhere.

But first I had to see the damage. I took off my clothes in the bathroom. The cut was long but not deep. I cleaned it as best

I could, then rubbed in some antiseptic cream that made it burn. My face was a bloody mess, the right eye swollen and bruised. Although it hurt, I had to clean my face, restore it to life.

The bedroom smelt of glue. It was too dark to see the walls; I guessed Min-seo had been busy. I looked at the small lump in bed; only the top of her head was above the blankets.

I was shivering, so I got into bed quickly. Though she was lying in the centre of the bed there was still plenty of space. The smell of glue seemed stronger, and I considered opening a window, but it was too much effort to get up. I snuggled towards Min-seo, hoping to warm myself against her, and felt something brush against my leg. I pulled it out. It was a feather. I felt around and found a long line of them stuck to the sheet.

'What's this?' I muttered. 'Are you sleeping with birds?'

I snuggled close to Min-seo, then put my hand on her shoulder. She felt cold. She was cold all over. When I shook her, she didn't respond. I got up and turned on the light and in the brightness my eyes kept blinking, as if they didn't want to see any more but couldn't close. Min-seo had traced her outline in black feathers. It was like the chalk drawing around a body at a crime scene. An empty pill box was on the bedside table. She hadn't left a note.

REBECCA

FELL asleep on the drive back. At some point I woke and saw a stream of approaching lights that seemed aimed at us. Then my eyes closed and all I felt was motion.

When I woke next the car had stopped and we were outside my building. I made a sound somewhere between a whine and a groan.

'Welcome back,' said Rajeev.

'Thanks. Sorry I left you, I was totally beat.'

'It's cool. I had a lot to think about anyway.'

'About the call?'

He nodded. 'Yeah. And other stuff as well. I got an email yesterday from a professor at Case Western. They want me to fly out for a meeting next week. They said they're looking for someone to head up a new unit linked to their prion centre.'

'That's great. Why didn't you tell me before?'

'I wanted to, but there was so much else happening. And I don't know if I want to live in Cleveland. Right now I like it here.'

He leaned in and kissed me, his tongue finding mine. It was great, and we kissed slowly, until I had a thought.

'You know, even if you don't want the job, you should still go. It'd be worth it just to meet with Cliff Sanchez. When I met him at a conference I got more ideas from talking to him for a half-hour than I got from my PhD supervisor in three months. Although he's not really a Werner's guy, I guarantee he'd be helpful.'

'Maybe. But it's not a Werner's unit they want to set up. They want to focus on avian zoonoses.'

'I didn't know you were interested in that.'

He looked uncomfortable. 'Sometimes we talk about it at lunch. Chris and Gulmera are writing a grant proposal.'

This was a lot to process; it took a moment to join the dots.

'Are you saying you want to stop working on Werner's?'

'No. Not immediately. Though I'd like to branch out. You know I was working on H5N1 when the epidemic started.'

He had mentioned this before, but only once or twice. I'd figured it hadn't been going on long, perhaps a few months. I thought it was nothing serious.

'Like I said, I'm not in a hurry. There's still a lot I want to do at the Institute, and my grant runs for another eighteen months. And most importantly, you're here.'

I wasn't reassured: if someone says they're going to leave you, the time frame doesn't matter. And my concern wasn't entirely personal. He'd be a huge loss to the field.

'Don't you think Werner's is more important? There's so much we don't know. The other day you were saying that the low infection rates in the Balkans are a total mystery.'

'I know I did. And of course it's important. But all I've done for the last nine years is think about the disease.'

'You and everyone else. Not thinking about it isn't going to make us safer.'

'I agree. You're totally right. I just don't want the disease to be the only thing in my head.'

He was being melodramatic. It was also ironic to hear Mr Concentration complain about being single-minded.

'Fine,' I said, though it wasn't. I was tired and my head felt like it was full of fluid pressing against my eyes. If we argued any more I'd get mean.

I reached for the door handle. 'Today was really great, but I'm knackered. I'll call you tomorrow, OK?'

'OK,' said Rajeev. Then he smiled. 'You know, you still sound British sometimes.'

'It's a chronic condition,' I said and wondered if I was letting him off the hook too easily. Perhaps it should have been a proper argument, with both of us trying to land a blow, trading punch for punch until we lost our shit enough to say stuff we wished we didn't mean.

As I got out he said, 'Wait.' Instead of taking a verbal swing he held out the bag of leftover food.

'I'll call you later,' he said, and I shut the door. I walked to my building, put the key in the door, waved and went inside. In my apartment I took off my coat then looked down onto the street and saw Rajeev still sitting there. He was probably wondering whether he should come upstairs, explain further, make certain things were OK. If he had, we'd have eaten the leftovers then had make-up sex even though we hadn't really fought.

I was hungry again so I put the quesadillas in the microwave. When I went back to the window, he'd gone.

While I ate, I watched TV highlights of the celebration with the sound off. It was OK to see people waving their hands in the air and laughing because I could make of it whatever I chose. They'd won the lottery. They'd bought the best home insurance.

I fell asleep and dreamed of climbing endless stairs. They kept going up and up and then I ate an onion.

When I woke my mouth was greasy. In the bathroom I flossed, brushed my teeth, washed my face and hands, then scraped cells from my cheek a little too hard. I sat on the toilet to wait for the results, my cheek stinging, feeling it was almost certainly a waste of a test. But the end of such a good day, after I'd turned a corner, seemed like precisely when I was going to test positive.

The tube was the yellow of new buttercups. I looked away, found a Q-tip beneath the sink, a bobby pin in a crack. I pictured Rajeev driving home.

The negative result was such a relief I threw the tube against the wall. My conversation with Rajeev must have upset me more than I'd realised.

The liquid was still trickling down when my phone rang. I let it ring until I had composed myself.

'Hi Dad.'

'Hey, Becky. How are things in the big city? Are you all still partying?'

'Oh yeah. It's crazy.'

I tried to laugh, but started crying.

'What is it, honey? What's happened?'

'Nothing. I'm fine.'

'Nothing doesn't make you cry. Have you been thinking about Matthew?'

'No. Not much.'

He sighed. 'It's a difficult time. Last night I was talking to Johnny Greene, you know I told you he's just come off the rigs in Alaska. Johnny and I were down by the lake, where everyone's idea of celebrating was to barbecue all night. There was so much mesquite smoke we had to go round the lake to stop coughing.'

I didn't know why Dad was telling me this, but I was glad of the chance to collect myself.

'Anyway, we went round as far as that huge rock you used to dive off. We sat on it and passed a bottle between us and told stories about Bobby. We kept on till the fireworks started, and then it was too loud to talk. Afterward, when it was quiet, Johnny climbed up to the top of the rock like he was going to jump off.'

As a kid it had been frighteningly high. When falling there was always an instant when I felt suspended.

'I told Johnny it was a bit cold for that, and he didn't say anything, just looked down at me like he had no idea who I was. After a minute he came down. He was quiet for ages, then he told me they'd had to shoot people trying to get on the rig. They didn't want to, but there'd already been an incident at a jack-up along the coast where a load of boats came in the night and snuck on and killed the crew. Johnny's crew had to deal with two small boats that were heavily armed and had some kids on board. Most of the crew were terrible shots, but one of the guys had been in Afghanistan. He shot three people, and then the boats exploded. When I asked Johnny if there were any survivors, he shook his head. He said they didn't look. Not even for the kids.'

Which was awful but sensible: someone who's been wounded is ten times more infectious.

'So honey, it's inevitable that you'd have difficult memories come up. You can't stop that, and you shouldn't try to. And like I've said before, there was nothing you could have said or done. Matthew wasn't himself at the end. The lovely guy I knew couldn't have done that to you. Sometimes I wonder why we didn't all—'

'Dad, I'm seeing someone.'

There was a brief stunned silence. I heard the dog bark twice.

'Honey, I mean, that's wonderful. Amazing. Who's the lucky guy?'

'Rajeev. He's a colleague at the Institute.' I wasn't sure what else to say except, 'He's an epidemiologist.'

'Great! So did this just start?'

'No, it's been going on a little while. I didn't want to say anything before – I wasn't sure how serious it was.'

'So it's serious?'

'Oh yes.' Hearing myself say this made me feel worse: it emphasised how much I had to lose.

'I'm so happy for you. If I wasn't hungover I'd celebrate again. Screw it, I'm going to have a Laphroaig.'

'Why not?' I said. He should enjoy this while he could.

After I hung up I went to bed. Despite being totally exhausted, I couldn't sleep. The room seemed too bright. Either the street lights had changed, or some final loss of leaves had allowed more light to enter.

Around eleven I got up and found an eye mask I'd taken from a plane. That helped, but there was too much noise from the street. Shouts, rumbling trucks, a car stereo's thumping bass, popping noises I thought might be gunshots. These sounds arrived then departed, and in the following quiet I nursed the delusion that now the rest of the city was finally going to sleep. Then there were new voices, car doors slamming, and I understood that no one else in my neighbourhood had any intention of doing anything so lame as going to bed before midnight on a Saturday.

I removed the eye mask and opened my bedside drawer; I was sure I'd also taken earplugs from the plane. There were so many layers of crap it was impossible to see what was in there. Out of impatience I ended up emptying the drawer onto the floor. I was then faced with a confusion of magazines, odd socks, gloves, souvenirs, old phone chargers, lipstick, combs, odd presents Dad had sent me (a key ring with a pink kangaroo and a woolly hat that said MAINE MAN), name badges from conferences, a can of Mace, a framed picture of Rajeev and myself at Niagara Falls, plus a three-speed vibrator I hated because it sounded like an electric drill. I put this mess back in the drawer, one item at a time, and found beneath the earplugs a small brown envelope that had been trapped in a copy of *British Vogue*.

I put in the earplugs, then got back into bed. After replacing the eye mask I could sense almost nothing. There was only the pressure of the pillow against my cheek, the comforter's soft touch. My mind was clear. I was relaxed. But I was completely awake. And eventually the image bled through the envelope. In the photo Matthew was leaning back from the table with a glass of red wine in his hand. His eyebrows were slightly raised; his beard partly concealed his smile. He was wearing a dark brown, single-breasted linen jacket I'd bought him on Oxford Street. Over his left shoulder Tower Bridge was blurred because it was being raised.

It was the last day of our trip to England. We were treating ourselves to an overpriced Italian meal by the Thames because it was our six-month anniversary. The first time we'd properly met was at the birthday dinner for Debbie, a mutual friend. We'd spoken enough for it not to be weird when he suggested we share a taxi going to Brooklyn. During the journey it didn't occur to me that he might make a pass at me, nor did I want him to. It had been interesting to hear about his work as a clinical psychologist, but he reminded me too much of my ex-boyfriend. Tom was an arrogant prick who invoked his Ivy League education like a protective deity. Matthew had the same confidence. His sentences came out finished. His long vowels and Cambridge degree made me think he was a British clone.

The cab stopped at his place; he got out and said goodnight. He was shutting the door when he shouted, 'Wait,' surprising both myself and the driver, who was starting to pull away. He asked if I wanted to come up for a drink, and I wasn't sure what to say. The cab driver's suggestive laugh didn't help. I still don't know why I got out the cab and went up to Matthew's loft. Maybe it was no more complicated than a sense of *why not?* I hadn't slept with anyone for four months. Though I suspect the main reason wasn't a good one. He seemed so much like Tom.

But during our two drinks Matthew didn't exhibit any of my ex's dickishness. When I spoke he actually seemed to listen, and there was nothing feigned about this (a lot of guys think women can't tell the difference). He was modest about his work. 'It's always a big challenge,' he said. 'The stuff you really want to ask is usually the stuff they don't want to talk about. You could say I'm like a policeman. My job is to persuade them to tell the truth, even if I have to trick them.'

'That's nice,' I said and reconsidered his beard, his eyes. I liked his mouth. He didn't need to say any more.

Next morning there was no talk of seeing each other again. It was just a hook-up. Over the following week I honestly wasn't waiting for him to call. The time we'd spent together was a perfectly self-contained experience. Matthew later admitted he'd felt the same way. If Debbie hadn't been knocked off her bike by a UPS truck, fracturing her skull and putting her into intensive care for twenty-four hours, we might not have seen each other again.

After seven anxious hours waiting together, freaking out about the number of tubes going into Debbie, how pale she looked, whether or not she had brain damage, it felt wrong for us to return to our separate homes. I don't know if I wanted *him*, but I didn't want to be alone. When the cab stopped outside his building I said, 'I'm coming with you.'

From then on we spent almost every night together. It felt weird being in bed without him. After six months I knew he loved me, and I felt the same. And yet I wasn't sure we had a future. He was having visa problems and didn't like the clinical practice he was working in. Though he never actually said it, I could tell he missed London. All this made me hold back from proposing we move in together. Something was missing but I couldn't say what.

So when Matthew suggested we take a trip to England, our first proper vacation together, I hoped it would provide clarity. The chance to observe him in one of his natural habitats was surely going to help me decide.

We spent the first four days with Matthew's parents in the Sussex countryside. There were a few awkward moments, like when his dad, after three gin and tonics, asked me if I found American culture crass, but for the most part it was good. We went on long walks and ate in pubs that were hundreds of years old. Although it was enjoyable, and it meant something that he'd introduced me to his parents, it didn't feel like what I was after, whatever that was. The only revealing moment was when I was helping his mother wash up on our last evening. She said, 'I think you'll be good for Matthew. He had a tricky time growing up, and he needs to be with someone confident.' I almost dropped a plate. I didn't think of myself that way; he seemed assured enough for us both.

Once we were in London I started learning a lot more about my beloved, most obviously that he had a much higher tolerance for bullshit than me. Whoever thinks the English are polite and good-mannered has obviously never eaten in a restaurant in London, used public transport, tried to buy something in a store, or walked down any main street. People bumped into me and said nothing. On the Tube a man with a coat on his lap stared at my breasts for four stops. Their rudeness made me feel like I wasn't a person. Matthew didn't seem to register any of this, and when I brought his attention to it, he laughed it off. He was equally unfazed by the almost constant rain. I went through three umbrellas that week (the first was too small, the wind snapped the second), and even the sturdy third couldn't stop me getting soaked below the knee.

After five miserable days I couldn't wait to get on the plane, preferably on my own. I had privately decided that Matthew was a fucking jerk for not being as miserable as me. His patient, valiant attempts to ease the tension made me feel like a childish American tourist who had to be placated. And if this was what happened on a short trip to a country where the worst hazards were rudeness and bad food, how could we manage the stress of living together? It made me doubt whether I could be with anyone.

On our last day the rain stopped, though for all I cared the whole country might as well have drowned. We were still in bed when Matthew suggested we walk along the river to Tate Modern.

'I'm staying here.'

'The views are great. It's one of the best walks in London.'

'I'm staying here.'

I knew I wasn't being reasonable, but couldn't help myself. Tom would have gloated if he could have seen me; when he'd broken up with me he'd said going out with me was like being put into the Kobayashi scenario every day. When I looked at him blankly he'd explained, with nerdish disdain, that this was a no-win training scenario from Star Trek. Tom was hateful, smug and almost certainly cheated on me, but he had a point. If Matthew had tried to argue, I'd have stormed out. If he'd pleaded or begged I'd have reacted with scorn. I could have met an emotional declaration with indifference. And if he'd done as I asked, and left me in the room alone, that would have been the end of us.

I don't believe in the idea of a perfect union. There are no soulmates. No one is able to complete anyone else. However, I can't deny that my boyfriend's ability to deal with difficult, self-sabotaging people was definitely an asset. After I had repeated my refusal to leave the hotel, Matthew rolled toward me and said, 'That sounds good. Let's stay in and get room service. I might have a bath.'

He'd said this calmly, with neither irony nor any hint of capitulation. As if he'd weighed up both our ideas and decided mine was better. And for this I had no answer. He'd signalled that he didn't care what we did so long as we were together. We stayed in the room all morning, eating smoked salmon and fruit, and though he did have his bath, once I joined him most of the water ended up on the floor. Around noon I stretched and said, 'I have a great idea. Why don't we go for a walk by the river?'

'Good idea,' he said. 'I wish I'd thought of that.' And his smile was more than just pleased, it was wry as well. Matthew appreciated the irony of the situation, but he didn't rub my nose in it.

Outside, the city was in the throes of its lunchtime panic. Office workers scurried toward sandwich places as if they feared rationing had returned. Walking at a normal, comfortable pace amongst them elicited mutters, sighs. Before I could get annoyed Matthew steered me down an alley that opened into a courtyard with a huge tree in the centre. Beneath it an elderly woman sat on a bench with a terrier in her arms. She was feeding the dog treats from a small tin while quietly talking to it. It was a totally ordinary moment that I liked more than all the famous buildings.

We crossed to the other side of the courtyard and went down another winding alley that deposited us on the bank of the Thames. Matthew took my arm and we joined the slow drift of families, dog walkers and tourists. Up and down the river I saw buildings with bright curves. Two young men were taking a selfie. An elderly woman swished by on rollerblades that made a quacking sound.

'I used to run along here,' said Matthew. 'Most days I'd go as far as I could, then walk back slowly, listening to the radio or a podcast. After a while this stretch felt so familiar that whenever I saw litter or broken glass I felt as if someone had dumped rubbish in my garden.'

'So did you pick it up?'

'No, but I wanted to. I also knew it would be going too far. If I started picking up litter, I'd never be able to stop. Eventually I had to force myself not to look at the ground.'

At the time I thought he was sharing a random memory. It was only when I lay in the dark, twelve years later, temporarily blind and deaf, that I realised he'd been speaking about how he coped with living in London (and I guess New York). He wasn't oblivious to the city's problems, he just was able to compartmentalise his annoyance, prevent it breathing too much. He could do that with his patients, his visa problems, his neighbour's week-night karaoke sessions, everything except an infected hair follicle or a spasm in his calf. These would produce an acute worry that sent him down internet rabbit holes. And yet at the start of the epidemic he wasn't especially worried, far less than me, and not because he was ignorant of what we were facing – it was pretty much all I talked about. I never stopped reminding him to be careful, to wear protective gloves when he was out, and usually he did. But like millions of others, he couldn't entirely believe it might happen to him.

LUKAS

DON'T know what the feathers meant. Maybe even Min-seo couldn't have explained why it was so important for her body to have a soft black frame.

She'd have been pleased by the result. The outline was wide enough to contain her body yet still preserved its shape. One of her arms was under the pillow; the other was perpendicular. Her legs were together and twisted slightly behind. She'd posed herself perfectly.

If she'd told me what she was planning I'd have tried to talk her out of it, but she was so stubborn. She'd have made me help her.

I wanted to run out and tell someone even though I couldn't, even though there was no point. All I could do was stand there and look at Min-seo lying on the bed. How long had it taken her to complete her work? What had she been thinking as she carefully placed each feather, stuck it down, saw her shape emerge? How had she been able to go through with it when every moment offered her the opportunity to stop, postpone, make another choice?

Unless she had treated it like any other piece of work. She'd feathered her walls. Now she was feathering her bed. Perhaps the frail and wrinkled object she was going to put there didn't seem like her body. She was making a frame for a piece of sculpture.

I switched off the light and got into bed. I snuggled up to her carefully so as not to move her. I didn't think about being in any other place or time. I stayed with her.

When I woke it was still dark. I hoped Min-seo was only sleeping. She was even colder.

Day began with a thick, grey light that made things look blurred. I'd have to leave Min-seo's house eventually, but I wasn't sure where to go.

I heard the front door open and panicked. I was reaching for a rock on the bedside table when Brendan entered. His smile shrank. He went up to the bed and picked up a feather from next to Min-seo's foot. He turned it over several times, then brushed his palm with it.

'She used to walk behind the canteen to see if any feathers had been dropped. It's a popular place with the crows.'

He put the feather back, then sighed.

'She picked a classy way to do it. I hope I do the same.'

I saw him lying next to her within his own black frame. Next to him Rustam, Ella and Sharnaz were similarly enclosed.

'Do you think you will?' I asked, as more bodies were added. Soon Valentina, Senk, Noor and Anurag would be gone. We could pluck every crow on the mountain and it wouldn't be enough.

'No, probably not. I suspect I'll cling on. Although I don't believe in God, I still think He might give me a miracle. You should get under the blanket, you're shivering.'

'No, I should go out. I can't hide in here forever.'

'True, but you'll have to stay put a few hours. There's a curfew until ten.'

'So how did you get in?'

He shrugged. 'I took a chance. And what can they do to me? Now come on. Before you catch your death.'

I moved close to Min-seo then said, 'There's room for another.'

'Do you think she'd mind?'

'No, she liked you. She said you knew how to cook eggs.'

He laughed. 'That I can do.' He eased himself in next to me, then snuggled up. I was holding Min-seo and he was holding me.

I closed my eyes. I asked if Edie was dead.

He pulled me closer.

'I don't know. But they shot her. After that, most of us got on the floor. They marched us back to our homes.'

'What about Alain?'

'He was in pretty bad shape. Even if he makes it, we won't see Dejan again.'

'I guess they'll have to lock him up.'

He tensed. 'They'll shoot him. They don't mind if we kill each other, but anyone who lays a hand on them is dead without even a trial.'

'You sound like Erik.'

'Well, after what happened last night, a lot of people will listen to him. They'll be angry about Mina.'

'What about her?'

'She got killed by one of the guards. Maybe it was an accident, and maybe it wasn't, though I bet nothing's going to happen to the bloke that did it.'

We didn't speak after that. As we drifted off I wondered if Brendan was right. In Rosa Khutor, when there were more of us, conditions had been stricter. Perhaps the authorities in Zaqatala had only been more permissive because up until now we hadn't challenged them.

Once the curfew was lifted Brendan accompanied me to my hut. A guard was outside my door. 'Where the fuck have you been? Get inside,' he said.

That afternoon I couldn't concentrate on my books, their words seemed irrelevant. I watched people passing. A lot of them stared at my house, and a few tried to come closer, but the guard sent them away.

At dusk I saw Brendan approaching. I went to the door and said to the guard, 'It's OK, he's a friend.' The guard hesitated, looked at Brendan, then nodded.

Brendan wiped his feet. 'I can't stay long. We're so far behind in the canteen I'll be there for hours. I just wanted to see how you are.'

'About the same. What's it like out there? What are people saying?'

'Well, some people really hate you. But you also have supporters. Erik's been trying to shift people's anger to the authorities. You're lucky he's on your side.'

'I know,' I said, though I wasn't sure that my welfare was his main concern.

Brendan told me that Mina and Min-seo's memorial services were going to take place the next day. He took a small step towards me. 'I'll send you some food later. Try to get some rest.' When he leant in, I thought he was going to kiss me on the mouth, but his lips chose my cheek.

The only alcohol I had was a bottle of quince brandy I'd been saving to drink with Edie on what she called her 'thirty-filth birthday'. It was even better than I'd expected, the flavour of the fruit so concentrated and excessive it was like a delicious poison. I should have been worried that it was necessary for me to be under armed guard, but after half the bottle it seemed pointless to be concerned. If they wanted to get me, eventually they would. It wasn't as if I had a long life ahead of me.

Even my unreflective brother had found a degree of calm during his time in detention. No one, including his lawyer, had any doubt that Tomasz was going to be found guilty. There were fingerprints and witnesses; he'd been caught in the act. After sleeping with Agata I didn't visit him for several weeks – I told his lawyer to tell him I had a lot of teaching. There was no way to postpone a visit any longer without it seeming strange. When I finally saw him I was amazed, and somewhat mistrustful, of how relaxed he appeared. Although Agata and I had agreed not to tell him anything, perhaps he knew and was trying to lull me into a false sense of security. But he didn't mention her. There was no more talk of escaping. His attitude was that he'd made mistakes and now was going to have to pay. This wasn't exactly a spasm of morality; I got the impression that what he regretted was the ineptitude that led to him getting caught.

But my surprise at his change of attitude was overshadowed by how easy it was to be talking to him. Several weeks ago I'd had sex with the only woman he'd ever loved. Guilt, remorse and anxiety should have been flooding through me. Instead I felt fine. I enjoyed hearing about the other prisoners.

At the trial two weeks later I took a seat far from Agata. A few minutes later she stood, came over to me and said, 'It would look suspicious.' She didn't say anything after that. For the next four hours she barely looked at me despite the bizarre twists of the proceedings. Somehow the arresting officer had messed up virtually every aspect of the case, failing to inform Tomasz of his rights and also not charging him properly. Two witnesses testified that at the time the officer seemed intoxicated. The DNA sample was contaminated. The strangest thing of all was that these facts had only come to light because during the trial the arresting officer's partner – who had been called as a witness by the prosecution – had an attack of conscience (or spite) that prompted him to denounce his partner. Unsurprisingly, this betrayal threw the court into chaos. Amidst the general confusion there were some excellent threats. When the arresting officer realised he couldn't get close enough to his partner to hit him, he took off his boots and hurled them. A mistrial was declared.

Two hours later Tomasz had his arms around us both. 'I must have an angel,' he kept saying. He bought drinks for everyone, and claimed he'd never been worried about the outcome. I imagined telling him what had happened with Agata, how abruptly his celebrations would end.

While I wasn't going to ruin his night, I was far less sure what Agata might do. At any moment she might whisper to him that I had got her drunk and seduced her. I was sure he'd believe whatever she said.

We drank more. People danced. Tomasz said it was the best night of his life.

'I can't believe it. But it's like Dad used to say, it's all about timing,' he said. I nodded, though I didn't see the relevance. Once again he'd just been lucky.

When we finally emerged into the dawn he hugged me so hard I felt all my organs being compacted. 'I love you, little brother,' he said, then staggered off to be sick.

During the following week I didn't have to do much to avoid him because he was either at Agata's or still in bed when I went to the university. At the end of the week I received a notice instructing me to report for a mandatory blood test for this weird new disease. It never occurred to me that I should be worried.

REBECCA

I SLEPT most of Sunday. Though I woke a few times, the eye mask and ear plugs meant I saw and heard nothing, which made it easy to go back to sleep. What I couldn't ignore was my bladder. Eventually I had to lift my mask to visit the bathroom, but I kept the earplugs in. Walking between the rooms, not hearing my steps, felt like floating through a dream.

When I finally got up it was dark again. Enough light was coming in from outside, so I didn't turn on the lamp. I lay on the couch and ate the last burrito cold. I got bored. I wandered between the rooms. I endured the noise of my vibrator. Afterward I lay on the couch and heard my phone ring from the other country of my bedroom. I was warm, comfortable, still relaxed from my orgasm. I didn't want to speak to anyone.

Then it was day. I didn't feel like I'd slept; the time had just been taken.

Rajeev had called three times. He'd also sent a text that said, 'Hope you're having a good day. Love you. Raj'. This routine, casual message had probably taken him an hour to compose. For a scientist he had a very romantic view of what language could do. He thought there were perfect words for every situation, and if he picked the right ones the other person would understand him completely. He wouldn't have liked what Matthew had said after a difficult session with a young woman who had a history of animal cruelty: 'You can be eloquent and incisive, you can say exactly what the person needs to hear, you can speak as well as you could if you got to script the session. But it's all fucking useless if they don't want to listen.'

I made coffee, then showered. I picked out a pair of black slacks and a cream sweater, then pictured myself wearing them in Damian's office while sitting in one of the worn green chairs. To be precise, I didn't really imagine myself there. I was watching a person with my face and body wearing those clothes. She had pretty good posture. She could have passed for twenty-nine.

I'd been planning to walk part of the way to work and then take a cab. When it began to pour I had to dash for the subway: the woman in Damian's office didn't look great with sodden clothes and bedraggled hair.

At 14th Street there were at least thirty people on the platform. It took almost two minutes for all of us to pass through the air-locks. By the time we got to 34th Street all the seats were taken. It wasn't pre-epidemic busy, but it was still a huge leap in numbers. None of the other passengers seemed nervous about having to sit next to strangers who might sneeze or cough. Those who chose to stand seemed fine with holding onto a pole or strap thousands of palms had touched.

At Van Cortlandt the sky was clear. The asphalt shone and a cold wind blew. I took out my last cigarette and was about to light up when the wind snatched it. This was annoying, though not a big deal; I had to buy another pack anyway. I walked quickly for two blocks, then was glad to see there was no queue by Carlos's kiosk. Once I was closer I saw the shutter was down. I'd never seen it closed before. On the rare occasions Carlos hadn't been able to open, his nephew had filled in. There was no sign apologising or saying when he'd be back. He just wasn't there.

I crossed the street and went into the Institute. I got out my pass, handed George my bag, and as he fumbled with its contents – one day he was going to break my laptop – a sudden terror overwhelmed me. Right then I was sure Carlos had killed himself. It wasn't the only explanation for his absence, and definitely not the simplest, but the thought had the plausibility of one of those ideas that pop out from raw data and immediately have the heft and shine of a fact. In the elevator I imagined Carlos sitting on his own at home hearing shouts from the street, loud music, explosions in the sky while remembering his family. There was nothing for him to celebrate.

When I met Chris in the corridor he started to say hi but a yawn interrupted.

'Sorry,' he said. 'Didn't mean to show you my mouth.'

'What time did you get in?'

'Early. I'm going out for a quadruple espresso, and if that fails, for some coke. Want anything? You look like you could use a bump.'

'Thanks but no thanks. I'm trying to cut down at work.'

I noticed a large bruise on his neck. He saw me looking, then blushed.

'I've no idea who did that. I just hope I did the same to him.'

It was a really nasty hickey, the bruise dark as old red wine. The thought of sucking someone's skin, bursting the blood vessels, the salty taste, made me so nauseous that as I entered the lab I didn't immediately notice Gulmera. She was standing at the bench with her back to me, her right arm raised while she wielded a micro-pipette. While she had to have heard me enter, I knew she wouldn't look round. Over the course of my career I'd probably done the same amount of lab work as her, maybe more, but the way I worked had none of her precision. Sometimes I sat, sometimes I stood, sometimes I listened to music. I moved my feet. I hummed. Even as I concentrated, I needed distraction.

In my office I checked my email and found a message from Damian suggesting we meet at one. I'd just replied when Rajeev knocked.

'Hey,' he said. 'How are you?'

He was wearing a long-sleeved grey top and black jeans, pretty much what he always wore, and yet it made me want him.

'I'm good. Close the door.'

He shut it. I stood up. He started to ask me about my Sunday but then I was kissing him. I put my arms round him. His mouth tasted of coffee and menthol. I was kissing him so fast it was hard to breathe. It felt like I was dehydrated and his mouth was water.

We pushed against each other. I pressed him against the desk. I felt giddy and wanted to laugh. How had I managed to go so long without this?

His hand cupped my breast; his thumb found the nipple. It moved in slow circles, then stopped.

'What if someone comes in?'

'They'll have to wait their turn,' I said, and leaned in to kiss him. Obviously I meant this as a joke, but Rajeev didn't get it.

'What do you mean? Wait for what?'

'I'm kidding, you idiot.'

'Why am I an idiot?' He stepped back. 'I don't get you. For almost a year you've made us use the screen and now you don't care about protection. What's going on?'

'Nothing,' I said, and was confused. Was he really pissed about us having normal sex?

'I don't believe you. You've been acting weird for weeks. What's going on?'

'How am I acting weird? Give me an example.'

163

'You push me away, then act like you're crazy about me. It's like being with two different people.'

He hesitated. Swallowed. I thought of a claw swaying as it descended to a bucket of words. He needed time to make another sentence, but I didn't give him any.

'Is that it? You're complaining that I have other things to think about besides you? What is it you want? We're not all blessed with your autistic concentration.'

He looked wounded, but I didn't care. He'd started this fight over nothing. Perhaps it was because I hadn't called him back. Or that I'd refused to have a little séance with that telephone.

'And you're not exactly easy to be with yourself. Half the time you're virtually mute. What are you thinking that's so amazing it can't be interrupted?'

'That's not fair,' he said, then got flustered. I'd already won the argument, yet was too annoyed to stop.

'Did you tell your amazing thoughts to your family when you were on the phone? You certainly don't have that much to say to me. Maybe you're only comfortable talking to people who can't answer back.'

Rajeev stared at me. His mouth opened but no sound emerged because I'd stopped the claw in his head. Although this was when I should have apologised, I said nothing. I waited. He left.

~

Damian had changed his screens. Instead of the Pacific there were redwoods. At first I believed it was a photo, until I noticed that the tops of the trees were swaying. I heard the wind's soft sough, the creaking of branches; against this background Damian's narrow body was almost another trunk.

'So did you have a good time on Friday?'

'I did. And that was a great speech you gave. Really. It was very brave.'

'Oh, thanks.' He blushed. And for an instant he could have been a man sitting near me at the bar, a man on his own, reading a paper, drinking bourbon neat. A man I'd ignore for one drink and then engage with during my second.

'I worked on the speech for weeks, and I thought it was done, then at the last minute I added all that stuff about us being lucky. It was actually you who made me change it.'

'Really?'

'Oh yes. Our conversation made me rethink what counts as protection. There's always going to be *some* risk. The question, the problem, is where you draw the line.'

Damian paused, glanced at his computer, then said, 'I suppose I could have gone further. But there's a limit to how much I can scare the donors. After a certain point they tend to want to keep all their money.'

He coughed, then took a drink of water.

'It seems like a good time to think about what's next for you. Assuming you succeed, and as I've said, I think you will, what will be your next step?'

It took me a moment to respond; although I knew Damian had faith in me, it was great to hear him state this so plainly.

'Well, then we start to think about how we might modify the vaccine to account for different strains of the disease.'

'Different *potential* strains. We really don't know what's out there.'

'Sure,' I said, though it seemed a little pedantic of him to empha-sise this.

'I mean, the big question is whether the variant you've made is anything like the strains of the disease that still exist. Given its high mutation rate, I'd be amazed if there aren't some new strains. So I want to reiterate that the Institute will continue to support your work. What you're doing is very important to us.'

Relief emptied my head of words. 'Thank you,' was all I managed.

'You're welcome. But, well, there's a but. You're going to need to establish the state of the virus that's currently in human hosts. Without that we won't know how to modify the vaccine.'

He was totally right, but as one of my professors used to say, 'The best experiments are usually impossible.' I couldn't imagine where I'd get that data from, given how much testing and vaccination had taken place. For all my fears, I didn't believe there were loads of infected people still out there. The camps in Alaska had been closed for two years.

When I asked Damian how I was supposed to gather that data, his face found an expression I didn't know how to read. He nudged a pen on his desk then said, 'Well, some of the rumours are true. There's still a few hundred people in Iceland. And there are a few other possibilities.'

My surprise must have been evident, because he quickly added, 'Of course, all this comes under Homeland Security. It's really for those poor people's protection. And in a few years' time all the camps will certainly be closed. So you'd need to go soon.'

I nodded, though my mouth was shrivelled. That data needed to be collected, but it wasn't a job for me. Having not left the East Coast for almost a decade, I certainly wasn't ready to go to the most frightening place I could imagine. Even the small amount of footage that had made it out of Alaska had given me nightmares. I didn't want to join the zombies.

'So what do you think?' asked Damian. 'Does that seem like something you might be interested in?'

And I, Rebecca, would have said, 'Go fuck yourself.' I'd have slammed the door. It must have been that other woman, wearing those nice clothes, who said, 'That would be a really interesting project. Let me think about it.'

I kept it together until I was out of Damian's office. The Institute had been my only constant since Matthew died; it was basically my home. Having to go to Iceland for a few months was like being sent into exile.

I went into the restroom to try to compose myself. As soon as I entered, my stomach lurched and then vomit was rushing up my throat. I barely made it into the stall. I immediately looked into the bowl; I was in such a state I thought there might be blood. Before I could feel relief I was heaving again.

In the laboratory Gulmera was in the same position, her right arm lifting and swinging like a crane. Once again, she didn't react when I entered. Her flat back was an invitation for a good, hard shove. She was like ice on a pond that's doing no harm and yet calls for a rock. Feelings seemed to be optional for her.

In my office I locked the door then stared at the virus spinning on my screen. I watched it turn, and I counted. After twenty rotations my breathing was slower. After thirty I was calm. I wasn't going anywhere for a while. I still had work to do.

∽

The next few days were pretty strange. My mind kept replaying the scene in Damian's office, but not from my perspective. I could see how I'd been sitting, my facial expressions, the way I held my throat. While I didn't doubt my memory of what he'd said – as much as I'd have liked to forget – the rest of it had to be invented. For some reason, instead of just remembering the scene, my mind had recreated it with my doppelganger in the lead role. So long as I was busy, I didn't see the images, but when I was sat on the subway, or in bed, I could see my lips trembling and then being compressed as Damian spoke about me needing to go away. The evenings were the worst, because I was on my own. Rajeev and I had had no contact since he'd left my office. Although it had been a nasty fight, I didn't think we'd broken up. I knew I was mainly to blame, yet I wasn't ready to apologise. Some time apart would help us figure out where our relationship was supposed to go next. Should we move in together? Should he meet my dad? Were we already too far down the slope that ended with him leaving me to go live in Chicago?

On Thursday I stopped to get cigarettes in a bodega near the subway, though it felt like a betrayal of Carlos. I was disappointed to see no one had placed flowers by his kiosk, then ashamed that I hadn't done so either.

I lit up outside the Institute. I didn't even try to look around. There was only the hot taste of each drag, the jet of smoke I released. Soon there was a little cloud that I wished was thicker. I smoked two more cigarettes. I really didn't want to go in.

When I entered the lab I saw Chris and Rajeev talking, or rather just Chris talking. Rajeev was looking at the floor so intently I imagined Chris was telling him to watch it closely because something incredible was about to happen.

They both looked in my direction, then quickly away; I was sure they had been talking about me.

'Hey,' I said.

'Hey,' they echoed.

I smiled and went into my office. As I shut the door I was relieved to have avoided a more awkward encounter with Rajeev. We had to talk and yet it also felt too soon. My relief disappeared when I realised that I'd trapped myself in my office. He could knock on the door any time. And of course he was also capable of waiting for me to emerge.

Though this was a distraction from thinking of that woman in Damian's office, it wasn't a good one. Out of desperation I picked up an old issue of *Virology* and mechanically read two papers from a special issue on zebra fish. I kept going, skimming papers that were of no interest, just to fill my head with the words. After two hours I'd finished the whole pile, and it felt great to have finally done what I'd put off for so long. Seeing the authors' affiliate institutions reminded me that I, like Rajeev, could also choose to leave. The idea of going to Cambridge or UCL, rather than Iceland, restored my sense of agency.

I was imagining myself walking by the Thames – on a sunny day this time – when I heard the knock I'd feared. I considered not answering, but then I went to the door.

Seeing Chris was a relief. It required no effort at dissimulation for me to cheerfully say, 'What's up?'

'I'm going to get lunch. Want to join me?'

On the surface this was a normal, friendly invitation, yet I suspected Chris was asking on Rajeev's behalf. Either I'd go down to the cafeteria and find Rajeev waiting, or Chris was going to try and broker peace.

'I'd love to, but I'm really snowed under. Maybe next week?'

'Cool,' he said, and I think he was relieved: Rajeev had put him in a difficult spot. After he left I stood in the doorway and listened until I was confident no one else was in the lab. I grabbed my coat, hurried to the door, then walked quickly toward the elevator. A few minutes later I was outside, walking fast, sucking in cold air, thrilled to be getting away.

Apart from the route from the subway to the Institute I didn't know the area well, so it wasn't long before the streets became unfamiliar. On one block there were a lot of Dominican stores; on the next it was all Korean. At first glance it looked like a rough neighbourhood – there were several vacant lots and the sidewalk was covered with broken glass – but there was also a place called Good Cup, Bad Cup that looked like it was run by coffee Nazis. Two doors down was a store selling vintage phones. These outposts of gentrification reassured me enough to go into a noodle place and order beef ramen with two eggs. When the food came I ate quickly, and probably disgustingly, because every mouthful made me crave the next. The bottom of the bowl appeared too soon. I put down my chopsticks and savoured the aftertaste. Then I ordered another.

I left the noodle place just after one. The prospect of having to spend the rest of the afternoon in my windowless office, waiting for Rajeev to knock on the door, made me want to cry. I walked to the end of the block, and as I stood on the corner, looking both ways, I realised I didn't need to rush back. The results of my experiment weren't due until Monday. No one was going to check up on me.

Friday was pretty much the same. I got in early, worked on a grant proposal, then left the lab at eleven. I had more noodles, then got coffee. I didn't go back to the Institute until three, and I was sure I wouldn't run into Rajeev as this was when he and Chris had their weekly meeting with Damian.

I was thinking that I'd managed things well when I saw him coming toward me down the long corridor that led to the laboratory. There was no way to pretend I hadn't seen him. When we got close both of us said hi; neither of us slowed down. It should have been an uncomfortable moment, but I felt fine.

LUKAS

IN the camp we often talked about last things. Last sunrises, last kisses, last meals, last fucks. We planned our final day, sometimes our final hour. But when the end approached, even those with plausible dreams, who just wanted to drink a beer and watch the sunset, were usually too sick to enjoy anything. Only those who chose to end things early were able to make their last day go as planned. Taking a last shower was something that I hoped would be possible right until the end. Under the water I could always forget.

On the morning of Min-seo's memorial I stayed in the shower until my skin looked sunburnt. Around noon I made coffee and sat by the window. I watched a lot of people heading towards the square for Mina's service. In other circumstances I'd have gone as well. Up until the judgment she'd been nice to me.

An hour later people started straggling back to their homes. The guard, whose name was Osman, said he'd have to escort me to the square. We set off twenty minutes later, with Osman slightly in front. He spoke several times into his radio. He was carrying a rifle, and had a handgun as well, but he wouldn't be able to protect me from a lot of people. If they attacked from all sides we'd be overwhelmed.

When we started down a row of houses whose windows were open I knew what was going to happen. In winter those windows should have been closed. Objects that could break an eye, a skull, were already being aimed. Even after we passed through safely, I didn't relax.

About fifty people had already gathered in the square. The air was thick with smoke from cigarettes and joints that hung over them like a cloud of bad thoughts. We took a place at the back among a line of mirrors propped against a wall, each of them turned back to front, as if they'd seen enough.

It didn't take long before people noticed me. A lot of them stared; a few shouted abuse.

'Let's stay here for now,' I said. I couldn't see Brendan or Erik, and didn't trust anyone else.

As more of us arrived in the square, so did more guards. Ten were lined up at the front, and there were almost as many on either side. By the time Stephan mounted the steps to the podium we were a crowd of a hundred.

Stephan thanked us for coming, then started telling a story about when he'd asked Min-seo to paint a mural on his bedroom wall. I'd heard it before but it still made me smile.

'I described the garden of my childhood home in Stuttgart in great detail. I told her all the flowers I wanted to see, the precise shade of green of the lawn. I listed the types of trees and the patterns of shade they cast. I didn't leave anything out, not even the bare patch of grass from where I had spilled a box of weedkiller. She listened very carefully, she took a lot of notes. I believed I had left nothing to chance.'

He paused and drank some beer, then continued.

'She worked very hard on it. She let me look at it for the first four days, but after that she wouldn't let me see. I wasn't concerned. I'd seen enough to know she'd understood.'

Osman's radio crackled. 'Affirmative,' he said. His eyes scanned the crowd.

'On the seventh day Min-seo came and told me she was finished. She told me to close my eyes, then led me into the bedroom. "Can I look?" I said, and after a pause, she said, "No. Wait a minute."

'I heard her take a few steps, then the sound of brushstrokes. "Alright, finished," she said.

'I opened my eyes. The wall could have been a window. I saw everything I remembered of that wonderful garden. But Min-seo had done far more than just provide what I'd asked for. She'd also put in what she thought was missing.'

'"What is that?" I said to her.

'"Ducks look good in a garden."

'"But why is it so big?" I asked.

'She laughed. "Because it's important."

'And it was a beautiful duck. If I had to have a monstrous, frightening duck in my garden, there couldn't have been a better one.'

Everyone applauded. Stephan stepped down from the podium and Senk and Aleksandr came up. Senk spoke briefly about the time Min-seo had brought her and Aleksandr rocks that looked like them. She was trembling so much her brother had to hold her up.

There were many other tributes. Lucia spoke about Min-seo's fear of spiders. Kobby told a surprisingly concise anecdote about helping her paint bark. After about half an hour Osman asked me whether I still wanted to speak.

'Yes, but not until the end.' I wanted everyone else to say their piece before I ruined things.

After Fatoumata offered her pithy summary of Min-seo's whole life ('She was good') no one else came forward. Stephan looked around, then moved towards the podium to conclude the service.

'Wait,' I called, and started forward. The crowd parted grudgingly. They stared at me in silence as Osman and I passed through.

I didn't feel any better standing on the podium. Everyone looked hostile. The only reason they weren't shouting at me was out of respect for Min-seo. I didn't know how to introduce what I was going to say, so I just started to speak.

'Min-seo was born in Seoul in 1995. Her father was a civil servant, her mother a librarian. She was an only child. During the day, when her parents were working, her grandmother looked after her.'

I looked up from my piece of paper. They were listening, for now.

'Min-seo's grandmother was so tall and thin she looked like she might snap. Her voice was a low croak. While Min-seo played she sat and watched without comment. She baked rice cakes and *yakgwa*. Every afternoon she swallowed a large red pill she refused to let Min-seo try.

'If the weather was warm they went to the lake to feed the ducks and geese. The ducks were brown and greedy but kept their distance. The geese did not. They didn't just want the bread Min-seo threw them, they wanted the bread in her hand, maybe the hand as well. She was frightened, but her grandmother was there to protect her.

'Then there was a morning Min-seo's grandmother did not arrive. Her father told her not to cry. Death was a long sleep.

'The following year, when Min-seo was eight, she found a broken crow. The crow could not fly or walk. It had given up. She took the half-dead creature home and for the next week she kept it in a cardboard box by her bed. She fed the bird peanuts from the tip of her finger. She did not give it a name. It was just The Crow.

'The first thing Min-seo did each morning was tell The Crow her dreams. The Crow was a good listener. Sometimes it made a squawk of comment. Mostly it was quiet.

'Although The Crow got stronger, it could not walk or fly. Min-seo's father wanted to take The Crow to a vet but Min-seo refused. The vet would put The Crow to sleep.

'One morning The Crow was lying very still. Min-seo ran her hand over its feathers but The Crow did not move. It too was asleep. When her father offered to bury it in the garden she screamed and locked herself and The Crow in the bathroom. They stayed in there for six hours. Only after her father promised not to bury The Crow did she come out.

'Next day an old man came to her home. He told Min-seo he could make The Crow stay with her forever. "Although first I must change it. Nothing I do will hurt your crow, but maybe you should not watch." Min-seo did not trust this old man who smelt of sweat and vinegar. She insisted on staying with The Crow. And so she watched the old man take a knife and cut open The Crow's chest. At first she wanted to make him stop, then she was curious to see inside her friend. The more she knew about The Crow, the closer they would be.

'The old man opened The Crow's neck. He cut into the head. The Crow's brain was a glistening jelly bean. Watching him peel the skin made her think of a tired person removing a coat. Afterwards The Crow's skin lay next to its body. The Crow looked different but it was still The Crow. There had been one part and now there were two. Nothing else had changed.

'On the following day the old man made The Crow a new body. It was a much better body for flying because it was so light. Inside, it was densely packed with clouds of cotton wool. When the old man sewed up The Crow it was whole again. "There," he said. "Now you can stay together."

'And they did. After her parents got divorced, The Crow went with Min-seo and her mother to Busan. There they looked out of a new window onto the Nakdong River. Neither had ever seen so much water before. Her eyes could glide on it for hours.

'The Crow went with Min-seo to Moscow. It followed her to Bishkek. It was present on her wedding night when she got infected. The last time Min-seo saw The Crow was from the street outside her house. The Crow was watching from the bedroom window. The room was full of smoke and flames but this did not affect The Crow. It watched her as she ran from the city, into the hills, as she roamed the woods, as she was captured. It saw her being brought here, it saw her hair turn grey. It didn't stop watching her. The Crow never blinked.'

After I finished speaking my eyes stayed on the paper. I didn't want to see their angry faces, but I looked anyway. I was relieved to see a lack of animosity; in fact, there was no discernible emotion on their faces. Which isn't to say their features conveyed nothing. There was an expectancy about the blankness. As if they did not think I had finished speaking, or rather, that I should not have finished. Because it was all very well to offer up some neat parable about the deceased, to shape her life into a story that made sense. But this left too much out. And so I told them about Min-seo's fingernail collection. I told them her favourite English words – *spoon, lemming, shut, pretend* – her dislike of Spanish, her love of white rice. There was no order or system to this information. I don't know what led me from one memory to the next, why the cluster of three moles on her shoulder made me recall the time she took all her plates to the edge of the fence then launched them, one by one, off the mountain; nor why this memory prompted me to tell the crowd that Min-seo believed most people were wrong about ghosts: you had to be a ghost before you could be a living person. Soon I was listing things without explanation. She ate apple cores. She had a green hat. Her balance was excellent. She liked Bulgakov.

176

She liked Calvino. She used a knife to sharpen her pencils. Her favourite numbers were eight and thirty-three. She often got the capitals of Greece and France confused.

When I came down from the podium Osman was waiting. 'Let's get you home,' he said. As he led me away I heard Lucia say, 'That was beautiful. But I still fucking hate him.'

We had almost reached the edge of the square when Osman's radio said, 'Fire in the north-east quadrant. All guards proceed to the area.'

'What's happening?'

'I don't know, but I have to take you back right now.'

Soon we saw the smoke. A grey, billowing cloud was rising ahead of us.

'I think someone's confused,' I said. 'That's in the opposite direction.'

'Yeah,' said Osman, then stopped. We looked to the north-east and saw another plume. Two voices spoke from his radio, talking over each other, sending him different ways.

'Come on,' he said, and we started running. People were milling around in confusion; a few were carrying buckets. No one wanted to spend the rest of the winter in tents.

We could smell the smoke by the time we reached my house. 'Go inside and lock the door,' said Osman. 'I'll be back as soon as I can.'

'Good luck,' I said. 'And thanks.'

He nodded and ran off. I went inside and locked the door. I wasn't worried about the fire. I just wanted to sleep.

I got a glass of water then went into the bedroom. Bob was sitting on my bed reading one of my notebooks.

'Very interesting,' he said, but before I could answer Kim hit me. Something in my jaw broke, then I was on the floor.

'Wait,' I said.

'For what?' said Kim. He kicked me in the stomach. He got me in the balls.

'Nothing to say?' said Bob as he got off the bed. 'I'm disappointed. I was looking forward to hearing you try and talk your way out of this. You probably think you're really persuasive after getting away with raping Valentina. You probably think you won them over with your clever arguments.'

'What do you mean?'

Bob laughed. 'That was all down to Erik. I've no idea why he chose to save you. I guess it doesn't matter. Kim and I will fix you.'

'Yes,' said Kim. 'We will.' He bent and put his hands round my throat. He brought his face close to mine. I struggled but he was too strong. I stared at his white Mohican. And then there was nothing.

REBECCA

I T was around six when I left the Institute on Friday evening
but it was so cold and dark it seemed much later. The train was
packed. In my carriage alone I counted seven people wearing
masks. It wasn't some act of collective remembrance because the
masks were all different, of such a variety of ages and ethnicities
that it was like a Benetton ad for the dead. I shut my eyes and
in that darkness I was nowhere, no one, an object being moved.
I realised that if I was going to be leaving, I had to sort out my
affairs, get everything in order.

When I got home I walked between the rooms, assessing what
needed to be done. I began in the kitchen. Leaks and spills had
left the shelves coated in a crunchy goo that had to be scraped off.
Rather than clean all the jars and bottles, I chucked them out. It
was wasteful but satisfying to be rid of spreads and condiments
I must have had for years. The empty shelves looked right.

With the crockery I was more restrained. I left a few plates and
bowls, some mugs; the rest I put in a box to take to the thrift store.

I spent all Saturday cleaning and decluttering. The more I took
out of the place, the less necessary the remaining stuff seemed.
Once I'd taken the pictures off the walls in the lounge it was obvious the couch had to go too. There was no need for it: I had a small
armchair and I couldn't imagine having guests. When Matthew had

done this with our expensive two-year-old couch, I'd been angry because he hadn't asked either my opinion or permission. He'd immediately apologised, then explained, and he was right that a lot of people had sat on it, but very few in the last six months – people already preferred to meet in open spaces. And as I pointed out, a soft surface was far less likely to transmit something infectious than a hard one. 'Oh,' he said, 'that's interesting.' The following day the kitchen chairs were gone.

Once I got rid of the rugs in the bedroom the furniture began to bug me. The huge closet and chest of drawers seemed like monuments. I took my clothes out and made two piles of them in the corner. Only then did I wonder how I was going to get the couch and closet down three flights of stairs. It was so frustrating to want them gone and yet be unable to shift them.

Eventually I remembered what century I was living in. I put the furniture on Craigslist and early next morning two huge Armenian guys came round, one with a beard dyed red, the other clean-shaven. They carried down the couch, then the closet, as easily as if they were stagehands preparing for the next scene. As they were bringing the chest to the door the bearded one said, 'When are you moving out?'

'I'm not. I'm getting rid of stuff I don't need.'

'If you tell us what kind of replacements you're looking for, we can maybe help,' said the other.

'That's nice of you, but I won't be needing replacements.'

They exchanged a look. The bearded one frowned. They started down the stairs. When they were almost at the bottom I had an idea.

'There's one more thing,' I yelled, then rushed back into the apartment. In the bedroom I hurriedly emptied my desk drawers onto the floor. 'Can you take this too?' I asked when the two guys came back.

I thought they'd jump at the offer, because it was a nice mahogany desk. Instead they conferred in a mutter, then the bearded one said, 'We can take it. But are you sure? It would be a shame if you changed your mind.'

'I'm not going to change my mind. I've decided.'

'Is everything alright?'

I laughed. 'Of course. I just don't need this any more.'

By early afternoon my place was looking great. I'd rented it unfurnished and it was almost back to that. Most of the rooms had the bare expectancy of a theatre set.

When I went outside and started walking I had a destination but not an exact route. I picked streets because they were sunny, because they were quiet, because a group of clowns was headed that way. I followed the red balloons south for ten blocks, long enough to wonder whether the clowns were going to a party or whether they simply liked being dressed that way. Some people crossed the street to avoid them, although to me their outfits were far less creepy than wearing a mask. After they disappeared into a brownstone I sat on a stoop and shut my eyes. I heard a whistle of birdsong, a skateboard's rumble, the squeal of a violin being roughly handled. Cars drove past so slowly their noise seemed delayed. I sat there a long time gathering the sounds.

The street was darker when I opened my eyes. I stood and walked to the intersection, then followed the downward slope. After two blocks the brownstones were replaced by low houses whose yards were either concrete or a dried-up lawn. Some of the houses looked so derelict I checked for a red cross on their walls.

I passed a tattooist, a chicken place, a store promising THE CHEAPEST MASKS. The dive bar had been between a laundromat and something that only felt the need to appeal to Chinese-speaking clients. Matthew and I had left after one drink because

181

it didn't meet our high standards of lowness. There was no sense of danger; it was virtually dead. There was just us, the bartender and two grizzled old men on stools. No music was playing, there was no TV, and no one was talking. Matthew said it felt like we'd walked in on a Pinter play that lasted seventeen hours and ended with a devastating shrug.

The laundromat and Chinese travel agency still existed but were at different ends of the block; there was no bar between them. None of the in-between stores had interiors that matched a memory I no longer trusted.

I gave up and resigned myself to the next bar I found. As I crossed the street, a red sign for a place called Greg's blinked on in the distance, which seemed fortuitous, even ominous, but I never got there. Sandwiched between a dry cleaner's and thrift store was my bar. I hesitated before going in. I felt like I was having to rip open a gift I'd wrapped myself. I knew what was under all that tape and paper, so what was the point? Whatever happened in that bar wasn't going to change my decision.

Inside smelled of dust and cigarettes even though bars in the city had been no-smoking for thirty years. Compared to my last visit, the place was packed. Three guys were at the bar, while a pair of probably underage girls were huddled in a booth. The bartender was now a gaunt woman with frizzy orange hair whose grey roots were showing. But the old hush was still present. Ordering two shots and a beer felt like an intrusion, yet the lady gave no sign that it bothered her. As soon as she'd poured my drinks she bent to a crossword that was two-thirds completed, its answers written in black, blue and red ink; as if many people, over many days, had failed to complete it.

I did the first shot at the bar, then carried my PBR and remaining shot to a corner booth. There I settled myself and made sure the big glass and small glass were equidistant from my hands. I kind of wanted to laugh, because I was doing something absurd. There was no need for me to sit in a shitty bar to think about Matthew's death. Doing so wasn't going to uncover anything buried or repressed. Even if something did float to the surface, there was nothing it could change. And yet I wanted to pick the scab from the wound. I was going to switch off all the lights to prove I wasn't scared of the dark.

I began at the end, with the four oranges rolling over the floor. The oranges were Californian, and very expensive. Originally I had wanted six. In the approved store near the Institute they were individually sealed, security tagged, perfect in their protection. Six would fill our fruit bowl. Six would be a pyramid, or at least a mound. The oranges would be a small, bright hearth on which we'd warm our eyes.

And it was normal to buy fruit for the sick. Matthew had had flu for eight days, not a long time, and it *was* just the flu. That morning he'd tested himself with one brand, then I'd tested him with another, and afterward he'd said, 'Alright,' and leaned back into the pillows.

'Have a good day,' he said. And I am sure he did not seem agitated or sad or in any way worse than the version of himself I'd gotten used to.

'I'll try not to be too late,' I said, and wanted to kiss him on the forehead but knew he wouldn't like it. We were taking a break from touching.

In the store I was only allowed five oranges, though this was enough, a large quantity, a generous amount. Five was a promise of oranges for a long time.

Five soon became four. When I got back into the car I gave one to Carl, my driver that week. He was paid well by the Institute, but I figured it couldn't hurt to be nice to someone who kept me safe.

There was still light in the sky as we drove. I don't recall the route we took to my apartment. Perhaps we veered south-east then doubled back. The army was camped around Central Park, and the whole Upper West Side was still a no-go area. Carl didn't speak during the ride, which wasn't unusual. The drivers gave all their attention to the road, the tops of bridges, open windows, parked cars, people carrying bags, people stood at the kerb. They couldn't protect us from everything but they had to try, just as we had to try to believe they could.

I recall seeing a wedding. A burned-out bus. Fifteen or twenty elderly people were marching, blowing bugles, their faces painted red. I don't know when or where these things happened because I was already in our apartment, arranging the oranges, taking them to Matthew as if they were a special present he'd wanted yet never expected to get.

I remember coming into Times Square then looking west to see the skyscrapers trying to trap the sun.

I texted Matthew to say I was almost home. I didn't expect a reply. The main thing was to give him notice that someone, i.e. me, was going to be entering the apartment.

We parked opposite my building and Carl got out quickly, opened my door and escorted me fast to the entrance, the whole sequence taking no more than fifteen seconds. He came with me through the first barrier but wasn't allowed through the second, and so he thanked me for the orange and left. When he said that, I put my hand in my bag to check the other four were still there. Matthew needed these oranges, and so did I, but they were just oranges. They could only do so much. Yet they were also a little song I could enjoy, a happy tune that let me imagine being five, ten years in the future and looking back to this day on which a few overpriced pieces of fruit were the start of us turning a corner.

I took the stairs from the lobby. I thought of my heart, my lungs. We were young and healthy. If we survived there'd be time for kids and all that.

It is hard to tell someone their behaviour is strange when normal no longer exists.

The long crack in the wall of the vacant apartment next to ours – they'd gone to try to sneak over the Canadian border – was exactly where it had been that morning, and every morning I'd lived there, and maybe would be until the day the building was demolished. Every time I saw the crack my eyes had to follow the diagonal from its origin, a foot from the floor, all the way up to eye level. It was a jagged yet determined line that was good or bad depending on how I labelled the x- and y-axes. Most days it was stuff like *Time* and *US deaths* or *Time* and *Global cases*, but there had also been a few days in the last month when I'd managed more optimistic labelling: *Dosage* and *T-cell count*; *Dosage* and *Immunity*. That day it was just a crack that signalled it was time to get out my key. My hand was already in my pocket when I noticed the hole in our door. It was the size of a quarter, about level with my throat, and though I could not recall seeing it before I wasn't certain it was new.

I unlocked the door quietly and closed it with care, because even before his flu Matthew had been sleeping more during the day. I went into the kitchen, washed my hands, then sprayed them. My fingers were still stinging as I washed the fruit bowl and dried it, but by the time I took the oranges out the bag they were fine. Though I was sure Matthew would prefer me to leave the vacuum-sealed plastic around each fruit, that wasn't how I'd imagined them in the bowl. Four plastic-suffocated spheres were no good; I wanted a mound of bright colour.

I removed the plastic. The oranges were so smooth and perfectly round they seemed sculpted. They had such a glow. Three formed a lower tier; the fourth perched on top like a winner about to be crowned.

I took the bowl and walked down the narrow hall toward what had been my study but for the last few months had been Matthew's room. I'd only gone a few steps before I realised there was a hole in the other door, which led to the lounge. That hole was also quarter-sized, and at about the same height as the one in the entrance door. Even then I did not properly connect this second hole with the first. The buttery light in the hole made me think of the sun sliding down the groove between the skyscrapers, the same sun that oranges drank.

I suppose that even in the best of times a gunshot isn't something people want to investigate.

The lounge window looked west toward Hoboken. The room was golden and red. And from then on I made choices without any sense of deliberation. I switched between kneeling by the body and being at the other end of the room. I chose to see the red patterns on the wall and floor, the couch and lamp, but I also chose to see a side of the room that hadn't been changed by a bullet opening a head like a sneeze. I went from being unable to look at a body that had been someone I loved to having a steady gaze for it. From the neck down, nothing was wrong with the man on the floor. He could have been sleeping or resting his spine. He could have been anyone, because what remained of his face had suffered a collapse and was thickly varnished with blood. In the man's very black hair the blood was almost undetectable except for where it had made spikes.

I do not think time passed. If it did, it moved in a circle. Every point was a start and an end.

I was mute or I was crying.

I had to see and not see.

Finally, there were no more choices.

Finally, it got dark.

~

When I left the bar I was half-drunk. I floated up the hill and saw lights in houses I'd believed abandoned. Dogs barked. A child screamed. Further up, amongst the brownstones, red balloons were tied to fences.

Back home I made coffee then attacked the crap from my desk drawers. I threw out invoices, bank statements, loyalty cards for cafés I'd cheated on, dead pens, clippings about the Institute, my Oyster card from London. All I kept was a Post-it note from Rajeev on which he'd drawn a heart, the photo of Matthew, and a copy of my will. It was so out of date Matthew was the main beneficiary.

I found a website offering a cheap codicil for simple amendments, and although I wasn't convinced this was as 'guaranteed 100% legally binding' as the website promised, it was better to do something that might be wrong than do nothing. I cancelled Matthew as the beneficiary, wrote in Dad's name, then signed every page. All I needed were witnesses. The easiest option was to ask my neighbours. I didn't know Sian and Tony well, despite living next to them for six years. For the first five of these we'd just said hi to each other on the stairs, but earlier this year I'd been woken at four in the morning by shouting. Then there was banging on my door, and when I looked through the peephole I saw Sian.

She told me Tony had drunk too much and it had screwed up his medication (for what, she didn't say). He'd had a nightmare about being infected and woken up in a panic. I couldn't figure out why she'd come to me – it wasn't like she knew my history. I guessed she didn't want to be alone with him.

Tony was already calmer when she and I entered the apartment. Immediately he went into the bathroom and got in the tub and closed his eyes. Sian asked me to sit with him while she phoned his doctor. When I started speaking Tony opened his eyes, but only for a second, he kept them closed after that, even when he started crying. I don't recall exactly what I said, though I know I tried to make him understand that it was OK to still be scared of the virus. I didn't go into the real reasons, I just spoke generally about hope blinding people to all sort of things. Sian must have misunderstood something I said because she rushed into the bathroom and told me to leave. After that our nods on the stairs were minimal.

So I wasn't sure what sort of reception I'd get when I knocked on their door. It was around nine, not late, though not exactly early. No one answered but I heard music inside, so I waited, then knocked again. The music stopped. Tony opened the door. He was wearing sweatpants and an old T-shirt and his face was red. I guessed he'd been working out, maybe rowing: three months before, I'd signed for the machine.

I apologised for disturbing him then told him what I wanted.

'Sure, come on in,' he said.

The place had changed a lot. Like me, they had tried for a minimalist look, but hadn't gone as far. The furniture looked new and the walls were mostly bare, though they had ruined this aesthetic by putting two paintings on the walls. One was of three Siamese cats wearing Confederate uniforms. The other was a sky done in pink and orange in which a black sun hung.

'Sian's latest,' he said. 'Take a seat. Let me find a pen.' He pulled open a drawer, then shut it. 'I don't know where they all go.'

The room was hot and smelled of sweat, deodorant, drying leisurewear. Half a grilled cheese sat on the coffee table.

'Here we go,' he said, and sat down next to me. I handed him the form.

'How much do I need to read?' he said.

'Just this bit about witnessing.'

'Cool.' He skimmed the passage, then signed it. 'I can do Sian's as well if you want. I mean, if you're in a hurry.'

'Really?'

'Oh yeah. Her signature's real easy. And I know she wouldn't mind.'

'Well, alright.'

He signed her name, then gave me back the form.

'Thanks, I really appreciate this.'

'No trouble. So what's brought this on? You taking up bungee jumping?'

'Nothing so dangerous. I'm just trying to get my life in order.'

'I hear that. Good for you. Listen, I was about to make coffee. You want some?'

He said this in a totally normal way, like we were friends, except we weren't. And so I wondered.

'Sure, thanks,' I said.

'Great,' he said, and stood up quickly. And that was when I knew. Not that he made things easy. While we drank our coffee he talked about Sian and how tough things had been, what with his anxiety and her health problems. I was the one who had to change the subject, to ask about his rowing machine, to say he looked like he was in shape. I had to suggest we make our second coffee Irish. Even then I had to take off my sweater slowly while I arched my back before he really started looking at me. But it was worth it. I hadn't had such a hard fuck since college. Afterward, he handed me my clothes and said I'd better go.

Around midnight I considered going to bed, but I was so close to finishing the apartment I decided to stay up. All I had left to do was the bathroom and the hall. The former took way longer than I'd expected; there was so much hidden dirt. I had to lie on the floor to reach under the toilet and sink. Even after the bathroom was objectively clean it retained a used appearance no amount of wiping and scrubbing could fix. It would always seem like someone had just been using the shower. The mirror would keep my face.

I didn't start on the hall cupboard until after three. That was far simpler. I threw everything out. It had been so long since I'd worn those shoes or used a tote bag. None of that stuff was mine.

After that I considered going to sleep, but there didn't seem much point. I made coffee and wandered from room to room, enjoying the free space. I read about Jonas Salk and the March of Dimes. Near the end of his life Salk had said, 'We are the co-authors with nature of our destiny.'

At six I showered then went to catch the train. It was mercifully quiet. For twenty blissful minutes there was a lack of thought.

When I came out the subway I paused to watch the sun rising over the park. Birds were working out a chorus. There was the cold that makes smoking better. I told myself it was my last cigarette and that I should savour it, which I did. I smoked it all the way down to the filter. Then I lit another.

I did the same with that cigarette until I turned onto the block with the Institute and saw a line of people by the kiosk. Finally I'd get to hear what had happened to Carlos.

From the back of the queue I couldn't see whether it was his nephew or someone else working inside. The line was moving slowly. I guessed everyone was asking the same questions. A lot of *when*s and *how*s but not many *why*s.

There were still two women in front when I was able to see inside the kiosk. And then I was confused. I was sick and delighted. Angry and relieved.

'And how are you today?' said Carlos to a blonde lady.

'Very well,' she said.

He handed over her change and when she left there was only one person between myself and the resurrected Carlos.

'And how are you, Mrs Rosen?'

'Fine apart from the state of this city. All this damn zoo is missing is a couple of lions.'

'And maybe a zebra,' said Carlos and laughed. Mrs Rosen stepped aside and then I was facing Carlos.

'Good morning, Doctor Rebecca.'

'Hi, Carlos. Where were you?'

'Antigua!'

'Why?'

My tone must have startled him, but he quickly pasted on a smile.

'For the weather! The sea! Have you been?'

'No.'

'You have to!'

'Do I?'

'Oh yeah. It's really something. Truly a heaven on earth.'

'Can I get two packs of Marlboro?'

He reached for them, then handed them over. I passed him a twenty, he gave me my change, and then I was walking away. He called out some bullshit pleasantry I didn't acknowledge. His friendly shtick was phoney. I'd been so worried about him and all he could do was talk about his fucking vacation after he'd gone off without even leaving a note. It didn't matter that some of us had been patronising his kiosk for years. Why would we deserve any consideration?

I finished my cigarette, then entered the Institute. The security check was very thorough. I had to empty my pockets, take off my shoes, even open my mouth.

'What's brought all this on?' I asked George.

He sighed. 'We've had a threat.'

'Do you think it's serious?'

'Yeah. They're saying it's forty per cent credible. That's basically fifty-fifty. Not my kind of odds.'

In the elevator I thought of Tony's hands round my throat. Maybe in a few days there'd be bruises I could not explain.

I took my ID out as I approached the lab. Before I could swipe in, the door opened.

'Hey, Rajeev.'

He stopped so sharply it was like he'd braked. 'Hey,' he said while looking to the right of my face.

'We should talk,' he said, and I let him. I wanted him to feel he'd left nothing unsaid.

'I don't understand what's been happening. I don't know why you said that stuff to me in your office. If I've done something to piss you off, just tell me.'

He went on to apologise for things that were not his fault. He said *love* several times. And this was hard to hear because he really wanted to make it work; he was willing to put up with so much of my shit. He had such terrible luck. Now I was eating and fucking like everyone else we should have had only normal problems. But it was too late. He was leaving, and so was I.

When he stopped speaking he looked to me for my answer. There were a lot of words in my mouth, most of them small and sharp. Telling him I'd met someone else would have been the simplest lie but this would provoke other questions. I suspected that if I told him about my infidelity, he'd forgive even that.

'There's nothing to talk about,' I said. 'We don't need to clear the air. We had a good thing, but now it's not working. We're done.'

He shook his head, and seemed about to speak, but he had used all his words. He looked at me and that was when I should have been crueller. It would be better for him if he hated me. Yet all I said was, 'I'm sorry'. Then I walked away. Someone else would have run after me, made me explain. Rajeev was too decent for that. For weeks, months, he'd be sitting on benches, stoops, the shore at Five Islands, turning the knife in this wound.

I barely made it to my office before I started crying. I sat and watched the virus turn until my eyes were empty. I felt awful; I was a monster. And yet I had no doubts.

My next task was to sort out my office. I wanted it to be as ordered as my apartment, which didn't seem difficult, given it was only one room. The old journals went onto the shelves, as did the pile of books on the spare chair. The hard part was clearing my desk. The easy thing would have been to sweep it all into one of the drawers, but I wanted a more permanent solution. That meant deciding what I needed to keep, and if so, how it should be filed. I wanted everything so logical even a stranger could make sense of it.

At noon I went down to the cafeteria and was faced with the usual difficult choice. Option #1 was chicken wrapped in prosciutto with wild rice and baby carrots. Option #2 was fennel and mushroom risotto with an orange and rocket salad. When Wanda asked what I wanted I said, 'I think I need to have both.'

She didn't find this strange. 'That's what I do,' she said. 'I have half of each. It seems such a shame to miss out on anything. I'm done with all that.'

I took my tray to an empty table right at the back. I didn't want to be distracted from the food.

I began with the chicken. I ate slowly, letting the food linger on my tongue, pausing after each swallow. Occasionally I thought about my experiment, but for most of the time my attention stayed in the right place.

After I finished the chicken I rinsed my mouth, then ate the risotto the same way. I must have had a cut in my cheek because the orange stung. I picked up my water to wash it away, then stopped: better to keep the sting than lose the taste.

It was half past one when I returned to my office. Its neatness surprised me; it was as if someone else had tidied while I'd been away.

I checked my email, then the *Times* website. Eastern Turkey had seceded. In Europe, wolf numbers were up. Some Afghan villagers had erected a statue of David Bowie made from plastic bottles. I sat and visualised these other places, their capitals, their position on the map. Although I had no idea where Damian was going to send me, nowhere seemed safe.

My computer reminded me it was time to check on the cells. I turned off the alert then went back to reading the news. The prospect of having to leave the country made everywhere seem relevant.

An hour later the alert went off again. I was sure I'd switched it off, so I went into Settings, but everything looked normal.

When it went off for the third time I stood and left my office. I sprayed my hands, rolled on my gloves, then went to see if there would have to be an experiment twenty-seven. If I couldn't infect human cells with the modified virus, there was no reason to leave. I pictured Damian nodding in front of his trees, their mighty trunks concurring.

My cells were in a little room at the end of a corridor. Inside the other rooms I saw Chris and Gulmera, both of them staring intently into a microscope. I thought about knocking on each of their doors, then asking, almost as a joke, if they wanted to come and see the results with me.

I entered my room, shut the door, checked my gloves again. The incubation chamber seemed huge. I switched on the ultraviolet light and stepped forward. In place of the single bright area I'd seen last time there were now three glowing areas, nowhere near the full blaze caused by the regular virus, but the jump in the infected population was like a leap from a village to a town with suburbs. For a long time I stood and stared at these signs of life.

LUKAS

I N the first darkness I floated in a morphine haze. I was conscious, and I could move; there was no sense of time passing. Nothing was changing, so there was nothing to count, no seconds to make a minute, no such thing as an hour. I could barely feel my body; it was drifting while remaining still. This was a lonely state and so I made myself company. Min-seo and I chatted while baking bread; Erik lectured me on the Scythians; Brendan showed me a card trick. Valentina beat the drums; Kobby read a poem. Like me, my mother and father were both in hospital, sick and yet eternal. This should have been a family reunion, except I couldn't make Tomasz attend. Even conjuring his face was difficult; there was no clear image, just the kind of flickering image you get when blinking very fast.

After a few days, or one long day, a stranger came to remove my right eye. The man had a Russian voice that made me think of long, red curtains being stroked by a cold breeze. I imagined him with a beard and glasses and two young sons. I stayed calm while he explained the surgery, but when the anaesthetic tried to drag me under I had to kick and swim to stay on the surface. It was the wrong darkness, not a sleep, its end not guaranteed.

When I came to, my eye socket was squeezing a stress ball, working hard, doing its best, yet the ball would not relax. It felt like I was perpetually trying to wink. They called it an orbital implant, which was funny in a science fiction way. At first it was a dead moon that tried to follow the left eye's lead, then it became a fixed point around which I was spinning. My remaining eye tried to assert itself but could only muster a grey sky that did not promise dawn. In answer the implant started to expand. Not satisfied with tenancy, it wanted dominion, perhaps the whole head. At least that was my supposition. *All theory is grey.*

The grey sky became the dirty white sheet we'd hung for privacy in the transport centre. None of us knew the name of that place. It wasn't on the map. 'Next, the cattle cars,' we all kept saying. We were right about that.

They kept offering food but I refused. Try closing your eyes and opening your mouth and then waiting to see what someone puts in there.

The first darkness ended with a hovering jewel on which a man was running towards stairs. The next thing I saw was my hand, its thumb, the fingers, all present and correct. I brought that hand to the dressing on my face, then found the tape keeping it in place. I removed that soft wall to be certain miracles had not occurred.

Sleeping, or pretending to sleep, became my priority. With a closed eye the left and right circles matched. With a closed eye Dr Nilsson wouldn't talk to me. All I wanted was stillness, silence, the opportunity to believe that if I waited, if I was good, eventually the bad dream would end.

My ribs were mostly healed when they removed my catheter. The toilet at the end of the ward was pointed out as if it was a reward. For the next three days I stuck to the bedpan until I was sure I had no audience. I sat up and put my left foot down, which was fine, but when I did the same with the right it disappeared from view. For that foot the floor could only be felt, not seen, and that didn't seem safe. I could only shuffle, and the room seemed smaller, as if it had been divided into cupboards I had to serially navigate. I went slowly, I was careful, I didn't trust the blank areas in my vision. My head turned quickly from side to side, checking walls had not crept up, that no one was lurking. Reaching the toilet did feel like a prize.

Even with my head fully to the right, most of that shoulder couldn't be seen. Touching it wasn't the same. Although I didn't ask for one, I was offered a mirror. This confirmed my shoulder's existence, but my face was gone. I didn't know that thin, pale man. He had the look of a victim whose attacker would never be caught.

Although I could remember being beaten by Bob and Kim, it was hard to connect my injuries to that event. They seemed more like the belated appearance of the visitor I had long been waiting for. Now he had arrived, other changes would follow. Liver spots; a mesh of wrinkles; a grey frame for my face.

The miracle occurred on a spring morning. I had just returned from the toilet when a rectangular patch of yellow appeared on my right. It remained for several minutes then faded. An hour later Dr Nilsson asked why I was so happy. When I told him I was starting to see again he said nothing at first, but I could tell he didn't believe me. I took great pleasure describing my shape, its attributes, how brightly it had shone. The doctor scratched his face then said it wasn't unusual after eye removal for patients to have hallucinations. Though this sounded true, I really wanted to hurt him.

The days got longer, lighter. I walked up and down the ward until I stopped bumping into things. I asked Dr Nilsson when I could leave.

'You're physically healthy enough,' he said, 'but there are safety issues. I don't want you going out there and being attacked. Let me make some enquiries.'

I laughed in his face. 'Yes, ask Bob and Kim if they still want to kill me.'

He shook his head. 'You don't need to worry about them. They're no longer a threat.'

The yellow rectangle did not return. Instead there were blue dots.

I was moved to a small, windowless cube that smelt of antiseptic, probably where they'd have kept me if I'd been found guilty at the judgment. All this time I could have been there, free to study, delivered from all temptation, just me and books to stare at until my eyes were sore.

When I asked Dr Nilsson if someone could bring me my papers and books, he looked at the floor. 'I'm afraid your home was destroyed in the fire. I'm sorry, there wasn't much left.'

'Fuck you,' I said, because I had to say this to someone.

Next day Nilsson brought me a pile of books. 'From Kobby,' he said, and I pretended not to be pleased. Predictably, there was fucking Tolstoy, though thankfully not *War and Peace*. At least *Resurrection* was shorter. On the title page of *Lotte in Weimar* he'd written 'Life belongs to the living', which was about as close as Kobby got to a joke.

I was grateful to him, but reading wasn't the same. I could see the words, but they didn't seem entirely present; it was like they had less substance, were printed in a thinner ink. It was hard to concentrate for longer than half an hour, and when I stopped reading, my mind had barely snacked.

Twice a week I was allowed onto the roof to walk up and down beneath half a sky. The mountains looked as if they were pasted on a wall. The guards let me go close enough to the edge of the roof to see the ground, which made me wonder if they cared whether I jumped off. Five storeys no longer looked like much of a drop.

Most days I saw the dots. There was once a red fog. These minor hallucinations began to bore me. I wanted landscapes, buildings, people. I tried to summon Tomasz's face in the context of a memory. Our last good moment had been when he was released from prison, that drunken night on which he was happy, believed himself lucky, said all kinds of stuff about wanting to be a dad. Agata had made no comment but I, in a soap opera moment, imagined her having my child. Though the memory was otherwise clear, and I could hear Tomasz's voice, he was mostly out of view, his presence in the memory more implied than actual. This strange effect, coupled with my headaches, made me wonder what harm Bob and Kim had done to my brain.

Time did not pass, or rather, time did not pass through me. I didn't scratch marks on the walls or table. Whenever Dr Nilsson mentioned the day or month it seemed like information from an obsolete form of measurement. The signs of summer I saw from the roof were as insignificant as a change of wallpaper in a room I wasn't allowed to visit.

My release took place late at night. It was warm enough for people to be sitting outside, perfect weather to enjoy a beer and a joint, but the camp was deserted.

'Where is everyone?' I asked the guard escorting me.

'Curfew,' he said.

Though I knew my hut had been destroyed, its blackened timbers were still a shock. While I had accepted the loss of my books and papers, I still foolishly hoped that a few possessions might have been spared. The five feathers from Min-seo; a doodle of Rustam's; one of Edie's teeth. All I found were ashes and the twisted metal of appliances.

'I used to live here,' I told the guard.

'Moving will be easy,' he said, and laughed.

He led me to the next row, in which all but one of the houses were burnt-out. The intact house had belonged to Mina, and when the guard opened the door, I almost objected, because she'd always insisted people knock.

'Wait here,' he said, and went inside. His torch moved through the rooms.

'All clear. And all yours,' he said and left me there.

Mina would not have liked the state of the place. Empty bottles, broken ones, a shirt covered in vomit. There was blood in the sink, but not much, the amount a person coughs up. A lot of the furniture was missing. I was surprised they'd left the bed. She'd hacked off so much of the legs it was almost as low as a futon: she'd told me she wanted to reduce the risk of falling out. I don't think either of us enjoyed sleeping together; we didn't communicate well. We only did it because it hadn't been done. Yet this was still a bed I knew, the closest thing to familiarity I'd had for half a year. I switched off the light, undressed, then got under the covers. Immediately I could tell that someone, or rather several someones, both male and female, had recently been enjoying themselves. I pulled the blankets over my head. It was good to have company.

REBECCA

A HEAD the mountains stretched so far it was hard to believe they could contain a destination. There was just more rock, more snow, until the horizon.

The first flash seemed to come from the morning sun reflecting off snow. When it repeated a few minutes later, the flash was larger, brighter, more like light that had bounced off metal. The flashes become more frequent until there was a near-constant blaze of white light along a distant ridge. Only when we were close did I realise it was a long line of mirrors.

'What?' I said out loud, but the pilot couldn't hear me. The mirrors remained a mystery until I saw the buildings behind them. The largest was a five-storey concrete structure surrounded by a high fence. Next to it a few hundred cabins were arranged in rows around a square. As we descended I saw some dots transform into people who were staring up at me.

We landed on the main building's roof. The pilot led me down a flight of stairs then we stepped into a strip-lit corridor with many doors, all closed. It was silent except for the hum of the lights. We stood there for maybe ten seconds; the pilot clearly had no idea where to go next. Then a door opened and a man with curly grey hair, thick glasses and a spade-shaped beard offered me his hand.

'I'm Dr Nilsson. Welcome to our camp. It's an honour for us that you're here. There's a lot to talk about, but you must be tired.'

'I'm fine,' I said. 'But thank you.'

'Then let's have coffee.'

I followed him down two flights of stairs, then along a short corridor where all the doors were open. Inside, bulky men in black uniforms were talking loudly. I got the stares you'd expect an unknown woman to receive in a mountaintop facility with a predominantly male staff.

The doctor brought me into a canteen that looked onto a yard and barracks. While he fetched coffee I watched two men practise some kind of mixed martial art, taking it in turns to kick higher than their heads. I was glad to have time to collect myself. Although Damian and I had prepared for the conversation I was about to have, in my travel-fatigued condition it would be easy to say the wrong thing.

'Here you go,' said the doctor and slopped a little on the table. It was sort of touching that he was nervous. He was probably going to tell me he'd read all my papers.

He took a sip, and I could see him thinking about how to begin, which was fine. I was in no rush.

'I hope you don't mind me telling you a little about the camp. Some of it you'll have heard already, but I'm old-fashioned and I like to think these things sound better from a person. When I came here, six years ago, it was much larger – there were about six hundred people, and it was very crowded. Originally I was just a physician, though I've had to be a lot of other things I'm really not qualified to do. Sometimes I've been a counsellor, sometimes a liaison, and I've also had to be an advocate for the people here. For the most part, I think they've been well treated, but given their situation, it's not surprising that they're often their own worst enemy. There's a lot of substance abuse, and all kinds of mental health issues. Right now, there are only a hundred and ten people left, and about a third of those are showing major symptoms. So the mood is very low. Which means it's good you're here. Although a cure will come too late for most of them, maybe knowing that someone is trying will give them a lift.'

'I'm grateful to be here,' I said, then paused. 'And I'm optimistic that the data I'm here to gather will help us make real progress in understanding the disease.'

This was a politician's answer that promised nothing. But it was better than saying there was almost certainly never going to be a cure. Attempting to reverse Werner's would be like trying to get smoke back into a fire.

We worked out some logistics: he'd arrange the inmates' appointments and assist me as much as his other duties permitted. He assured me that all my equipment had arrived safely.

'They've made some of the other machines feel old,' he said, and when I laughed it became a yawn.

'Sorry,' I said.

'No, I'm sorry. I've gone on too long. I'll let you get some rest. How about we meet again at four? That's a good time to tour the camp – they'll all be up by then.'

I stared at him in confusion. I wasn't there to inspect the place. There was no reason for me to meet the inmates before I took their samples.

'Or we can leave that for tomorrow,' he said obliviously. 'Although the sooner they see you the better. Obviously you need their consent to take part, and my job will be a lot easier if they don't think of you as some anonymous official. Things have been tense over the last nine months and there's not as much trust as there was.'

It seemed like a very bad joke to have travelled so far to be told my access to the inmates was in doubt. The sensible thing would have been to take it easy for the rest of the day, then go into the camp next morning. But whether I went into the camp today, tomorrow, or the day after, I was going to be afraid. The more time I had to think about it, the worse the fear would get.

'What about now?' I said, and the doctor looked surprised.

'Well, we could, although it's a little early for them. And I have to do my rounds in the clinic. How about in two hours?'

'That's fine.'

'Good. I'll show you to your quarters.'

He stood up and led me to the end of the corridor, then up a different flight of stairs. I was expecting something spartan, like a Travelodge, but the suite bordered on fancy. The bed was large and topped by a canopy. The furnishings looked antique.

'We had your vice-president here two years ago,' he said and handed me the key card. 'They must have looted a dacha for her.'

After the doctor left I went to the window and looked down onto the camp. From the helicopter I hadn't noticed that a lot of cabins had been destroyed. A slight slope to the plateau made the little buildings seem at risk of sliding off.

I opened my suitcase but didn't unpack. If I was only going to be there a few weeks, there wasn't much point. I lay down. I took deep breaths. Little cracks in the ceiling became rivers seen from space.

The ceiling went blank. There was silence. I hovered over mountains whose soft, deep snow lovingly promised to catch me. There was a gentle knock, but I could ignore it. There were no doors in the mountains.

The second knock made me fall and there was no longer snow to cushion the impact, only jagged black rocks that hated visitors. The impact of waking was hard.

'Just a minute,' I said, then let the details of the room solidify. I got up and adjusted my clothes, and as I did so I glanced out the window. More people were outside. A man was jogging. It might have been a vacation camp, a health spa, an alpine sanatorium.

When I opened the door the doctor smiled, then asked how I'd slept with a professional solicitude that made me think I looked awful.

We went downstairs then left the building, and the cool air revived me. At the fence we were met by a guard holding a rifle. As he went to unlock the gate I noticed he had a limp.

The nearest building was a round structure with small windows that made me think of a community church.

'This is our meeting house,' said the doctor. 'It's very pretty inside, but unfortunately I can't show you because it's closed at the moment. There was an incident last year and ever since then the authorities have forbidden big gatherings.'

I heard something being dragged. I turned and saw a small white-haired man moving slowly toward us on crutches. Every step he took seemed to require such effort it was as if he was having to plan and execute each one from scratch. He couldn't have been less threatening and yet I backed away.

'Don't worry,' said the guard. 'If he comes too close I'm allowed to shoot him.'

'But you won't, Alain,' said Dr Nilsson. 'You know he isn't a threat.'

I wanted to believe the doctor. Although I knew it was irrational to be frightened of this poor, broken man, he was the first infected person I'd seen for six years. Even if I was immune, he was still contagious.

The doctor walked towards the man, perhaps to shield him, then said, 'How's the hip today, Kim?'

'The same,' he said, but he was looking at me when he spoke.

'Well, why don't you come in tomorrow afternoon for a shot. And if that's alright with you, could Rebecca' – he gestured at me – 'run a few tests as well?'

Kim nodded and seemed too shy to say anything else.

'See you tomorrow,' said Dr Nilsson. I realised he'd found me my first participant, and while I was grateful, the knowledge that this quiet, unthreatening man would soon be near me made me feel sick.

I was glad when we were joined by another soldier. Ahead of us five inmates were standing in a circle, occasionally glancing at us. Rather than engage with them, even at a distance, I kept my eyes on the huts. In the first window I saw a man with a black beard staring up at the sky. The next few were empty, and then there were several windows painted black. I guessed it was a gesture of mourning, but when Dr Nilsson saw where I was looking he sighed.

'I should warn you that there will certainly be a few inmates who won't cooperate. The Gnostics won't even let me treat them. The last two who died had been ill for months without my even knowing. The others just left their bodies in the square.'

Hearing their name was like remembering a brand of soda that had been discontinued. They had had their moment, done their damage, but thankfully it had passed. In ten years' time kids would find it funny that we'd been so dumb.

As we got nearer to the circle of five I saw there were three women, who looked drunk yet otherwise healthy, and two men with the frailty that suggests an organ close to failure. Even though they were objectively not much more of a threat than Kim, I was trembling. It was the like the fear I'd felt as a kid when I went to the zoo and saw the crocodile enclosures. No matter how strong the glass, how high the fence, somehow they'd get out.

When Dr Nilsson greeted the inmates they were friendly, but he didn't stop to introduce me and I wasn't sorry.

Over his shoulder the doctor said, 'I think it's best to approach only a small number of people at the start, the ones who I'm sure will agree. That way they can reassure the others.'

'Sounds like a good idea,' I said. I couldn't tell if he knew I was scared. I hoped I wasn't that easy to read.

Any sense of reprieve vanished when we reached the square. About twenty inmates were drifting around, some of them grouped around a cluster of chess tables. Two of the spectators had oxygen canisters. A woman was being pushed in a wheelchair by a bald man with very large forearms. Any path through the square would take us into their midst.

As if sensing my worry, Dr Nilsson hesitated on the edge of the square. But he was just waiting for the woman in the wheelchair to come closer. She was extremely thin, and perhaps had once – or rather, recently – been beautiful, although now her gaunt face, with its prominent cheekbones, made me think of all the people I'd seen lying in alleys, stairwells and vacant lots with a plastic bag over their head. It wasn't that she looked old, more like she was lacking some essential nutrient. She was hunched so far forward she seemed on the verge of falling from her chair.

The man pushing her stopped ten feet from us. The woman raised her head with the slowness of someone trying to feel each of their vertebrae. Even when she was looking in our direction, I doubted she could see us.

'Is this your wife, Lars?' she said, and her voice was as deep as a two-pack smoker. The noise that followed was either a gasp or a laugh.

'We're divorced,' said Dr Nilsson, then introduced us. Valentina said, 'Pleased to meet you,' then asked where I was from. When I told her she wanted to know how things were in my country.

'Normal, except when it isn't.' I told her about our new subway, the masks people were wearing.

'You were already a strange place,' she said, and I couldn't argue. For those first few minutes I felt comfortable talking to her, but when she spoke of her life in Madrid, going out dancing, playing Frisbee in Retiro Park, it made me remember this was someone my age or even younger. It was like some cruel spell had been cast on her. The worst part was the calm way she answered Dr Nilsson's questions about the loss of sensation in her limbs.

'Not much feeling in the right hand,' she said. 'I can sense heat but not pressure.' From her easy tone she could have been talking about a failing shower system.

After we'd left Valentina I asked Dr Nilsson if she was heavily medicated.

'She's not taking much. She's been able to find relief in other ways.'

'Such as?'

He hesitated long enough to get my attention. 'I've been trying some new treatment options for the terminally ill. It's a kind of counselling. I think it's helped Valentina and a few others.'

He didn't say any more, and I didn't want to pry. I liked that he was withholding something; it made it easier for me not to tell him why I was really there.

We left the square and skirted the edge of the camp. The mountains hanging over us were already casting shadows. Within their gloom we walked between two rows of burned houses.

'Was there an accident?'

'No, this was from the incident last year.'

'Was anyone hurt?'

'Three people died. The authorities were more concerned with putting out the fire than checking whether people were inside.'

Although he said this with the level tone of someone trying not to show anger, his voice wavered as he continued. 'And this was what most of them had come here to escape. They gave up being free so they could be protected.'

We walked on, but the tour seemed over. I couldn't wait to be back on the right side of the fence. We had just turned a corner when Alain, who was in front of us, yelled at us to stay back. We did as he said, although all I could see was a row of huts with no one in sight. The only unusual thing was a bathtub outside one of the huts. I watched Alain move towards it with his rifle raised. When he got close to it he shouted, 'Clear.'

He beckoned us forward.

'The usual crap,' he said to Dr Nilsson.

In the bathtub there was a naked man, bleeding from small grazes on his arms and legs. He was in his mid-thirties and without obvious symptoms, except for a patch over one eye. To me he looked dead, but after Dr Nilsson checked his vitals he said, 'Lukas hasn't killed himself yet.'

'Shouldn't someone help him?'

The doctor shook his head. 'Believe me, I've tried.'

LUKAS

S UMMER was the worst season. There was little shade and the nights were too short; dust got everywhere. Mina's bedroom faced east, so on my first morning I was woken early by the sun. In the next room smoke was curling through the light.

Erik was at the kitchen table. 'Morning,' he said and grinned. In front of him was a bar of soap, a bottle of vodka, three apples and some bread.

'Brought you a housewarming pack,' he said while inspecting my face. 'Fuck, those brutes really went to town. I always knew Bob was a psycho – he had that frustrated little man complex that makes people torturers. Or drama teachers. But Kim was one of us. I think he's bloody sorry about what he did, though that's probably no comfort to you.'

'He's alive?'

'Just about. And you're in no danger from him, or anyone else. They all know who the enemy is now.'

While I didn't think of Erik as a friend, I'd always enjoyed our disagreements: they were like the cordial but vicious attacks that senior faculty used to inflict on a new member of staff. He'd really stood up for me during my trial, no doubt for his own reasons, which didn't mean I wasn't grateful. It was good to see him.

'So what was it like in there? Did you see Dejan or Edie?'

'No.'

He banged the table. 'The fuckers must have killed them.' He muttered something under his breath then said, 'Do you want to get some clothes on and come out? A lot of people have missed you.'

I hesitated; six months ago some of them had been trying to kill me.

'What are you worried about? I told you, that's all forgiven. You'll be safe with me.'

On the way to the square I asked Erik who had died in my absence. I expected to hear a lot of names, but after he'd said thirty it was hard to listen to the rest. The final tally was double what I'd expected. There were only a hundred and twenty of us left.

'It's bloody grim. But not all bad,' he said. 'Now we're a lot closer. Although they won't let us meet in large groups, it's not going to stop us.'

'From doing what?'

He laughed. 'Forgive me for not telling you everything after you've been in there six months. For all I know they brainwashed you or offered you a trip to a tropical island. You might not even know they got to you.'

'Oh yeah. And my fake eye is really a bomb.'

At least he laughed at that.

The first people I saw were Enzo and Stephan, who both looked healthy, but Stephan said he had pains in his legs. I asked him if there had been any more judgments in my absence. 'Oh no,' he said. 'We don't need those any more. Erik's helped us to be more disciplined.'

For the rest of the morning people kept turning up in twos and threes. Even those who had voted against me at the judgment expressed sympathy for my injuries and asked about my captivity. They listened and nodded but most of them couldn't wait to tell me what I'd missed.

'Now this is just a prison,' said Yasmin.

'No, it's a concentration camp,' said Mikhail.

He said the guards had used nerve gas during the riot; she said the guards had opened fire and tried to kill them all. It was as if they'd forgotten I was there. There was a moment when I wondered if I looked so different that they'd mistaken me for a stranger.

Dejan and Edie were the heroes of the riot. Their bravery, their sacrifice, had apparently saved the others. Even Kobby, the most well-read person in the camp, wasn't immune. 'Did you know that "martyr" comes from the Greek for "witness"?' he said, then went into a paroxysm of blinking.

I didn't contradict their versions of that night. It would have been my memory against theirs, and despite Erik's assurances, it was hard to believe they'd forgotten, or forgiven, what I'd done. I also couldn't help noticing that although they were saying terrible things, most of them seemed happy. There was a sense of camaraderie. All the deaths had reshuffled people's relationships. Kobby was with Lucia; Aleksandr and Khunbish were holding hands.

Meeting so many people, after months on my own, was exhausting. After two hours my fake eye began to dig its way towards the back of my skull. A blue blur ghosted across my vision while Khunbish gleefully told me how stupid the new guards were. 'Isn't that right?' he kept saying to Erik, who nodded sagely like a teacher satisfied with his pupil. Nothing about Erik seemed different to me, but the others were treating him with far more respect, wanting his approval.

There were eight or nine people around me when two guards started shouting. 'Move along,' they said, and one of them lifted his gun. Alain had grown a beard, which meant I didn't recognise him at first, nor did I remember the harshness in his voice. Erik and the others exchanged glances before dispersing. As I walked away I raised my hand to Alain. In the look he gave me there was no acknowledgement.

My feet automatically brought me towards Min-seo's cabin. I knew she wasn't there, but if I could go in, sit a while, it might be some comfort. I'd push my hands through feathers, gently part them, glimpse the underworld.

But her hut was also gone. I sat in the wreckage and tried to reconstruct the melted things that remained. There was a door-knob, a ruptured kettle, one of the bath taps. Anyone could have lived there.

I went back to Mina's hut, opened the vodka, then drank for the rest of the day. When I eventually went to bed I discovered that someone had pissed all over it.

∼

During the next few days I wandered around the camp. I sat in the square; stood at the fence; trudged through *Resurrection*. I didn't know what to do with myself. Reading wasn't the same;

the people I'd been close to were gone. Sometimes I managed to attach myself to a group for a few hours, yet I was never at ease. I imagined how I must look to them, what they must think. At best they might feel pity.

I didn't want to go in the canteen and not see Brendan, but it was inevitable. Fatoumata was now in charge. Though apparently no one had been enthusiastic about her getting the job, there had been no other volunteers. This was the only positive change that had happened since I'd been away. Brendan had cooked simple, stodgy meals that made us fat and sleepy. Fatoumata, using more or less the same ingredients, created subtler, lighter food. The rice that day was sweet with carrots. The lamb was flaked and pink. When I complimented her she bowed. It was the first time I'd seen her smile.

I ate quickly. Although I'd have liked to savour the food, I was worried it was going to get busy. Being in a large group made me uncomfortable, and the canteen was the only place exempt from the six-person rule. Nobody was grateful for this. There were cameras on the walls. Guards wandered in and out. We couldn't be trusted to eat.

The food sat easily in my stomach as I walked round the camp. While I didn't like the constant sense of seeing through a telescope, occasionally there were moments when this restricted view worked like an iris shot in a film. Something that might have been ignored demanded attention. Two crows stared at each other as intently as if their counterpart was a mirror. A forgotten pawn was the unchallenged ruler of a chess table. This was also how I saw the wheelchair next to the fence that looked over the valley. The person had their back to me. When I got closer, I saw the long scar on her neck, but I still wasn't sure. Although Erik hadn't said Valentina's name when listing the deceased, I had just assumed. After four days back in the camp, having neither seen her nor heard anyone say her name, I was sure she was gone.

I breathed deeply as a yellow square strobed in my periphery.

Her grey hair was now shoulder-length. Her hands looked like children's gloves.

When I said her name she turned slightly. I walked around to face her. There was the same shock I'd felt when I saw Kim on the floor, his hair bright white, apparently tumbled from some precipice of health. This was the grandmother of the young woman I'd last seen half a year ago, though the transformation wasn't only in terms of age. Some other force had warped her body. Her left shoulder was pushed forward, as if she was trying to turn round, while the rest of her torso seemed to want to go the other way.

'Good weather,' she said. 'Good clouds. Just look at them hang. A lot of coins in that purse.'

At first I thought she was high, except there was none of the febrile energy she'd shown in Rustam's house. She asked if I knew what there was for lunch. When she heard she clapped her hands together soundlessly.

'That woman is a genius. You could give her two rocks and she'd make a cake.'

She obviously didn't recognise me, so I told her who I was. I expected many reactions – anger, fear – but not for her to shrug.

'Don't be silly. Lukas has two eyes. He's also in prison.'

'No, it's me. I've been injured. I was in the hospital, not prison.'

She looked confused, though not upset.

'Oh, it must have been prison after what he did. Everyone knows he's a rapist.'

'The judgment found him innocent.'

She laughed. 'By one vote! What sort of innocence is that?'

The yellow square was now a constant presence, luminous, awake.

'I didn't do that,' I said. 'But I'm sorry about other things I did. I shouldn't have, I just lost control.'

'He was terrified,' she said. 'And we were only talking. Even though I know some men are like that, it always surprises me when they become abusive. He wasn't even drunk. I wonder why he didn't kill me.'

'I'm so sorry,' I said. 'I know that's useless. I want to make excuses, but there aren't any.'

The yellowness burnt to a white pain. I put my hand over the patch, which did nothing.

'Are you alright?' she said with genuine concern. 'It's nice talking to you, but if you need to go, I don't mind. Even if we're all dying, it's still important we take good care of ourselves. Is there anything I can do?'

'No,' I said, then walked away. I couldn't apologise to her.

∼

Although the others hated the curfew, I preferred those early nights. After the second bell had rung I could sit at the kitchen table in total confidence that for the next ten hours I'd see no one. Most nights I read, but not for long. After three or four drinks either the blue dots or some other shape would appear to keep me company. I drank for both of us, letting my mind wander, sometimes through unfamiliar territory. Even if I didn't have brain damage, the contents of my head seemed to have been shaken up. Memories of my mother – her kindness, her illness – kept repeating, until what had been a solid block, welded by grief, had become separate piles which could be examined. She had been a secretary, sometimes a cleaner, but whatever her work she had preserved an air of dignity. While my father would be gregarious during his stay in hospital, my mother kept herself apart. Visiting her on the ward was like stepping into a private space. I couldn't remember what we talked about during those two weeks, only that every day she asked how Tomasz was, and I'd say he was fine, and that he'd said he was going to try and visit. He was off in Warsaw, apparently working on something big, and unlike the rest of us, didn't think she was in any real danger. He did call on the day of her operation, when she was already under the knife. She'd been asking for him as they wheeled her in.

Apart from when I had to go out to get food or alcohol, I stayed home. This seemed the safest place for me; the downside was that it made it easy for people to find me. Dr Nilsson came by once a week to check on my eye, and probably me, but at least I knew what he wanted. To tell him I was feeling fine wasn't difficult, and although I was sure he didn't believe this, he thankfully didn't have much time to spend with me.

Erik's visits were more complicated. A week could pass without him visiting, or he might show up two days in a row. He never stayed long, and did most of the talking, telling me who was sick, who'd pissed him off, the minutiae of some petty victory he'd scored against the authorities. I didn't believe he visited because he cared about me; I suspected he found the sound of his own voice as reassuring as a heartbeat. But as summer began to fade I felt that Erik was, perhaps for the first time, giving me his full attention, weighing my replies, parsing my silences. I suspect he didn't believe I was really so broken. He distrusted simple truths. Perhaps he thought the loss of an eye, a broken nose, the recent deaths of several loved ones, would not have affected him as much.

For a while I had other visitors. My absence (and perhaps my injuries) must have made me seem less familiar, less known. I can't think of any other reason why those people took a sexual interest in me. With none of them did I have much of a history. I tried to go through the motions, but my body refused to perform. The only three people I wanted to sleep with were dead. Having another person close to me, seeing their face, wasn't just uncomfortable – I found it disgusting, and also ridiculous. So much grabbing and gasping for a little moment that would soon be forgotten. Even when I closed my eye I couldn't escape their desperation. Enzo wouldn't stop talking; Mikhail's grunts were bestial. The only moment I came close to enjoying was when my flaccidity angered Clara so much she slapped me with her knuckles. That shocked me into a sudden tumescence she was too apologetic to exploit. Neither she, nor the others, made a second visit. No doubt word spread quickly that I was too broken to be used.

At the start of autumn I began blacking out. The first time was frightening, but after that it was interesting to find myself in the square or amid burnt houses with no idea of how I'd got there. I liked that the preceding minutes had been thoroughly erased. It became sort of a game to look at a place – the chess tables; an abandoned bath – and wonder if I might wake up there, and then a few days later find myself, sometimes clothed, sometimes naked, in that exact spot. It was like I'd crept there so stealthily I hadn't noticed myself doing it.

So there was nothing unusual about the day I woke up in the dark. I'd had three or four drinks at lunch, then gone for a walk to ease a cramp in my leg. After a short while I felt lightheaded and sat down next to a hut. Since it was dark, five or six hours must have passed, much longer than I was usually unconscious, which meant I was outside after curfew. The stillness made me think I was inside, though not in my hut, because none of my rooms were so dark. I could smell shit, very strong hash, and a coppery scent that at the time I couldn't identify as blood.

In that darkness I wasn't alone. There were four or five people breathing softly, two of them lying close to me. 'Hello?' I said, but no one answered. I lay there for a long time in silence: it seemed pointless to speak if no one was going to answer.

Eventually someone moved. There were sounds of friction, skin rubbing against wood. A hollow, choking noise went on for a long time before it burst into a gasp. The person on my right began to masturbate in a way that told me they were a man. When he came, a little touched my thigh, but this did not seem deliberate. Despite our proximity I had no sense that his act had any connection to me. When the woman to my left began her own routine it seemed equally unrelated to my being there.

She was making a low moan of climax when the bell for curfew rang. Even in my discombobulated state I realised it was earlier than I had believed; it shouldn't have been dark. I had the panicked thought that I'd been blind for hours. I stood up, then felt myself falling, but didn't. Although I was on my feet I was scared to move because I was surrounded by bodies I couldn't see. There was no way out.

'You can leave,' said a man's voice, and I didn't know if he meant this as encouragement, the granting of permission, or a simple articulation of what was possible.

'But I can't see,' I said, and the silence that followed made me think that once again I did not deserve a reply.

After a long time the man said, 'There is a light within a man of light, and it lights up the whole world. If He does not shine, He is darkness. It doesn't matter if we can see. God is the only eye.'

Now I knew his voice. Brendan and I had called him Rasputin, but his preferred name was Seth. While I was grateful to him and the other Gnostics for declaring me innocent at the judgment, that didn't prevent me from replying, 'Where there is much light, the shadow is deep.' If he was going to throw absurd scripture at me, I was free to quote from a better source.

Seth paused for long enough that when he spoke it didn't seem like a response to what I'd said. 'He is light to those who see him,' he said, and then, as if this was some kind of call and response, the woman next to me intoned, 'He is a mirror to those who know him.'

Someone lit a cigarette, and that brief illumination was enough to show me the room. There were two people on the floor between myself and the door, both of them naked, one with blood on his chest, the other lying on her front with faeces placed at intervals down her spine. Then it was dark again, and though I was careful, on my way to the door I stepped on what was either a hand or arm. The person didn't protest. All I heard was a sigh.

I made it home just as the second bell rang. I washed, got into bed, then fell into the arms of the bottle. In the twilight a small pain woke on the right side of my face but didn't move about. I lay awake for a long time, exploring the shadows, trying to reconcile what I could see with what I could only guess.

When, a week later, I woke up in the dark again, there was, despite the silence, an atmosphere of welcome. I took off my clothes and waited. Eventually I felt a hand.

REBECCA

After the tour I went to my room and lay on the bed until my heart rate came down. I told myself I wouldn't have to go into the camp again. The next time I saw the inmates it would be in ones and twos, in a safe environment.

That night jet lag wasn't a problem. I got into bed just after eight and then I was dead for ten hours. When I showered the water pressure was so much better than at home I could have stayed under all day.

I was demolishing a mountain of eggs when Dr Nilsson came into the canteen, looking like he'd barely slept. He raised a hand in greeting, then went and got coffee. He brought it over and we exchanged some morning pleasantries. After I praised the shower, he said, 'A triumph of Soviet engineering. It's verging on hydrotherapy.'

Behind him a group of guards was sitting at a long table. They were speaking Russian and English, switching between the two so freely it was sometimes hard to work out which was their first language. Aside from Dr Nilsson, I guessed they were probably the only people with whom the inmates had regular contact.

'So this morning I have my rounds, and you're welcome to accompany me. But if you have a lot to get ready for this afternoon,

I completely understand. So far I have five people scheduled to come in – Kim, Valentina and three others.'

'I'd like that. Would it also be possible for me to run a few tests on the guards this morning? I want to make sure the protocols are running smoothly before I see the inmates. It'll only be the regular test I'm sure the guards are used to.'

'Well,' he said and looked embarrassed. 'We haven't done much testing in the last few years. We've been so busy. And all the staff are vaccinated.'

'Of course,' I said, but his answer made me more determined to test them. 'I don't want to put you to any trouble. Five or six will be enough.'

And I didn't feel bad about this sleight of hand. It *had* been a while since I'd stuck a needle in someone's arm. I could use the practice, and it wouldn't hurt them, much.

Dr Nilsson's rounds didn't take long. A pale, silent woman was having dialysis. Next to her a tall, thin man with an aristocratic face was reading a book in German. Stephan paused to introduce himself then kept reading while Dr Nilsson changed the dressings on his legs. The venous ulcers covered so much skin they looked like garish leggings.

Neither of the inpatients was conscious. A large woman was on a ventilator. In the next bed a man with reddish hair was whimpering in pain. His face and hands were horribly burned but the damage didn't look recent. Whatever was causing him such agony was happening internally.

'There's not much more we can do for him,' said Dr Nilsson. 'If he gets any more morphine he'll stop breathing.'

'What's wrong with him?'

'Chondrosarcoma. Though the burns didn't help.'

'What happened?'

'Jorge was the one who set those fires last year. He thought he was making a statement, but he just made things worse. In my opinion he wanted some attention. Jorge wasn't popular.'

We stared at Jorge in silence. Given how much pain he was in, I hoped he wouldn't regain consciousness.

After Dr Nilsson finished his rounds we went to my lab, which was a small room off the clinic. We'd sent them a new thermal cycler, a few gel chambers and a couple of centrifuges. I'd have sent more but Damian said it might draw too much attention.

I thanked the doctor, and reassured him I had everything I needed. He nodded and seemed about to leave, then lingered.

'I was wondering,' he said with an almost boyish shyness, 'do you think it's possible that some of them might never become symptomatic? Could the ones who've had it for eight or nine years only be carriers?'

And there was so much hope in his voice I didn't want to shut him down, at least not completely.

'It's not impossible,' I said, which wasn't much of a concession. 'Although I think we'd know that by now. Even the most generous projections don't give more than ten years between infection and becoming symptomatic.'

He nodded, but his mouth was small. I saw no way to sugar-coat the truth. The best I could do was to say, 'Of course, we don't know. Only time will tell.'

This was almost certainly not the answer he'd wanted. But perhaps I'd left him hope.

Arranging the syringes and tubes felt good. Getting ready for an experiment, assembling equipment, always brings me calm. Laying everything out is both a beginning and a statement of purpose, the first step toward an answer.

Although I'd only asked for five or six volunteers, twelve guards showed up. From the way they leered their motivations were clear. As I stuck the first one he asked if I was married or had a boyfriend.

'Both,' I said, which got a big laugh. Their arms were tattooed with symbols and dates. They had a lot of scars. In the best tradition of Melanie, I made small talk while I scraped cells from their cheeks and took their blood. The majority were Chechen or Russian, though there was also a German and a Serb. Most had been working in the camp for several years. They liked the pay but also couldn't wait for the camp to close.

'I want to do some living,' said the German. 'Get married, build a house, have babies.'

'In that order?' I said while coaxing a vein.

'The house could come first,' he said. 'And maybe I have just met my wife?'

Despite their very clear intentions, none of them suggested we meet again. While I certainly wouldn't characterise them as shy or sweet, they seemed content with achieving proximity to an unknown woman who fulfilled their doctor/nurse fantasies. I didn't mind their crude attempts at flirtation; I wanted them to be happy, at ease, not thinking about the results. To be on the safe side, after taking each swab I put it in a container.

They departed happily. I closed the door. I was sure that each of those twelve had friends, lovers and family that they saw on leave, people they kissed, hugged, shared cups and cutlery with. Thinking about their journeys home made me picture a map of Europe on which big red dots were pulsing.

When I lifted out the first tube I gave the longest exhalation. The rest were yellow too. I sat with the relief for the next twenty minutes, wanting to tell someone, knowing I could not. But as soon as I imagined myself presenting these findings, asking for questions, too many hands shot up. *How much bodily contact did the guards have with the inmates? How frequently did they interact with them in a confined space?* By the time I'd finished clearing up, I wasn't sure what I'd learned. It could have been a false negative.

~

I wanted to skip lunch but made myself eat some puffy bread and pungent cheese. When I came back into the clinic Jorge was silent. He had gone deep enough to escape the pain.

At two o'clock I was ready. Kim was supposed to be first. I was picturing his face and hearing myself speak when the guard brought in someone else. The man was tall, in his mid-fifties, and though overweight, looked strong. His reddish beard had streaks of grey. His nose looked as if it had been broken several times.

'I'm subbing for Kim,' he said. 'I'm Erik.'

'That's fine,' I said, then looked to the guard for confirmation. He stared at me blankly.

'Ragnar doesn't speak much English,' said Erik. 'But he'll stand in the doorway to make sure we play nicely.'

'That's alright,' I said, although the substitution had thrown me off balance.

'So who are you then? You're American?'

I explained who I was, and that I'd come to do some research. Since I would have said this anyway, it made me feel we were back on track.

'Very interesting,' he said and smiled. 'You know, before I came here, I used to be a bit less stupid than most other people. I was a professor at Canberra. So I hope you'll forgive me if I ask you a few more questions before I let you have my blood.'

'Please,' I said, because that was entirely his right. I suspected he wanted a little mental exercise, a chance to stoke his ego, but that was a fair exchange.

'Do you know a place called Flinders Island?'

'No.'

'It's in the Furneaux Group. In the Bass Strait.'

I nodded.

'Know where that is?'

'No,' I said. If he wanted me to admit that my geography was terrible, that was OK by me.

'It's north of Tasmania. You've heard of that, I'm sure.'

I nodded.

'Alright then. Well, back in the good old nineteenth century, all the Brits who didn't yet think of themselves as Australians decided that, after killing and raping most of the aboriginal Tasmanians, it would be good to protect a few of them. So they persuaded the last few hundred of the poor bastards to go into a camp on Flinders Island, and they told them it was just for a bit, that when it was safe they could come back. They put them in a bunch of huts and made them go to church on Sundays. And in that safe place disease and depression finished the job. Ten years later there were only forty-seven of them left. Sound familiar?'

'Maybe. On a superficial level,' I said, then regretted this swipe: I didn't want to get drawn into an argument that was really nothing to do with me. Erik didn't seem annoyed. He leaned back in his chair, then said, 'For sure, there are differences. The Brits taught them to read and write and let them send letters back to the mainland. We can't even send a text. And in the end they did take those forty-seven people back to the mainland. There's no chance of that for us.'

It wasn't my place to argue with him about his situation. There were probably good arguments for why the camps still had to exist, though I doubted that any of them could offer convincing reasons for why it was best for him. But he deserved a reply.

'I'm sorry this happened to you. I can't pretend I have any idea what you've gone through. I don't know anything about how this place works, I just arrived, and I'll be gone in a few weeks. I didn't ask to be sent here.'

He laughed. 'Thanks for the bullshit. So you're only following orders? That's what the doctors at Gusen said when they got caught cutting off heads.'

I must have looked confused, because he snapped at me.

'Another fucking scientist who doesn't know any history. You've probably only heard of Auschwitz. And since you're just visiting, let me tell you some things they may have left out of your welcome pack. In the last year they've shot four of us. They've been holding two of us in detention for almost a year. Yes, we came here voluntarily, but now it's our prison and we all have a life sentence. We have no legal representation. All we can do is give you lot the finger sometimes. So that's what I'm here to do.'

'Wait,' I said, because I could see what was coming yet had no idea how to stop it.

He stood up and said something in Russian and the guard stepped forward.

'You won't be getting my blood or anyone else's. Why should we help you? Have a nice flight home.'

After he'd gone I sat there for the rest of the afternoon. I rearranged the syringes, lined up the tubes, watched the clock, and waited. I hoped Erik had been making an empty threat.

At four o'clock Kim entered the clinic. I saw Dr Nilsson give him a shot. Afterward the doctor looked in my direction and said something, and Kim shook his head. The doctor looked confused. I watched Kim leave, and as Dr Nilsson started walking toward the lab I got really scared. He was going to come in and say how sorry he was and then there'd be no avoiding what had happened. So long as I was on my own, the sense of failure could be like a splinter buried deep. The doctor's sympathy would just make it bleed.

LUKAS

WITH the Gnostics it was neither night nor day. I was present yet invisible. I didn't need to speak. Most things happened without anyone needing to ask my permission. Being there was a tacit acceptance that every now and then a mouth would press itself onto mine and offer a tongue or a rich stream of resinous smoke that would blur my thoughts. Fingers had free access. I took what I was given.

At the start I slept at home most days. A morning and afternoon with the Gnostics left me tired and sore, craving my own space. But there was less and less to interest me outside that room. I had no desire to speak to people whose hatred of the authorities was boring and futile. It wouldn't change anything.

This indifference seemed to be mutual. After being absent for so long, my second, lesser disappearance was barely noteworthy. Though they can't have missed the scratches on my face and hands, the bruising round my throat, amongst us these marks were not uncommon.

Only Erik had something to say. He was outside the canteen with his acolytes, bragging about a history lesson he'd given to some scientist. As soon as he saw me he came over.

'So you've joined their club,' he said. 'Is there a lot of pillow talk?'

'Not much.'

'Do you know why Gnostics don't play chess with each other?'

'No.'

'Because they both want to be black,' he said, and laughed with vicious delight.

He asked what we did, what they talked about, but I just said, 'Nothing special.' I thought I knew why he was so curious – it was one of the few aspects of the camp from which he was excluded.

Though Seth did not deliver sermons, he often made pronouncements. Sometimes he repeated the same sentences throughout the day, the most frequent of which were 'Wealth has made its home in poverty,' and 'The spirit gives life, but the flesh is of no use.' These repetitions usually elicited only silence, except for when the woman said, 'Nor does the perishable inherit the imperishable,' which made Seth say, 'What I am saying, brothers and sisters, is that flesh cannot inherit the kingdom of God.' Given the way they talked about the body, and the rough ways they treated theirs (and mine), they seemed to have a particular hatred for it. Growing up Catholic I'd heard plenty of people go on about sinful appetites, the desires of the flesh, the need for abstinence. The Gnostics seemed to have drawn the opposite conclusion. Everything was permitted. Their heavily scarred bodies resembled maps from which the names were missing.

I cannot say it felt *good* to be with them. *Appropriate* would come closer. It wasn't that I wanted to be there, more that all the other places in the camp were worse. It certainly wasn't about the sex, which was cold and mechanical, an exercise routine that required a partner. Even at its roughest there was no sense of passion. When they cut me it felt surgical.

Sometimes, after many hours, I was barely there. My arms and legs were part of the floor; my back had merged as well. Breathing was a local movement that required no control or effort. My senses, deprived of input, explored an apparently limitless space, journeying outwards with the calm of scouts in peacetime. I saw no shapes, no dots, no lines; no phantoms visited that room except for when memories of Tomasz offered themselves for inspection. I saw him at our mother's funeral, but only as a silhouette, an outline, not fully present. He stayed in my periphery while I stared at the coffin and the priest spoke of the mysteries of our time on earth. At the wake he and I were at opposite ends of the room, and I could not remember us speaking during the whole event. He was surrounded by a large group of people, and although he had his back to me and I couldn't hear him, I could see their sympathetic nods. Three years later, we were back in that room, standing in the same places, and it was now our father that was missing. People offered me their condolences but did not stay to talk. I stood by the buffet and watched his audience grow.

Most of the Gnostics had been in the camp for two or three years, and yet no one knew much about them. Seth had been that way since he arrived, four years ago, but the others had all spent a few weeks or months doing the same thing as most new arrivals – i.e. fucking and having fun – before suddenly disappearing from communal life. While I knew that the other men's names were Hassan, Quanguo, Salambek and Steve, those people seemed to have left the camp a long time ago. As for the woman, she'd refused to tell anyone her name, which didn't stop people giving her one. She was Sunny, Headache, Rhianna, The Nurse. Once she joined Seth and the others she was just The Gnostic Woman.

I couldn't tell how much of Seth's teaching was directed at me. His questions seemed aimed at no one in particular. When he said, 'Where is heaven?' it was followed by such a long pause that one of the men had time to choke another while the woman slapped them both. Five or ten minutes must have passed – though in there it was hard to tell – before Seth answered his own question. 'If you think it is in the sky, the birds will arrive before you. If you think it is in the sea, the fish will be there first.' I found it surprising they believed there was a better place and that they were headed for it, given that they viewed our disease as a punishment for either something we'd already done or would do in the future. When I did eventually ask a question, it wasn't out of theological curiosity but a vestigial student reflex: hearing an authority figure talk triggered a need to argue.

'If we've been punished with this disease that's going to kill us, doesn't that mean there's no forgiveness?'

Seth's reply was unusually swift.

'Punishment requires its crime, and then the chain is complete. Sin dies with the body. No one who fears death will be saved.'

In the dark I didn't have to worry about keeping a straight face.

'And so how are we going to be saved?'

Again, he didn't hesitate.

'As was revealed to Thomas: if you bring forth what is within you, it will save you. If you don't bring it forth, it will destroy you.'

The choir joined in.

'The revelation of what is.'

'The transformation of things.'

'A journey into newness.'

They went on like this, talking over each other, until I began to grope the man nearest me. He kept talking as I jerked him off; I took him in my mouth but it made no difference. Only when he came did he pause for three or four seconds, then he resumed his litany about the pure, eternal life of the soul that was waiting for all of us once we had broken our chains, looked within, sung a hymn in silence, made the two one, the outside like the inside and the inside like the outside, the above like the below, the male and the female one and the same. The man's cum tasted strange.

The Gnostics believed they possessed secret knowledge and wisdom, which was insane yet comprehensible. What I didn't understand was why they had accepted me so readily. I suspected it was something to do with why they'd declared me innocent at the judgment, though this idea wasn't much of a help, since that made even less sense to me now I knew a little more about their notions of suffering and punishment. I tried to think of ways to bring up the subject naturally, in conversation, but since there was almost none of that, it didn't seem possible. Eventually I just asked. The rain was hammering on the roof when I said, 'Why didn't you find me guilty at the judgment? Aren't we all?'

'Yes, we are,' Seth said. 'You, we, all of us. Imperfect beings made in the image of an imperfect spirit. You were guilty then, and you're guilty now. But that was not a judgment. No truth was spoken there. Anything said or done in that place was written on water and sand, not in the great book that shall be read at the end. Everything else is a lie. Good works make no amends. Our mission in this place has always been to expose the wound. The greater the chaos, the more that can be seen.'

'You sound like Erik. Why not send him an invite?'

It was one of Seth's best pauses.

'He is not one of us, and never will be. But we watch him. He is useful. Despite his ignorance, he can be an instrument. When he changed his mind at your judgment, he was being guided. If you had been found guilty, the others would have been happy. Nothing would have happened.'

Hearing that their stupid ideas had cost me an eye made me take a swing at Seth's voice. I connected with nothing. I imagined punching him in the face, the throat, then being attacked from all sides, us fighting blindly in the dark until we couldn't move. I didn't try again.

The days were getting cold when I noticed the smell. It was sweet, a little fruity, not unlike old grapes. Amid the miasma of our scents – a large ensemble production in which faeces and sweat assumed the main roles – this new smell was unremarkable, at most a cameo.

Over the next week the smell acquired more lines. That reek became the first thing I registered on entering the room, and although I didn't like it – it had turned cloying – the smell was just another unbearable thing to accept.

I was emerging from a deep, stoned trance when the choking began. It seemed like more of the usual until the man lying next to me started making desperate sounds. The woman was talking to him very softly, the way you might lull a sleepy child, and despite his strained noises I didn't hear him resisting. None of the others seemed concerned. My high was so perfect it all seemed like a dream. If the man sounded like he was dying, that was only because choking always sounds that way. Yet he was also kicking and making a squealing noise I hadn't heard since a man was strangled in Rosa Khutor for stealing. I couldn't imagine why she might want to kill him. Given what we'd already done to each other, it was hard to imagine what could still provoke her. Though she was hurting him, killing him, at any moment she was going to stop. Then there would be scrabbling, grunting, more gasping, and of course I'd join in.

I was approaching tumescence when I heard a little crack. The room acquired a deeper quiet, as if we were all holding our breath. Then there was moisture on the floor and then we were all blinded. For the first time I saw them all properly. Two of the young men had grey hair. Her face was a nest of wrinkles. It was Salambek that she'd killed. He was pale and thin and had so many infected wounds on his arms and legs that they looked like copies of the same tattoo. Yet this did not seem like a mercy killing, more like a ritual in which both he and she understood their roles. The woman was calm, her face unreadable. The others were staring at his body without surprise. The moment, the act, meant something to them all, but this was one mystery they didn't offer to share. And I refused to ask. I stood up and put on my clothes and none of them tried to stop me. As I left Seth said, 'Let us say goodbye to our brother,' and I wasn't sure who he meant.

REBECCA

S CIENCE is mostly failure. No one's right all the time, or half the time, which isn't surprising: if you knew the answer there'd be no reason to ask the question. What makes this bearable is that there are plenty of do-overs. You get to guess again and again. Of all the things that had scared me about coming to the camp – the long journey, its remoteness, the risk of infection – the work itself had been very low on the list. I wasn't attempting to do anything complex, just take samples then use them to try to infect vaccinated cells. In methodological terms, it should have been a slam dunk.

Erik's refusal meant I'd failed before I'd even started. Dr Nilsson tried to soften the blow by saying that in time they might come around, which was possible, though neither they nor I had much of that to spare. Right then what I needed was unqualified sympathy but the only person I'd get that from was my dad, and he believed I was off with Rajeev on a grand hike along the Appalachian Trail.

The person I should have called was Damian. That night I composed multiple draft emails to him in which I tried to spin what had happened. At first it seemed safe to talk about 'minor logistical problems' and 'a few hiccups with subject access', but soon his imaginary replies, with all their questions, were flooding my inbox. Whatever I wrote, however I portrayed my failure, he'd end up saying, 'Come home.'

I watched dawn break over the camp. In the shower I became aquatic. I spent a long time flossing. At breakfast I chewed slowly. I only went to the lab because I couldn't think of anywhere else to go.

The clinic was quiet. The nurse on duty was holding the hand of the woman on the ventilator. 'Lucia, it will all be better soon,' she said, and I wanted to believe her.

In the lab I set out the equipment, and although it was pointless, the routine was comforting.

Once that was done I had nothing to do except stare at my surroundings. I considered an air vent; a sleek door handle; I fully appreciated the compact lustre of machines that would probably never be used. But I couldn't really focus on anything except the dull sensation of futility that lay on me like fog.

When Dr Nilsson entered the clinic he conferred with the nurse, then spent a long time checking on Jorge and Lucia. To look busy, I switched on my laptop and opened the spreadsheet in which I'd been planning to record data. I stared at the blank cells until the virus began to spin on the screen; it was strange to see this familiar sight in a new place, but at least on my laptop the image didn't get stuck. A keystroke and it was gone.

The knock on the lab door startled me.

'Sorry,' said Dr Nilsson. 'I have a bad habit of creeping up on people. I've been thinking, and I've decided it would be acceptable if you had a sample from Jorge and Lucia. I'm sure he wouldn't mind. He's a pretty contrary soul.'

Relief flooded through me. Before I had time to thank Lars, he offered me two labelled tubes of blood.

'I know it's not much. But it's a start.'

Both tubes were still warm. I held Jorge's in my right hand, Lucia's in my left, and though I was used to holding human material, I couldn't ignore that the donors were dying in the next room. Soon these little tubes would be all that was left of them.

I put the tubes carefully in the rack, then thanked him.

'You're welcome. There's one other person who might say yes, though that's a little more complicated. You'd have to ask her yourself.'

'Of course,' I said, then realised this would mean going back into the camp. But I had no choice.

He scratched his beard. 'She's currently in protective custody. While we don't like to keep inmates confined for a long time, we think she might harm others if she was released. Not that you'd be in any danger,' he added quickly. 'She'd be restrained and there would be a guard present. I just wanted to prepare you.'

'Alright,' I said. 'It's worth a try.' Knowing that she might get violent didn't make her more scary.

Lars was about to walk away when I remembered what Erik had said about there being two detainees. I asked if anyone else was in custody.

'Not now,' he said and looked grim. 'But there was last month. He was also too much of a risk to release, even after he became ill. Dejan needed far more help than I could give him.'

'I'm sorry,' I said. I felt like I was saying this a lot, yet couldn't think of what else to say.

It probably wasn't necessary to test the samples for the virus but I did anyway. It seemed important not to make assumptions. While I waited for the results I checked the centrifuge, then the microscope. I prepared the dye. Ten minutes later there was confirmation that the impossible hadn't occurred. Jorge and Lucia were still infected.

The next question was whether their virus was similar to the one we'd based the vaccine on. First, I had to see it. I put the samples in the centrifuge to isolate the virus, then negatively stained the sample. I had to wait for the slides to dry, which was going to take twenty minutes, plenty of time to go and eat, but that would have been an interruption and I wanted to stay focused. And so I sat and waited. I didn't watch the clock or the slides. My mind had the surface tension of a still lake.

When I lowered my eyes to the microscope I saw two separate monochrome circles, then they fused into one. There, in a dark nimbus, almost like a halo, was the virus. As if I were meeting an old acquaintance, I looked to see what had changed. My first impression was that it looked squatter, larger, but that was probably an artefact of how the sample had been taken. Until I sequenced it I wouldn't know how closely the two viruses were related, whether this was a twin, a close cousin, or some even blacker sheep.

$\sim$

They were keeping her in the basement. Most of the walls were bare rock, but it was not dark or damp or dungeon-like in any other way. The plain grey door was more suggestive of a small office or storeroom than a place of detention. And yet there was no denying the fact that the authorities viewed this terminally ill woman as sufficiently dangerous to need locking up. Lars hadn't been forthcoming about what she'd done; all he was willing to say was that she'd hurt a guard and another inmate.

Two guards went in first. Through the half-open door I saw a couch, a table, some generously padded walls.

One of the guards beckoned to me while the other stepped into the corridor. 'Watch out, she's a crazy bitch,' he said, and then I entered.

The woman was about my age, my height, a little prettier than me. I'd had my hair like that once. Her hands were secured by a plastic loop that went through the table. There were a few shelves with books, a photo of a sunset, and some origami cranes. Behind a curtain there was a toilet, basin and shower. Apparently this had been her world for almost a year.

'Hi Edie,' I said. 'I'm Rebecca. I think Dr Nilsson told you why I'm here. Do you mind if I sit down and tell you a bit more?'

She stared at me in a way that felt more appraising than hostile, though it was still uncomfortable to be inspected like that, because she took her time. She tilted her head and sucked in her cheeks, while I struggled not to fill the silence.

She worked her jaw a little. 'Is that a Philly accent?' she said.

'A bit. My dad's from there, but I grew up in Queens.'

She nodded. 'Well, I was about to head out, but since you've come all this way,' she said, and used her thumbs to indicate the chair.

I sat down and left a large gap between myself and the table.

'Good for you,' she said. 'That won't help you if I spit.'

Although she was obviously trying to scare me, if she really wanted me to leave she'd have already done something.

'So. Give me the pitch,' she said. 'Are you here to check me for VD?'

Despite the situation, I laughed. She looked very pleased.

'There's more where that came from. I don't mean to be rude, but you look like someone who hasn't laughed for ten years.'

'I've laughed,' I said. 'At least three or four times. It's a real non-stop party at the Institute for Infectious Diseases.'

'I bet it's almost as much fun as here,' she said. She reminded me of girls I'd known back home, the ones who would thankfully never take no for an answer when I said I had to study.

She listened to my spiel. She didn't interrupt. When I was done she stayed quiet for a few moments, then said, 'I get why you want to study the disease, and why you're here. But why now? Is there a problem with the vaccine?'

'No,' I said. 'It's working fine.'

'Everyone's fucking and drinking in dive bars and pushing to get to the counter in Zabar's?'

'They are,' I said, and swallowed my reservations about this normalcy.

She puffed out her cheeks. 'Thank the God I don't believe in. And not to keep you in suspense, I'll be glad to help.'

'Great, thank you.'

'Sure. Why not? I have nothing against you.'

I could have left at this point. I had what I wanted, and we'd already talked plenty, so it wouldn't have been rude. But my relief that it had all gone fine made me think it would be OK to stay. I was curious about her, and the best (and perhaps only) way for me to show my gratitude would be to keep her company.

'So how did you end up here?'

'I was writing a food blog in Osh when it all kicked off. My first camp was somewhere in the Pamirs and, let me tell you, it made this place look like a country club. You couldn't blame the locals for trying to burn it down. The first few years of that were shit. I'd had all these plans for my life, and now they were impossible.'

'What did you want to do?'

'Oh, you know. The usual stuff. To have a one-woman show on Broadway based on my bestselling erotic memoir. To be on the *Tonight* show and lead the Macy's Parade. I also wanted to experience weightlessness and work in a monkey sanctuary. The only goals I've got to fulfil here are sexual ones. I know that most of my fellow prisoners don't look hot, but it's a regular Baskin-Robbins. Any flavour you like.'

She chewed her lower lip, then raised her gaze to the ceiling. 'I have found one new thing I want to do. There's someone I want to kill. He did something awful and he's not going to be punished and I don't mind being the one to do it. I don't want to say he's *evil*, that lets him off the hook, but that word fits him so well. Even talking about him makes me feel a cold fire in my gut. The worst part is that I got it all wrong at the start. I thought this guy I was seeing had done it and tried to kill him. That's why they put me in here.' She brought her gaze to meet mine. 'And if you haven't already guessed, this "it" was rape. And no, it didn't happen to me or a friend of mine. I barely knew the woman.'

'But how do you know the guy you were seeing didn't do it?'

She laughed. 'It's not that Lukas couldn't have done it, more that he's a terrible liar. He has such a guilty conscience about everything he'd have ended up confessing. And then the poor bastard ends up getting accused of something he didn't do. That's some nasty irony. After I'd been in here a few months I realised there was only one other person who could have done it, and then my hate didn't just transfer onto him, it became a whole other thing, this cold burning feeling that I picture as the blue bit in a gas flame.'

She was trembling slightly; I wondered what I was supposed to say. *I agree* or *You're totally right*. Perhaps she wanted an argument. The way she then changed the subject made me realise she didn't care what I thought. When you're totally certain you're right, other opinions don't matter. It's not your problem if others are wrong or don't understand. What you know is enough.

'So who else have you talked to in the camp?'

'Not many,' I said. 'Kim and Stephan and Valentina. A few more, but I don't remember their names.'

'What about Erik?'

'Yes, I've met him,' I said, and this delighted her. She clapped her hands as much as she was able.

'I knew he was still alive,' she said. 'I mean, I was sure he had to be if I'm still in here.'

It took me a second to understand. 'So you're saying Erik's the one you want to kill?'

'It had to be him. I'm certain.'

'Can you prove it?'

'I don't need to. Haven't you ever been sure of something without having proof?'

'I don't know,' I said, although the truth was more complex. As a scientist, I had hunches, which I then tested, but that wasn't the same. I made progress by admitting when I was wrong, albeit usually more in terms of method than the actual hunch. It's fine to do twenty-six experiments if your basic idea seems right.

'You spoke to Erik. What do you think of him?'

'He was pompous and condescending. He seems like a dick.'

'For sure. Can you tell me how he looked? Has he gotten sick?'

'Not that I can see.'

She sighed. 'That means I'll be in here a while longer. He got infected a few years before me, so it will probably happen soon. You're the expert – what do you think?'

'On average, you're probably right, except that most of you have already survived far longer than the vast majority of people who got the disease. So I think all bets are off.'

'Oh yeah, we're the chosen ones,' she said and rolled her eyes. 'It would be just my luck for me to get sick before that fucker. If I hadn't blabbed about what I was going to do to him I'd have been released by now. But once I figured out it was him I got so angry. I have a great mouth, but it's a big mouth too.'

Behind me the guards were restless. It was probably time for me to go, but I was curious about what else she might say. For all her breeziness and snark, she was obviously obsessed. Although this was why she had to be locked up, maybe it was also what had allowed her to survive being on her own for so long. That blue flame kept her company.

She yawned and her jaw clicked. She inspected her fingernails; I felt like I was being dismissed. When I stood up she said, 'Oh, are you going? Thanks, this was fun. And if you see Lukas, tell him I'm sorry. My bad.'

The guards escorted me back to the clinic. Lars asked how it had gone.

'Fine. She said yes.'

'Good for her. When do you want to take a sample?'

I was about to suggest the following day but then I changed my mind. I asked him if he'd do it for me, and was glad he didn't ask why.

LUKAS

I CONSIGNED myself to bed for the week after I left the Gnostics. By switching the patch to the functioning eye I was able to abolish the days. There was also a satisfaction in following the logic of my decline from two eyes to one, then none, from half a world to blindness. For long periods I was awake but sensed nothing, had no thoughts, no memories; there was only the imperturbable entry and exit of breath that repeated like a mechanism someone had forgotten to switch off.

I was in bed when Erik told me. At first I didn't believe him. It had to be a sick joke, another provocation: after hearing him say so often that no one was looking for a cure, his sudden conversion was too much of a volte-face to be plausible.

'Fuck off' was the only response this deserved. I was sick of him coming into my house without asking. He was a manipulative liar, nothing but trouble. I turned away from him and stared at the wall, hoping he would leave.

He didn't. He also remained quiet, and for him that was strange. We stayed like that for ages. I convinced myself he'd gone. I tried to fall asleep.

'It's not because they care about us,' he said eventually. 'They never have and never will. There are plenty of other reasons. Someone in Washington may have made the issue into a stick with which to hit the other party. Or some drug company thinks it can raise their share price. If any of us benefit, it will be just a side effect. So yes, it's more bullshit. But sometimes we can use them a little while they're using us.' He stood up. I was still trying to find a reply when he left.

Although I tried to forget what Erik had said, over the next few days it was the only thing people were talking about. Suddenly the authorities weren't trying to kill us. It had been a long time since I'd heard anyone start a sentence with *When I get out of here...*

I wanted no part of this. I kept to myself. But I'd quarantined too late.

At first the spread was slow, barely noticeable, a thought every few hours. Swimming in Morskie Oko. The long shelves of a bookshop.

I fought the infection. I made it through an entire day without symptoms, then dreamt about skiing. I travelled in slow motion. Powder hung in the air.

I had a short remission when people switched from saying the scientist had come to research a cure to saying she'd come to administer it. Seeing another patient whose disease is more advanced can make you think you're well.

The fact that Erik was sick should have made us more sceptical of his claims. Although he tried to hide it, we'd all seen him twitch.

He was obviously desperate to believe there might be a cure for him. Seeing him shake and tremble gave me no satisfaction. He wasn't being punished; it had happened to the best of us. We were all in that queue.

It was Dr Nilsson who pushed me over the edge. Before he started spreading the good news I was only having two or three fantasies a day. Long lunches with almost-lovers; big nights out in Brooklyn; crossing Russia by train. In between these daydreams were periods of remission when I could acknowledge the possibility that this new doctor might not succeed. But after seeing Nilsson in the camp every day for a week, smiling and answering questions, making no promises yet being optimistic, saying, 'Rebecca's one of the best in the world,' all my defences collapsed. Though I had issues with him, he'd never lied to us. He kept saying what we wanted to hear with more conviction than any of us would have dared.

Joining in with the talk of destinations, restaurants, the first thing we'd buy, made me feel included. Between us we achieved a critical mass of leisure planning that in any other situation would have been banal. Are there death row prisoners whose most fervent wish is to eat a kiwi fruit or get a puppy or shoot down a water slide?

Now we had a reason to get up and brush our teeth and not be drunk all day. We cut our hair, we swallowed our pills. The men took turns shaving at the few remaining mirrors. While I didn't know the face I saw, afterwards it looked better. If I saw that face sitting on the ground outside a supermarket, I'd flip it a coin.

I thought a lot about my first meeting with Rebecca. I pictured her with short brown hair and glasses, wearing a white coat, looking tired but pretty. Not that I had any sexual aspirations towards her. Although the days before meeting her did resemble the anxious, giddy preparations of someone about to go on a date with a person obviously out of their league – I worried about what to wear, how to style my hair, whether to go with my black or brown eyepatch – my most serious concern was how to express my gratitude. Finding the right words was crucial because I had to make the best possible impression. She had to fully comprehend what this meant to us. The better she understood, the harder she would try.

REBECCA

W ITH Edie's sample, plus the other two, I could have started testing. Instead I spent the next few days sequencing the genome of each sample. It's probably childish to have a favourite lab technique, but I still take great pleasure in watching ladders of DNA being slowly revealed. When Matthew first saw one of these images on my desk he ran his finger down the black and white rungs and said, 'What's this Super-Rothko? It belongs on a T-shirt.' After I told him what it was – life at its most fundamental – he liked it even more. 'And so this is everything?' he said, and I laughed. 'Not unless you think proteins are people.' It became one of our in-jokes. In a crowded place he'd mutter, 'Lots of protein here.'

When I compared the three samples to the original strain there was almost no difference: they had the same overall structure, the same sections that repeated like a chorus. There were a lot of small mutations, but I had no reason to suspect these were significant. My concern was the part of the virus I'd modified. Any changes in that region would be a red flag.

Rather than watch the progress bar I went outside for the first time in three days. The sky was overcast and despite the wind the clouds didn't seem to be moving. A few of the guards said hi to me as I orbited the building. As I walked my eyes enjoyed the pattern of the fence, the intertwining helices that kept it together.

Back in the lab there was good and bad news. The virus from the inmates had mutations in the crucial region, but they were different from the ones I'd engineered. The question was whether, as Damian would say, these mutations changed the virus's behaviour. Could these mutations allow it to beat the vaccine? I really had no idea. Even after ten years of intensive study, much of that section of the virus's genome was a mystery. There were many theories about its functions. Some thought it did nothing. I guess this was what first attracted me to exploring that section. It was almost a blank slate.

There wasn't much left to do except start testing these new strains against the vaccine. And yet I was reluctant. I spent the next four days with my eyes glued to the microscope, zooming in and out, exploring the cellular terrain. Every time I switched to a different level of magnification I believed I was going to discover something with this new perspective. But I found nothing. If those mutations did anything, it could not be seen.

I had almost accepted that conclusion when I went into the canteen late. The place was empty and the staff glared at me so resentfully I felt as if I was solely responsible for them still being at work. They gave me a plate on which a grey mass sat; I didn't dare ask what it was. I'd sat down before I realised Lars was at the far end of the canteen. He was on his own, with his back to me, and was staring at the same mass that occupied my plate. I got up and went over to him, and though I registered that he was hunched over, and on his own, that didn't prevent me speaking with a cheerfulness I couldn't have summoned ten seconds ago.

'Answers on a postcard,' I said, which was dumb, and I didn't expect a laugh, but the slowness with which he raised his head, showing a tired, sad face, made me feel as if I'd chuckled at a cremation.

'Sorry,' I said. 'I didn't mean to bother you.'

I started to turn away, then he said, 'It's alright. Please, join me.'

I put my tray opposite his. I waited for him to speak. After too long a pause he asked how things were going. While I told him about the sequencing, the small mutations, he nodded and ate the awful-looking pap.

'I'm glad things are going well,' he said, although I hadn't said they were. He pushed his plate away. 'We lost Jorge this afternoon.'

'When?'

'About three o'clock.'

I'd been in the lab but had seen and heard nothing. Worse, I'd walked past his empty bed without noticing.

I offered my condolences.

'Thank you,' he said. 'I don't know why it's hitting me so hard. I wasn't close to Jorge. Sometimes he was very annoying. And then of course there was the fire. That did so much harm.'

It was my turn to nod and eat. The grey stuff tasted grey. It had the smoothness of mucus.

'Maybe it's because he made me promise to tell his mother and father that he loved them. And there's no way that can happen. No one outside this camp will ever know what happened to Jorge, or any of them. It's like they've been erased.'

'Will there be any kind of service?'

He shook his head. 'We used to have those, but now they're not allowed. It was during one of those, when everyone was distracted, that Jorge started the fire.'

'What do you know about him? I mean, from before he came here?'

'Not much. He was from Brasilia. He loved Formula One. He was some kind of digital artist for films. He told people he'd been married twice, but I don't think anyone believed him. He said that when he was very young both his parents died in a car crash, and I think that was true. You know, he was often thoughtless, and he liked to play the fool, yet he could also be very kind. He spent a lot of time visiting people too ill to leave their homes.' Lars nodded in approval.

'What about Lucia? How is she?'

'She may survive the night. The nurse and I will take turns sitting with her. So I need to get some rest now,' he said and stood up.

'Sleep well,' I said.

After he'd gone I went outside and stood by the fence. No stars were visible. In almost every direction there was darkness so total it seemed to prohibit the existence of anything. Pretty soon I was freezing, but I wasn't ready to go inside. It was better to feel cold than sadness.

Only when I turned to leave did I see the small squares of light; they were orange, yellow and white, glowing like those fluorescent creatures that live in deep, dark waters. I wanted to view these lights as markers of activity, signs of occupation, but as I watched them float in that black sea all they inspired was caution.

∾

That night I couldn't sleep; I was both eager and anxious. Dawn was a beautiful purple bruising I wanted to hurry. I was there when the canteen opened at seven, and in the lab at half past. On my way through the clinic I saw Lucia had made it through the night.

I vaccinated three trays of cells, then prepared a viral sample from Jorge, Lucia and Edie. In two days the cells could be exposed to the virus; the results would take another six. I could be home in less than a fortnight.

For the rest of the day I messed around with some new graphics software that claimed to be able to make a three-dimensional model from a small number of electron micrographs. I don't know what I did wrong, but it was a real shitshow. All I got were blurry images in which the cellular structures were obscured by a haze that lay over them like a smokescreen. I recognised almost nothing.

That night I gave myself permission to drink a few shots of vodka. I slept better, but when I woke I had a hangover that was disproportionate to what I'd drunk. While getting dressed I tore the sleeve of my shirt; I dropped a glass in the bathroom. As I was picking up the shards I wondered if I was only going through the motions of an experiment that would tell me nothing. Relying on three viral samples was like trying to come up with a theory of canine behaviour based on a trio of dogs.

I was not exactly my best-self when Lars visited the lab that afternoon.

'Hello,' he said. 'Well, this is strange. I've just seen Erik for his check-up and now he wants to give you a sample. I think I know why, but to be on the safe side, I think we should have an extra guard in here.'

'Fine,' I said. 'Perhaps he just wants to call me a Nazi again.'

'Maybe,' he said, and a few minutes later two guards brought Erik in. When I said hi, he didn't reply. He sat down, rolled up his left sleeve, then offered his arm in silence. I recognised the guard standing behind him from my tour on the first day. Alain had his hand on his holster, which at first made me suspect that Erik was being compelled. He didn't look at me until I was about to select a vein. Then he flicked his eyes up to mine and held my gaze. Although he wasn't smiling, I didn't see any resentment. I was glad he'd chosen to be there, but I suspect I'd have still taken the sample even if I thought he was being forced.

We watched Erik's blood enter the tube. He closed his eyes and for a moment I could inspect his face, note a scar on his chin, think of him as just a man asleep. Then the tube was full and I was applying a Band-Aid. He rolled down his sleeve, then stood. He'd kept his other arm tightly by his side throughout, but now it was hanging freely I could see it twitching violently.

Four more people came that afternoon. Valentina was first. 'Nice to meet you,' she said, then introduced herself. She asked where I was from, and when I told her, she said, 'Such a strange place.'

I rolled up her sleeve. 'This won't hurt much.'

'Oh, I won't feel it,' she said. She was as cheerful as on our first meeting, and didn't seem confused about what was happening. Her clarity and elevated mood made me suspect this wasn't simply the product of her early dementia. I wondered what she believed.

Next morning six more inmates came to give a sample. I guessed this was solely due to Erik's influence until one of them wouldn't stop thanking me. Mohinder did not elaborate, and I didn't ask, but it made me wonder what he thought I was doing for him.

Lukas clarified their motivations. Were it not for his eyepatch, I probably wouldn't have recognised him. Despite the broken nose and the scars on his cheeks his lean face was clean and eager.

'Good morning,' he said, and his gappy smile immediately made me uneasy: no one should be cheerful at the prospect of having a needle stuck in their arm. He was rolling up his sleeve before I'd asked him to.

'Thanks for coming in,' I said while prepping the syringe. His laugh startled me. He spoke rapidly.

'Since when do doctors thank their patients? That's a one-way street. It's probably the same for chefs. And artists. I doubt that Goethe ever thanked his public, at least not sincerely.'

I wasn't able to pay much attention to what he said next because I was hunting for a vein. I had to give up on his right arm. The flesh was pale and doughy and offered nothing I fancied trying to access. The left wasn't much better. Both the cubital and cephalic veins were like string. Only the basilic vein seemed possible, and that was going to really hurt. I figured he'd need a distraction, so I asked him why he'd chosen to come in.

'Because I don't want to die. When Dr Nilsson told us why you were here, I wasn't surprised. I knew people still had to be looking for a cure.'

He didn't flinch when I pricked him. I wasn't sure whether to be angry or grateful to Lars. I hadn't asked him to lie.

Lukas's blood was sluggish.

'You should probably drink more water,' I said, and he smiled.

'Yes, I will. Definitely.' The prospect seemed to excite him.

Gradually, in no hurry, the tube filled like a watched bath. The only other person I'd seen in the camp who looked as contented was Valentina. But I suspected they'd done different math to get that result. She had an air of acceptance; Lukas was high on hope.

LUKAS

O N the way to my appointment I passed Mohinder, who gave me a thumbs up. In his cloudy eyes there was a small, bright light like a candle behind a curtain. 'This blessing,' he said, and I nodded. As he moved away he was singing.

Rebecca didn't look how I'd expected. She was taller and didn't wear glasses. Her face had a hardness that made me think of the few teachers at school that were immune to Tomasz's charms (when he was expelled for starting a fire, one of them resigned in protest). After I said, 'Good morning,' I tried to mimic her sombre expression, but when she thanked me for coming in, a laugh bubbled out. Her being grateful was such a strange inversion – I should have been on my knees – that I had to joke about it. I wasn't trying to be irreverent; on the contrary: the joke was a way to underline my thankfulness. Yet I immediately regretted comparing her to a chef and so I compared her to an artist, and since that was vague, I got specific. I wasn't sure she got my Goethe reference, and so I qualified it – he was not an *ungrateful* genius, just not always entirely humble.

While she explored my right arm, testing its veins, I said some of what I had prepared. It was fine to joke, break the ice, but it was time to be serious.

'First, I want you to know how happy we are that you're here. We've had a dark time recently and we really needed this. If there's anything you need, if there's anything we can do, you only have to ask.'

I paused because I could see that my right arm had failed. 'Sorry,' I said, and rolled up my other sleeve. I felt bad that I'd wasted her time when she had so much to do. As she tested the veins on my left arm I decided it was best not to speak; I didn't want to distract her. Although it had seemed important to convey my gratitude, now that I was with her, watching her work, it didn't seem necessary to say more.

So it was a surprise when she asked why I'd chosen to volunteer for the study. And that really *was* an excellent joke – as if we had a choice! – but I didn't laugh because she was playing it deadpan. I followed her lead and said, 'Because I want to live. I can't wait to get out of here, I've got so many plans. When Dr Nilsson told us why you've come, I wasn't surprised. I've always believed someone like you was looking for a cure. None of the others believed me, they kept saying I was wrong, but I never gave up hope that some incredible person was going to try and save us.'

She accepted this praise with remarkable humility. There was so little reaction that at first I worried she hadn't heard. For a weird moment I even thought she was angry, but since she couldn't possibly be upset, I decided she was one of those really good people who find it hard to be thanked.

She made a small noise, perhaps of sympathy, as she drove the needle into the vein. It was painful, but I'd had worse.

I wasn't sorry my blood was slow to emerge; it gave us more time to talk. I asked if she believed in second chances.

'For what?'

'For everything. I've made a lot of mistakes,' I said and hoped it didn't sound like boasting.

'Who hasn't?' she said, then adjusted the angle of the tube. 'And as for second chances, most of the people I know have blown theirs. They've learned nothing. Where I'm from it's business as usual.'

'And where's that?'

'New York.'

'That's on my list,' I said. 'I've got a whole trip planned.'

'Have you?' she said, then stared at my blood. There was a long silence that felt very comfortable, but it also seemed OK to break it.

'After New York, I'll go to Mexico, then Korea, then Paris. And some other places on the way. I'm not sure what I'm looking forward to more – seeing those places, or the travelling itself. I think we've all got plans like this. Of course we all want to go home, try and find family and friends, and then get back to living.'

She made a slight jerk of the head I took for a nod. She slipped the needle out.

'All done,' she said. I watched her label my sample, and even though she'd done all the work, I nonetheless felt proud to be playing a small part.

I was rolling down my sleeve when she said, 'Edie says hi.'

I stared at her, and although I didn't speak, she answered my question.

'We talked a few weeks ago. She was one of the first people to give me a sample. We spoke about all kinds of things. She's very interesting.'

She signalled to the guard. 'OK, we're done here.'

REBECCA

T HE next five days were pretty vampiric, just arms and veins and blood. I tried to focus on the task but the inmates wouldn't stop thanking me for something I wasn't going to do. From that there was no protection. But it was their choice to be there. Whatever their reasons, whatever they believed, they were still volunteers. And when, each night, I lay awake and faced an ethics committee, I kept telling them I was doing no harm.

By the end of that week I had ninety-seven tubes. At lunch Lars said there probably wouldn't be any more.

'A few of them just want to be left alone. And the Gnostics are probably against the whole idea of a cure,' he said, and snorted. 'Of all the terrible things that have happened over the last decade, for me the resurrection of an early Christian sect is still one of the strangest. I suppose it probably happened through the internet. Though I'll never understand why people chose Gnosticism.'

I nodded. My lunch was more than edible. There were worse topics.

'During times of crisis people look for answers, but it's not as if there is any shortage of active belief systems, most of them optimistic. All the major world religions have a lot of useful things to say about suffering. Any of them could have brought comfort and yet instead millions chose a twisted version of Gnosticism – which in its original form wasn't so bad. People chose a set of ideas that made them wish for the worst outcome. They actually prayed for it, even after we had the vaccine. It's as if they thought humanity should end.'

'They were nuts,' I said, then opened my yogurt.

He paused to consider my profound contribution.

'Maybe,' he said, in exactly the same way Matthew used the word when what he meant was *No*. 'There's probably some kind of logic at work, even if you or I can't follow it. My best guess, based on what I've read, is that a lot of them got so traumatised that they found living more terrifying than the prospect of dying.'

'So why didn't they kill themselves? Plenty of others did,' I said, and swallowed hard. Speaking in general terms had quickly gone elsewhere.

'Well, that's a good question. I think that must be a taboo even for them. Maybe they're all just trapped. If that's the case, I feel sorry for them.'

'I don't. They were superspreaders. It would have been better if they'd killed themselves.'

He looked a little shocked, perhaps as much by my tone as what I'd said: my mouth felt as if the words had clawed their way out. He let a few moments pass before saying, 'Beneath their esoteric mumbo jumbo, maybe they're like a lot of people who've spent the last six years trying to adjust. Fear was what kept us all alive, it was very useful, and it's a risk to give it up. It's one of the reasons I came to the camp. Even with the inmates, it felt much safer here.'

It was my turn to be shocked. That really made no sense. Sometimes a single statement is enough to undermine a person's credibility. No wonder he believed I was there to cure them.

'I'd better get back to it,' I said, and returned my tray. I felt the awkwardness you get when you see a friend naked and it doesn't bother them.

Back in the lab, I got on with preparing the rest of the viral samples, of which there were about sixty remaining. It was like singing 'Ninety-Nine Bottles of Beer', only the countdown was slower; I did ten samples an hour. When there were forty left I told myself I'd stop at thirty, and when I got there I thought I could do another ten, and once there were twenty remaining I decided to go all the way. I did consider taking a break, because my back was sore and all the pipetting had made my thumb joints feel like rusty hinges, yet the idea of stopping, even for a short period, wasn't acceptable. The task had to be completed and I'd delayed enough. I remembered Gulmera's tireless, robotic arm swivelling like a crane. During my absence she'd probably make a move on Rajeev. They would be a good match.

Eleven samples were left when my trapezius muscle began to spasm. I almost dropped one of the tubes, but then I was counting down again and this brought me a strange excitement, as if reaching zero would make something amazing happen.

My hands were shaking at T-5. I'd been working for over six hours and had already missed dinner, but my mom always said that the end of the race is when winners don't quit.

There were three left when I fumbled and almost dropped the tube, and in catching it knocked the remaining two onto the floor. In the old days, with glass tubes, this would have resulted in a big dramatic mess; thankfully the plastic ones were much tougher. Now it was only the contents that were fragile. If the blood vessels had ruptured, the samples would be useless.

Although this was annoying, it was only two samples. I could ask Lars to have the donors come back in. After I checked who they belonged to, I decided it wasn't necessary. I didn't want to see Lukas again.

I finished the last sample, tidied up, then went straight to bed. I couldn't wait to have a major pause in my consciousness like one of those computer restarts that go on so long the machine seems stuck. Falling asleep was no problem, but at 3 a.m. I woke and didn't seem to be breathing. Fists were in my chest. My lungs were taking such small sips of air it was like they were trying not to be heard. It was a classic fight or flight episode, even though there was no obvious threat. I hadn't been dreaming of being chased or wrongfully accused of a crime. *I'm safe*, I said to myself, and encouraged my lungs to take deeper breaths. They were reluctant and I had to force them, yet even after they were inflating properly the fists remained. *I'm safe*, I said again, but my body didn't believe me. I remembered what Lars had said about the camp being safe, and his naïveté made me angry. Someone who was responsible for the well-being of others had no right to indulge that kind of optimism. If I was right, the camp was probably the most dangerous place in the world.

When I finally got up a couple of hours later I felt and looked like crap. My face was lumpy pizza dough on which the mouth, eyes and nose were awkward, stupid toppings. It took ten minutes at the mirror before I could kid myself that my reflection was presentable. In the thin light my features seemed about to slide off.

In the lab I began immediately. It was like speed dating. Forty-five different couples were introduced to each other. Could they interact, exchange information, form a real connection?

I worked all morning without a break, but made myself stop for lunch. Despite being hungry, I forgot about food when I saw Lars was alone in the clinic. I knocked on his door, he beckoned me in, and all the words I'd prepared in the dark were ready to come out my mouth. They had the urgency of bees and it took a great effort to begin gently. I tried to channel Matthew, and said, 'Can we talk about why I'm here?'

'Of course,' he said and looked eager.

'I know you've been telling people I'm trying to find a cure, and I understand why you might think that, but that's not something I've ever said. All I've said is that my work might help in that direction. Frankly, it might not.'

In my imagined version of this moment he'd had few lines. So when, after a weighty pause, he said, 'I see,' I was ready to go on.

'To the best of my knowledge, no one's working on a cure. It's not a political priority, and no pharmaceutical company is going to see a few hundred or even a few thousand patients as a worthwhile market. I'm sorry, but that's how it is.'

He sat very still. I waited for him to argue, call me a liar, a heartless bitch.

'Yes,' he said. 'I have wondered about all that. I preferred to think otherwise, even though I had doubts. But thank you for telling me.'

He smiled so nicely I wondered if he'd understood. Either he didn't get it, or he thought the facts I'd told him were just my opinion. I suspected he was going to carry on in his little bubble of hope, and it was infuriating. He should have been asking me why I was in the camp, if not to find a cure, and when this question didn't seem forthcoming, I gave him the answer.

'I'm here because of the vaccine. There may be a problem. It's possible that the vaccine doesn't work against some strains.'

His mouth opened. He took a slow breath. It was a big build-up, but all he said was, 'Oh.' He brought his hand to his mouth as if he was going to throw up. Finally he said, 'Are you sure? I mean, how likely is it?'

'I really don't know,' I said. I could see the idea sinking into him like a ship going under. When I asked him not to tell anyone else, he quickly agreed. He must have realised what would happen to the inmates if the guards no longer thought they were safe.

In the canteen I ate some passable lamb. When I returned to the lab Lars wasn't in his office. I wasted no time introducing the remaining viruses to their prospective partners. The results would take another three days, and as I considered the rows of Petri dishes I felt what I can only call a patient sense of impatience. I wanted the results immediately; I could have waited weeks.

LUKAS

THROUGHOUT my time in hospital, then in captivity, I'd often thought of Edie with a nostalgic fondness made possible by the belief she was dead. Our greatest hits were not disrupted by memories of her wielding a knife or cigarette. I could safely recall her third night in camp, when she came to Bob's variety show, got up on stage and did a passable soft-shoe shuffle despite not knowing anyone. Although I admired her nerve, I didn't speak to her, but something about my performance in Bob's latest one-act play – what he called 'Chekhov with fist fights' – must have appealed to her. The first words she spoke to me were, 'Can I take you home?' Her confidence attracted me; after that, I borrowed it whenever I could.

Her being alive complicated these memories. From then on she lurked in the background, stalking me and her former self. Recollections that had seemed safe suddenly had dimmer lighting, a more ominous soundtrack, the potential to go off-script.

Inevitably, I worried what might happen if Edie was released. I pictured her confined in a small room like the one I'd been in, only in hers everything was broken and the walls were covered with writing, smeared with awful stuff. She pulled at her long, unkempt hair as she paced back and forth muttering my name, clenching her fists, feinting with an imaginary knife at my back, my chest, my balls. Occasionally I indulged the fantasy that she might be calmer, less convinced of my guilt, until I remembered how depressed and frustrated three months' captivity had made me. She'd been in there three times as long; she'd probably gone way beyond stabbing.

But if Dr Nilsson had told Edie the good news she might see things differently. She could also be saying, *When I get out of here…*

And so there were moments when I thought of two cured people walking along a pier, going to the cinema, having a naked picnic. Meeting each other's parents, siblings and cousins in the cemetery.

I hoped they released her as soon as possible.

I hoped they never let her out.

Dr Nilsson was no help. Though he admitted that Edie was still alive, he wouldn't tell me anything about her. He refused to give her a message. I asked him about her for five consecutive days, but on the sixth, when I cornered him outside the canteen, he lost his temper.

'Stop asking. And don't get everyone stirred up about this. If there's any trouble in the camp she definitely won't be released. Don't you think you've done enough? Between you and Jorge I'm amazed there's anything left.'

I was about to reject the comparison, but he cut me off.

'Look, I'll tell you what you want to know and then I don't want to hear any more about this. She isn't going to hurt you. OK?' He walked off, muttering in Swedish.

Kobby had been watching from a distance. 'What was all that about?' he said.

'Nothing. He's just in a bad mood.'

While we ate I struggled to pay attention to Kobby explaining his theory of dialectical imagery in the works of Krzhizhanovsky. When he said, 'Fire follows water, and if there's a man, there's a woman,' I saw a couple walking along a pier. They were feeding each other candyfloss, and she was laughing, putting it in his hair.

'The great man made mirrors for us,' said Kobby, then nodded his approval.

～

Next morning there were bodies in the square. Six laid out as neatly as if they were the latest item we had rejected. Salambek was already rotting but the others were fresh. Seeing the Gnostics all together in daylight was almost as strange as the circumstances of their deaths. No one would ever know how they had managed to sneak out during curfew, whether some of the deaths had occurred in the square or taken place earlier. We speculated on their motives, the timing, why they had chosen to display themselves. I guessed that this was the Gnostics' answer to the prospect of a cure. They had put themselves beyond temptation.

After the guards removed the bodies I left the square and went to the Gnostics' hut. Perhaps they'd left a note, a final sermon, a denunciation of those still determined to languish in a perishable prison. I wanted to make sure they were really gone.

Inside it smelled like the lair of a carnivore. I gagged and had to go outside and throw up. When I went back in I covered my mouth and tried to open a window but they'd all been nailed shut. I wanted to run out of there: in the dark, and with that smell, I didn't feel alone.

I don't remember what I grabbed, only how I used it. The window broke with a high note and the room was revealed. The floorboards were stained and scratched. There were piles of rags. A lot of shit. What looked like a toe. I went from room to room, smashing every window, letting cold light in. Next to the bathtub, which contained three inches of urine, there was a row of cups. When I went back into the main room I noticed that the walls were covered in tiny writing. At the start, close to the ceiling, it said, 'THESE ARE THE SECRET SAYINGS THAT THE LIVING JESUS SPOKE AND JUDAS THOMAS THE TWIN WROTE DOWN. WHOEVER FINDS THE INTERPRETATION OF THESE SAYINGS WILL NOT TASTE DEATH.' As I read my way down I recognised things I'd heard. 'WHOEVER HAS COME TO KNOW THE WORLD HAS DISCOVERED A CARCASS' had been one of Seth's favourites. The woman had been fond of saying, 'NOW, WHEN YOU SEE YOUR APPEARANCE, YOU REJOICE. BUT WHEN YOU SEE YOUR IMAGES WHICH CAME INTO BEING BEFORE YOU, WHICH DO NOT DIE AND DO NOT SHOW THEMSELVES, HOW WILL YOU BE ABLE TO BEAR SUCH GREATNESS?'

I left feeling sick and dirty. As I was walking away I looked back and the structure seemed to rush towards me. The prospect of having to see their empty-eyed hut for the rest of my time in camp made me so angry I started back towards it, as if the building could be argued with, insulted, made to leave.

It took a lot of kicking to make a hole in the wall. Afterwards I was tired, my anger spent, unsure it had been worth the effort. The Gnostics would have had something pithy to say about the destruction of earthly temples.

I was about to leave when Enzo and Mikhail came running up.

'Good idea,' said Enzo. 'You know, I used to work in construction. I think the three of us can do it.'

'The whole thing?'

'Most of it.'

I had my doubts, but I wanted to try. Once we'd disconnected the bath it became a battering ram we used to punch through the walls. It didn't take long for the guards to turn up, though by then the place was just a shell.

'We'll finish it another time,' said Mikhail as we prepared to leave. One of the guards walked up to us and I expected him to be angry, but all he said was, 'Why are you stopping? Do you need some tools? We fucking hated them.'

They brought us hammers. I struck doors, walls, cupboards, the floor. We cheered when the roof collapsed.

REBECCA

R AJEEV would have been proud of how I waited for the results. On the first morning I sat on my bed and stared at the mountains until I was among them. The peaks were clean teeth, some of them whitened. Although my laptop was next to me, it seemed an inert object that could offer no rewards. Occasionally my eyes closed, but not for long; it was only to partition the flow of time into separate scenes.

In the afternoon I sat amongst the ninety-five couples as a sort of chaperone. I felt responsible for what was happening, or not happening, in each of those Petri dishes. There were moments when me sitting there mutely made it seem like an art installation. *The indifference of cells. Ninety-five weddings. An American woman in the dismal company of her life's work.* I always used to wonder how people could sit so still, for so long, in galleries, like they were just another thing that had been made.

Midway through the second day I couldn't shake the feeling that what I'd made was incomplete. There should have been ninety-seven couples, and while the lack of two of them was of no statistical importance, it was also not impossible that one of those samples might tell me something.

But in order for Lukas and Dirk to come in again I had to speak to Lars, and for the last two days we'd only been nodding at each other. I couldn't imagine how our next conversation might start.

When I knocked on his door Lars's face didn't offer much in the way of welcome. I wouldn't say he looked scared, but he definitely tensed. I was going to apologise until he said my name without any hint of bitterness; then I granted myself an absolution I didn't deserve. Before I could speak he started apologising for telling the inmates I was there to find a cure. Although this was a relief, I felt like a coward.

'What harm did it do? You said they needed hope.'

'Yes, that's true. But it was like me telling them that the sun is never going to set.'

I told him about my snafu with the samples and he said he'd ask Lukas and Dirk to come in later that afternoon. 'After what I said to them, they won't need much persuading.'

'You did nothing wrong. I should have been clear. I could have done that without saying anything about the vaccine.'

'Thank you,' he said, and then there was one of those rare, satisfactory pauses when two people have both said what they need to. Rather than ruin it, I thanked Lars and went outside. A large bird was circling the camp. Three of the guards were having an argument in Russian about something that alternated between sounding serious and them breaking into laughter. It must have seemed like I was eavesdropping because one of them came over and said, 'We cannot agree on the snow. One of us says it's coming here in one month, another says three weeks, and I say next week. And for us it is a big question. Last year the helicopter couldn't get here for four weeks and that made us very boring. Do you know when you will leave?'

'Very soon,' I said, and he nodded approvingly before returning to his debate.

I resumed my chaperone duties. The room tone was the electric hum of busy machines. Every time I glanced at the clock it was just a sequence of numbers. I imagined getting into the helicopter, rising up, the camp diminishing.

When Lukas arrived I had everything ready; even with his sleepy veins we could be done in five minutes. And yet I found myself saying, 'Before we start, I need to tell you something.' I'm still not sure what my motives were. You could say I was simply trying to ensure I had his informed consent. However, I suspect I was either doing the wrong thing for the right reasons or vice versa. While it couldn't have been both, I'm sure it could have been neither. Doubly wrong or doubly right.

'Lukas, I know Dr Nilsson has told you I'm here to find a cure, but that isn't true. I'm doing essential research on the virus, and although your participation is very important, it shouldn't be because of a misapprehension.'

His smile faded yet I wasn't sure he believed me. How could he?

'Oh, fuck off,' he said and laughed, but it sounded hollow. He stood up so suddenly he startled the guard, who grabbed him by the shoulder. Lukas went limp then dropped heavily onto his chair.

'Shall I take him away?' said the guard.

'No,' I said. 'Not yet.'

'I think he needs to be secured,' said the guard, who wasn't asking my opinion. While Lukas's wrists were being tied to the arms of the chair he stared at the floor in silence. His lips were open, moving slightly; the only expression I could read on his face was confusion. Although I wasn't sure he could hear me, I had to speak. The content of what I said was so unthought it was like hearing another person talk. In some ways they were other people's words, a version of what I'd heard so often during the months after Matthew's death. Stuff about acceptance, moving on. Platitudes about time being a healer, which, given Lukas's circumstances, were definitely in poor taste. For several minutes I blundered on. Having denied him one form of hope, I offered him several other kinds I made up on the spot.

When I stopped speaking Lukas was still hunched over, seemingly reading the floor. His face looked like a wet mask. I saw a kind of despair I didn't want to recognise. There had been a time when every day began with me checking to see if this was the same despair as the previous day, and if I saw the same dull fear, I took a bleak comfort that Matthew hadn't gotten worse. At that point I still believed that words and oranges could help.

LUKAS

O n my way to see Rebecca I had the delightful anticipation that you get on a second date having kissed on the first. I couldn't wait for the confirmation that she still existed, was still working, still cared. If she wanted more blood, she could have a litre. I'd donate a finger, a toe.

Passing through the clinic, I saw Stephan having his bandages changed. He raised his hand, displaying the palm, in a greeting that seemed Roman.

Rebecca looked tired and her face was pale, but if she'd been overworking that was maybe good for me. I was rolling up my sleeve when she said she had something to tell me. Her face was serious, and her pause was long, yet this didn't concern me. I didn't believe she could say anything bad.

There was only one good response to what she told me. Though this wasn't a tutorial, the gambit might still work. 'Fuck off,' I said, then tried to leave – as a joke, of course – and the guard hit me. I fell rather than sat. A blankness began to expand in my head with the confidence of spilled paint.

After that she talked and talked but said the wrong things. It felt like I was screaming and she couldn't hear.

The worst part was that I believed her. Over the last eight years, whatever I'd said, I'd never been truly certain there was a cure. It had always been safe to discuss the idea because none of us knew anything for sure; it was an argument I could sometimes win but never really lose.

I cried in silence except for when a cough of grief emerged. My tears gave the linoleum the vital sheen of a shell returned to water.

'I'm sorry,' she kept saying, and at least that made sense, because the refusal to look for a cure had to be someone's fault. This outcome had not just happened. Healthy people had sat round a table and made that decision.

'Thumbs down,' I tried to say, but it came out as a slurred mumble. I imagined Stephan, clad in purple, the silence following the verdict, the Coliseum crowd rising in approval. Meanwhile Rebecca kept offering me new and shiny thoughts to play with. She spent a long time telling me about an experimental treatment for slowing the disease that had almost worked. She floated the idea that some of us might only be carriers. 'And you're not symptomatic, are you? You might have a long time left. You might be transferred somewhere better.'

This didn't sound like a promise. For us, there were no prizes. It was like she'd pushed me off a high bridge and was now calling out that there was a chance I might bounce.

'Just don't give up,' she said, and her pleading tone jolted me into eye contact.

'Why not? Are you saying there's *hope*?' It was good to see her flinch.

And she could not say *Yes*. And she could not say *No*. I dared her to say *Maybe*.

'All I'm saying is, we don't know what's going to happen.'

'Nice truism. That's a great comfort. Thanks.'

She obviously had no idea what to say; I couldn't have done any better. But she clearly felt responsible for my distress, and that suited me. Her being there meant I could maintain a saving fog of anger.

'Did you really think I'd be willing to give you more blood after what you've said? I know scientists are supposed to be cold, but that's stupid. You must be really desperate. Is funding still that bad?'

She brought a hand to her throat. When she spoke it seemed effortful. 'I just thought you should know,' she said. 'I think I would.'

'Is that right? And what else do I want? Maybe you can tell me, because Christmas is coming soon. Last year my friend got a brain tumour. This year I'm sure we're all going to get presents.'

Thinking about Brendan made a gap in the fog. I wanted to throw his name, and all the others, at her, while knowing it was futile: for her these words weren't sharp. I couldn't understand why she kept sitting there, holding her throat, failing to comfort me.

'Please. I'm sorry. I wish there was something better I could tell you.'

'You've already said too much,' I snapped, but it was too late. The fog was lifting fast. I had made the mistake of wondering about her. She didn't strike me as a particularly sensitive person. Though maybe that was how things were now amongst the free and healthy. Maybe that was the kind of face they'd needed in order to move on.

'How did you get here?' she asked. I wanted to say, *By train, then bus*, but couldn't manage humour.

'Bad timing. Or maybe bad luck.' I tapped my eyepatch. 'A few bad choices too.'

'Edie told me something about what happened. She said she knows it wasn't you.'

I was glad to hear this, but I knew Edie.

'Maybe she's just saying that,' I parried, which was a pointless remark, because Rebecca didn't know Edie well enough to adjudicate.

And yet I couldn't help being pleased when she said, after a long pause, that she thought Edie was telling the truth.

'Why do you think that?' I asked.

'She spent a long time blaming someone else.'

'Who does she suspect?'

Rebecca hesitated, then said, 'Erik. Though I don't think she has any proof.'

After what the Gnostics had said I couldn't dismiss the possibility. Maybe Erik's lack of sexual interest in women was irrelevant. He'd certainly had the opportunity. Although I couldn't guess his motive, that didn't mean he lacked one.

I asked Rebecca how Edie looked, how she seemed, and for the next few minutes it was like we were talking about a mutual friend. While she went through Edie's list of great ambitions – a few of which were new to me – I briefly forgot that Edie and I were never going to walk along a pier together. And perhaps Rebecca thought she'd fixed me. Her face relaxed, and although she didn't smile, her relief was obvious; I couldn't tell whether it was me or herself she felt better about. When the guard said, with clear impatience, that he'd have to take me back in five minutes, the interruption wasn't welcome.

I waited to see if she'd ask for my blood, and when she didn't, I prompted her. She looked surprised but recovered quickly. My veins were slightly better. I suspect that one person taking another's blood, with or without their consent, is always going to be strange. Knowing why it's happening doesn't make it any less odd for one person to stick a sharp object into another and then for the two of them to wait while a vital fluid is taken. It was during this voluntary wounding, when we were each other's captive audience, that I said, 'And what about you? If you're not looking for a cure, why are you really here?'

The pause that followed was long enough to make my question seem rhetorical. Then she sighed and said, 'I just need to check something. And I have nothing else in my life. Out there it's like they all have amnesia. OK, all done.'

She removed the needle, then applied a plaster. The guard undid my wrists. I felt a little light-headed as I wondered if she was going to say any more about herself. But the tension was back in her face. We were out of time.

REBECCA

I N college I used to follow three or four shots of bourbon with a huge coffee. The resulting tug of war between sedative and stimulant made me feel both wiped out and fizzing, ready to dance like crazy so long as I could shake it lying down. None of my friends were into this; I sometimes got the impression the idea made them uncomfortable, perhaps even scared, like they feared a kind of chemical whiplash. And they weren't totally wrong; I threw up a few times. But when it was good the thrilling, delicious feeling was more than just the sum of the two. The caffeine buzz was sharper, the alcohol calm, more mellow. Together they made me levitate while sinking into the ground.

I felt something similar after I talked with Lukas. A heavy sadness accompanied a light sense of relief. Gravity seemed altered, not entirely consistent. Going downstairs, I had to clutch the handrail.

Waiting for the results felt like one of those anxious childhood Christmases when nothing under the tree seemed the right size or shape. I'd get presents, but the wrong ones, and then wonder why. On the final night I didn't think I'd be able to sleep; I lay down anyway. Rather than count sheep I imagined all the people sleeping in the camp, first the guards in the barracks, then the inmates in their huts, and finally the canteen staff and office workers. During my month in the camp I'd amassed a lot of faces I couldn't put names to. By the time I fell asleep I was surrounded by a crowd of them.

My alarm was set for seven; I woke at five. I got up, dressed, then went downstairs. The building was silent, the corridors empty. My footsteps seemed so loud I wanted to take off my shoes.

The lights were on all the way to the clinic; inside there was only the faint wash of the emergency lighting. There was no one inside, not even a nurse. What with the quiet, and the shadows, it was the perfect setting for a scary movie. But there was nothing in that room to frighten me. I stood there a while before I went into the lab.

When I sat down by the cabinets it was not as a chaperone – it was too late for that. If coupling had occurred it couldn't be reversed.

People love to say science is a team effort, though in my experience the moments that really count are inevitably solitary. Microscopes and computers are designed for one person. You still have to tell others, give presentations, but the actual finding-out belongs to individuals. Whatever you discover you have to process, consider, before it can be spread.

It would have been a good moment to pray, but despite everything – or rather because of everything – I addressed no one. If we had survived this far, it was only because of our efforts. If there must be blame, there must be credit too.

Sunrise was two hours away. A burst of light on the eastern horizon and everything would be changed. It didn't matter where I went, how I was occupied. Light and heat would find me.

I wished that all I had to do was wait for dawn to reveal what was hidden. If nothing else was required of me that wouldn't be so hard. I had been practising.

But no ordinary illumination would make the cells show themselves. Only in an extreme of the spectrum would all be revealed.

Can the world really be destroyed with a flick of a switch? Is that idea terrifying or just insulting?

I felt as if my eyes were shut as I stood. I took small steps. I switched on one ultraviolet light, then another, until the room was like the bottom of a pool. It was time for the cells to yawn, stretch their limbs, confess their transgressions. A single infected cell would be a bonfire on a hill.

I turned in a slow half-circle. Saw that in the watery glow all my cells were dark.

I got closer, went door to door, found neighbourhoods that seemed abandoned. Just like in a power failure, I expected the lights to blaze on.

I waited.

I waited.

I set a new record for holding my breath underwater.

When daylight took over I was still on guard. My bladder was killing me but I couldn't desert my post.

There were noises in the clinic. Shapes that didn't matter. Apparently I ignored one wave of a hand, then a second one an hour later. It took Lars knocking on the door to get my attention.

'What's wrong?' he said, and when I said, 'Nothing,' that was only the truth.

'But you're crying.'

He was right.

'Is there a problem?'

'No.'

He looked baffled, and I felt the same. He put his hand on my shoulder and for the next few minutes I cried in a slow, wrenching manner that seemed to empty my chest.

At some point I explained. 'Oh,' he said, and closed his eyes. His smile took decades from him. In my head a voice was spouting qualifiers – *a small sample*; *replication*; *the virus will keep changing* – but it was only a whisper. We were safe, for now.

∼

I slept the rest of the day. As soon as I lay down I was seized with the sensation that I was falling from a great height, at incredible speed, yet this was fine because I was headed toward a soft surface that promised to catch me. There were no dreams, bad or otherwise. Waking was a gentle melting into consciousness. It felt like a Sunday, though I had no idea what day it actually was.

There was more snow on the mountains, and a light powder all over the camp. In the bright sun the snow wasn't going to last, but it was still a thrill to see. My first impulse was to run outside and push my hands into the nearest patch. I wanted to form a hard ball to throw off the mountain, a little thing that might gather mass and speed until it was unstoppable.

Instead I opened my laptop. It turned out to be a Thursday. It was 10 a.m. local time, which meant 2 a.m. in New York. My message to Damian didn't need to be long – I only had to tell him about testing the guards, the differences between my viral strain and the virus in the inmates, and then the final results. Yet what should have taken three paragraphs was still unfinished two hours later. I'd got bogged down in the details when I should have cut to the chase. I took a break and saw the snow had almost melted, which pissed me off so much I switched to a new paragraph. I wrote *In conclusion* then told him the vaccine was still the boss.

I started to check through the email – Damian hates typos – but after only a few lines I felt as if a balloon was inflating in my skull. The words seemed to bend and bloat, refusing to be read.

'Fuck it,' I said out loud. It felt so good to press Send.

This was at about 4.30 Eastern, so I expected to have at least four or five hours before his reply. I showered, then put on clean clothes. I was putting on socks when my computer informed me I had mail.

Sometimes after I open a long message I can't read it at first. For a few seconds it's like I'm staring at symbols and spaces whose only function is to act as a barrier against the white space behind it. My eyes freeze; I can't look away; then there is text, punctuation, usually my name. But once I was seeing clearly I found that Damian had begun by saying, *Thank God*. What followed was a reply whose thoroughness embarrassed the rambling screed I'd sent. I was past being surprised that he could do this at so early an hour; the rest of us were mortals.

He ended by asking when I'd be back. The sentences formed in my head at once. I hit Reply. The white box begged for text. My fingers hovered on the keys for five, six seconds. Then I closed the window. Having stared at the screen for so long that morning it seemed impossible to write a few additional sentences. There was really no rush.

That afternoon I walked round the main building twenty-seven times. When I ran into the guard who had correctly predicted the snowfall he pointed at the ground triumphantly. 'You see?'

'Congratulations. What's the prize?'

'First pick for vacation slots. I'll be on the next flight out, in three days' time. You should join me,' he said.

'Good idea.'

That time frame was pretty much what I'd been planning to tell Damian.

I walked around the building ten more times. On the eleventh the guard said, 'You know, if you want to stop going round like a goldfish, we can take you in there.'

It took me a second to understand.

'Are you sure?'

'It's no problem.'

'But is it safe?'

'Oh yes. Things are very quiet right now.'

I couldn't think of any more objections except the feeling that my heart was being royally plucked. This was a needless risk, it was asking for trouble, and yet I let it happen. He unlocked the gate and we went through. A second guard followed.

'Just a quick loop,' I said too loudly. As we approached the meeting house the sun made one of its windows blaze like a stop sign, but we carried on.

In the square four people were gathered around Valentina, and the fact that there were five of them against our three was enough to scare me. When they offered me a friendly wave it was as if they'd given me the finger.

Passing between the burned huts didn't make things easier. Those blackened structures were like a row of monsters. I couldn't understand why the authorities left them there.

As soon as we were back through the fence I thanked the guard, trying hard to hide my relief and unfortunately succeeding.

'No problem,' he said. 'Same time tomorrow?'

'Maybe,' I said, and he said, 'Great.' He must have thought I was being coy. But I hadn't agreed to anything.

Back in my room I drank two shots of slivovitz then checked my email. There was a message from my dad. He hoped I was enjoying the Appalachian Trail and wondered what my plans for

Christmas were. He'd written, *And it's just a suggestion, but why don't you bring Rajeev too?*

I replied immediately. I said I'd try to make it, then told him that things between me and Rajeev hadn't worked out. Having to mislead him about where I was, and what I was doing, didn't give me carte blanche to lie about everything else. Typing those few sentences was exhausting. I had nothing left with which to write to Damian.

For the rest of the day I drank and napped and stared at the mountains. Dinner was something brown. In the dregs of the night I lay on my back and imagined the long trip back, the helicopter, then a car ride, the waiting in Grozny's militaristic airport. I imagined adding my presence to the minimal rooms of my apartment.

I spent the morning in the lab packing up the samples. At minus seventy they could sleep for a long time. Whether they came back to the Institute wasn't my decision.

When I went to speak to Lars he wasn't alone. He was in his office talking to Lukas, who was doing a lot of nodding but not saying much. I wondered whether Lukas had shared what I'd told him with the other inmates.

They were in there a long time. I expected that Lukas would come and speak to me afterward, but when he left he didn't even glance toward the lab. I waited a few minutes, then went and knocked on Lars's door. He looked tired but managed a smile.

'How is he?' I said.

'Not good. Perhaps we've made a little progress. We're going to try something tonight. What I did with Valentina.'

'Some kind of psychotherapy?'

It was the first time I'd seen him look evasive.

'Yes and no. Something more immediate.'

I couldn't blame him for being cautious: I hadn't been straight with him. But Lars's ethical calculus worked differently from mine. That I had, eventually, been honest with him, must have counted for more. There was also the fact that I was leaving.

'They take hallucinogens,' he said eventually. 'And then they listen to music. And for some of them, it helps. Valentina and a few others have been much less anxious and depressed since then.'

'Because they're high all the time?'

'Oh no. The amazing thing is that they only need to take it once.'

'How long have you been doing this?'

'A few years now.'

I wasn't sure what else to say. I couldn't see how getting high could help, but I hoped it was true.

Lars may have misinterpreted my silence.

'And you should know that although I have the patients' consent, I don't have official permission. I won't ask you to keep this a secret, but I'd certainly prefer you not to tell anyone. Whatever you decide, it won't affect my promise not to tell anyone about your work.'

I didn't see this as blackmail; it was more like a gentle reminder of what he was owed.

'Also, we probably don't need to keep all that equipment. Would it be alright if we donated it elsewhere?'

'I thought you needed it?'

'We do. But to be honest, I probably don't know how to work most of those machines. The hospitals in Grozny would get more use from them.'

'Can't you just hire a lab technician?'

'Believe me, I've asked. The budget for this place keeps shrinking.'

'That's insane,' I said. It made me really angry. This was wrong for so many reasons. The inmates needed proper diagnostic facilities, plus there were all kinds of measurements that should be taken regularly. While I didn't want to promise anything, I was definitely going to ask Damian if the Institute could cover a salary. That work needed to be done. Someone had to be there.

That night I was woken by the sound of a crashing plane, a crashing that went on and on. The windows were vibrating like crazy; a nose or wing was going to tear off the roof, slice through my room.

The noise stopped and then there was silence. I was about to get up and look out the window when everything was erased by a phosphorescence that blinded me. It was as if the nuclear switch had been flicked. When the next wave of thunder broke I was no better prepared. The walls were no protection. But neither was being afraid.

At breakfast everyone was talking about the storm. The man in front of me in the line called it 'a good bit of thundersnow' then promised me bigger ones in the next few weeks. He said, 'You'll think you're in a lighthouse during a tsunami,' in a way that suggested there was nothing better. I didn't bother telling him I'd be gone by then.

The sky after the storm was a pale, scraped blue that made me think of the upper atmosphere. My leg muscles felt tight, and I wanted to stretch them, but it seemed ridiculous to circumnavigate the building for twenty minutes when I could walk normally through the camp. I looked for my previous escort, and was told he was apparently packing, so I got one of the other guards to take me in. 'We should give you a key,' he said and laughed.

When I'm going to leave a place I like to take a last look round, try and store all the details, fix the memory. That day it seemed as if there was some sort of interference whenever I stared at something, a conflict between what was in front of me and how I wanted to remember it. For some things, like the meeting house, I tried to get closer, really zoom in, but that made it hard to pay enough attention to the overall structure. The guard must have thought I was a total idiot as I walked backward and forward, tilted my head, crouched down, trying to find the right perspective.

A few people were outside, and when a few of them waved at me I suspected that Lukas hadn't said anything. I couldn't decide if I was glad.

When we reached the square I asked the guard if he'd mind if I sat for a while: from there I had clear lines of sight in several directions. If I could really look, and do nothing else, maybe that would fix the memory.

The sky had a pregnancy that made me anticipate snow dropping heavy and fast, falling for many days. I'd only been sat at the chess tables for a few moments before I wanted to stand up and keep moving. Being stationary made me feel exposed, and I wasn't sure I had the right to sit there. Only by telling myself that this was completely normal, the kind of thing I'd do in Washington Square or Bryant Park, was I able to remain. And in many ways that square was better than those places. It was quieter and cleaner and I had someone to protect me from a random guy who blamed his unemployment, divorce and drug addiction on the toxic vaccine the Hitler government had forced him to take.

I saw a few people walking along the edge of the square. Most of them were too far away to recognise, though there was no mistaking Valentina's wheelchair. The bald man pushed it toward us, and the guard went to meet him. They spoke briefly, then the guard came and asked if I was willing to speak to her. When I agreed, he said, 'The man will have to keep his distance.'

The bald man pushed Valentina close to me, then walked away.

'Nice to see you,' she said. 'I know your face, but not your name, so you must be new.'

'Sort of,' I said, and felt no need to correct her. It was true I hadn't been there long.

'You'll get used to it. I didn't think I would, but now I like the view. Before this I lived in a flat place and couldn't see very far.'

'Me too,' I said and tried not to stare at her tiny, twitching hands. They were poking out of her sleeves like the snouts of small creatures. I asked how she was feeling.

'Thank you for asking. Today I am mostly feeling my shoulders and neck, and occasionally my knees. I know this body will soon be asleep but at least these parts are dreaming. There's still a silly black cloud in my head that thinks it's the king but soon there'll be a big wind and whoosh!' She laughed and pointed at the sky. 'Just like there. All the plates will be clean.'

We sat quietly for a bit. I thought I felt snow, although when I checked, there was nothing.

'Would you like more blood?' she said and smiled. 'I think I have plenty more.'

'No thanks.'

'Alright. You just let me know.'

She lapsed into a low humming that sometimes seemed like a tune. Sitting with her, in the cold sunlight, was relaxing. I wondered if the guard was getting impatient; when I glanced over he was smoking what looked to be a joint.

'There aren't many rules here,' she said. 'But I advise you to sleep with as many people as possible. I didn't do that and now I really regret it. It's friendly and very good exercise. Do you like sex?'

'Yes,' I said, perhaps a little defensively.

'That's very good. But watch out for Erik. Although he's getting sick, apparently he raped me. I don't remember, but that's what

295

I've been told. I think he's always had a black cloud in his head. It's a shame he can't be happy. I think you can, you have the right face. Good ears.'

'Thank you,' I said, and must have blushed at the compliment, because she then said, 'How lovely! You're going to be very popular here.'

'I'm not part of the camp,' I said gently. 'I'm from the main building. Remember, that's where I took your blood.'

She looked at me calmly. 'That's right, you did. And you can have more whenever you want. Just ask.'

'I will,' I said without thinking, but it didn't feel like a lie. Our conversation wasn't following the usual rules. Although Valentina was saying weird things, and getting stuff wrong, I never regarded her as crazy or confused. She was the first infected person I wasn't scared of.

'Do you like being in the woods?' she said. 'I visited them two months ago.'

'Here?'

She laughed. 'Oh no! We can't leave. The ones I went to are very far away. Do you know Ordesa?'

'No.'

'There are beech trees and silver firs. The canyons are long and there are cold shadows but at the end is a waterfall. It was wonderful to swim.'

This could have been only a distant memory, though I suspected that whatever drug Lars had given Valentina had allowed her to visit.

'Did I tell you about the sex?' she said.

'You did.'

'In that case, there's one other thing you should know about this place,' she said. 'Up here we're very safe. There could be a war down there and it wouldn't matter. That's why they put the camp here.'

Of course, it was not their safety that had been paramount: lepers go on mountains; lepers go in pits. But in some ways she was right.

She yawned and looked around. 'Where's Enzo? It's time for my siesta.'

The bald man appeared from behind a hut, buttoning his trousers.

'This was very nice,' said Valentina. 'Shall we meet here tomorrow afternoon?'

Without thinking I said, 'See you then.'

As the guard took me back to the main building a stillness fell on me with the lightness of first snow. I could look at the huts without being concerned about how I'd remember them.

Inside I went directly to the clinic. Lars was washing his hands with the casual thoroughness of a surgeon. When he saw me I said, 'I've been thinking. You should hang onto all the lab equipment. At least until spring. I'm sure someone will find a use for them.'

I wasn't sure he understood. I wasn't sure he'd agree. But then his smile was sudden, bright.

LUKAS

AFTER I left Rebecca I walked around the camp and hated all the buildings. The huts, canteen and meeting house were going to be my whole world for the rest of my life. There'd be no piers, no restaurants, no bookshops, no brothels, no slow walks in Central Park. No pierogi. No goulash.

I paused at the wreckage of the Gnostics' hut. Some of the wood had been scavenged, and judging by the smell, a lot of people had pissed on the debris. It was a good thing they were dead. If they'd still been alive, I'd probably have joined them.

The others kept making plans to go on safari and ride in hot-air balloons. I envied their ignorance so much I wanted to tell them they were going nowhere. Why should they get to talk about sailing a yacht around the Cyclades or adopting a tiger? The idiots seemed to think their cure would come with a million dollars.

Erik's plan was to write a memoir and then go on a global book tour. If I told him it was all a lie he'd certainly deny it, but the truth would nonetheless weigh on his chest so heavily his ribs would perpetually feel like twigs about to snap. No matter what he said, he'd know.

But despite my anger, and my wish to hurt him, I knew it was much safer for Erik to have hope as long as possible. He needed something to lose. And I liked knowing something he didn't, which didn't stop me wanting to tell him.

I wondered which of the guards would be willing to shoot me. Having saved me, Alain had earned the right. I'd make it easy for him. So long as I was holding something while I ran at him he could say it was self-defence.

I considered hanging, suffocation, a handful of pills. As soon as I imagined tying the noose, or swallowing, I knew I'd stop myself. It had to be immediate, with no chance for take-backs.

It was almost funny to be on top of a mountain and yet unable to jump off. After the riot the fences had been heightened, even those that led to a sheer drop. The razor wire alone was enough to put me off attempting to climb them, even though it seemed stupid to be frightened of the pain of getting cut when that pain would end seconds later. If only the Gnostics had been alive: they'd have gladly strangled me. Perhaps when they released Edie, she'd do me the kindness.

I dreamt my good eye froze then melted. Crows took it to their nest. I popped it out then launched it over the fence, off the cliff, and it saw all the way down.

The first snow usually inspired delight in the camp: it reminded us we'd survived another year. But when the first flakes fell I watched the others walk around as calmly as Christmas shoppers who'd bought their gifts in September. Perhaps for them the snow was no cause for wonder, just another thing they deserved.

And then one morning I woke in the clinic. Above me the man was still running for the stairs. There was a tube in my arm. Years had passed. Now I was old, wise and kind, deserving a good death.

Dr Nilsson said my name. He must have thought I could see him, but he was in my blank zone.

'The guards found you outside last night. You had hypothermia, and maybe if you'd been out there another hour you wouldn't have made it. If this happens when the real snow comes, you'll die. Although I don't want that to happen, I can't stop you. I know you've had a difficult time, and things must seem bleak, but you're not yet showing any symptoms. You still have some time. There are things we can try.'

'Will these things be like our cure? Or do they actually exist?'

I moved my head so I could see his face. I saw what I'd hoped for. His mouth drew in; wrinkles ate his eyes.

'She told you?'

'Yes.'

'I thought she might. Have you told anyone else?'

'No. But I still could.'

I didn't mean this as a threat: it was just a fact I liked saying out loud. Still, I was disappointed by his measured response.

'That's your decision,' he said. 'And I want you to know that when I told you all I believed it too. That was my mistake, and I wish I hadn't, but I don't think telling everyone the truth will fix anything. Whatever you decide, I'll help you, if you want. Although it's not a cure it might change how you feel about your situation.'

I left a suitable pause before saying, 'Alright.' I had no faith in whatever he was going to do, but when it failed I'd get to gloat.

'Good,' he said. 'You should take it easy for the rest of the day. Drink a lot of fluids. Get a good night's sleep then come and see me tomorrow afternoon.'

When he told me what he planned next day I laughed. I'd taken every drug I could get for the last seven years and none of them had helped. No matter how high I climbed, I'd had to come back down.

He warned me there could be adverse effects, especially at the start.

'But I'll be monitoring your vitals. It's really very safe.'

'Don't worry, I've done this before. I took some mushrooms at a party in my second year at university. I threw up and talked to a plant for an hour then went home. I didn't have any great insights.'

My scepticism didn't bother him. 'We'll be doing this in a more relaxing way. And I think we can avoid the nausea. It's best we do this at night so we won't be disturbed. I'll get one of the guards to bring you in just before curfew. Make sure you don't eat too much.'

There were a lot more instructions I nodded through. I appreciated that he was going to so much trouble, but no drug could change reality. I was dying. End of story.

∼

The guard and I walked into a cold wind as the first bell rang. People hurried to their homes without glancing at us. I could hear though not see a tarpaulin slapping against concrete, over and over, like a punishment.

In the clinic, Dr Nilsson told the guard he didn't need to wait. 'I'm running some overnight tests,' he added, but the man was already turning away. 'That's sort of true,' he said and smiled. My face made no answer. I trusted the doctor without liking him.

We went upstairs, past floors I'd never been to, all the way to the top. He unlocked a door and then led me down a carpeted corridor that seemed to have been transplanted from a hotel. There were little lamps. The rooms were numbered. He opened number seventeen. Inside was a room my mother would have said was very cosy. The bed had many soft pillows. There were paintings of hills and sunsets. A tall plant was dropping its leaves.

He told me again what was going to happen. He was only trying to be reassuring, put me at ease, but it annoyed me. He wasn't saying the important stuff.

'So what am I supposed to do? What should I think about?'

'Just let it happen. And if you experience something that's difficult or negative, don't struggle against it. Don't try to be in control.'

He'd put honey in the tea but it was still bitter. 'Taking it this way should reduce the nausea,' said Dr Nilsson. 'It may also make you feel the effects much quicker than the last time. They may be more intense.'

I put on the eye mask. Then the headphones. I lay back and heard some cheesy flute music I hoped wouldn't go on for the next seven hours.

Soon I got hot. My forehead was damp. It felt like I was running, and I wanted to stop, though since I wasn't moving there was nothing

I could do. This wasn't like the last time I'd taken mushrooms. Something was wrong. I was either having a bad reaction or he'd poisoned me. Which was the smart way to get our numbers down. Not through a cull but individually, two or three extra deaths a month.

In the left portion of my darkness a jagged red line glowed like an electric heater. If it reached me there was going to be something worse than pain. Not a burning, not a cutting, but an instantaneous vaporisation that would erase me totally, a death so hygienic the sheets would not need to be changed.

When I was touched, I screamed. My life label was used. As I panicked, the only thing I understood was the doctor's hand on my shoulder, its eloquent presence. Thanks to that little speech I did not die alone.

Many kinds of relief happened at once. Gravity stopped; there was no need to breathe; two moons rose with a popping sound and then Dr Nilsson said the operation had been a success and I could go home in my new body that he promised would be excellent at jumping. My laughter was a fizzy drink leaping from a can. I was tumbling down a grassy hill, rolling faster and faster, the sky flashing blue before each rich new hit of soil. If an orgasm counts as a five, that rolling was a hundred. It was a great achievement, a personal best. And still the bubbles rose.

When the air thickened it was confusing. I seemed to be sinking into very clean mud. This thick substance was rising up, absorbing feet, legs, stomach, neck, my corpse was soon entirely covered, nicely embalmed. But this wasn't preservation. The goal was to dissolve.

Whiteness. The Tatras. Freshly fallen powder. Dots elongated into spruces. My skis led the way. This was our default blue run. Tomasz was ahead though not by much, perhaps fifty metres. He was moving fast, but this was not his top speed: my brother wasn't trying to get any further away from me. When I wanted to, I could catch up, so we could speak face to face. For now it was easy to keep following him up the slope into the trees that flanked us like spectators. Deep in them I glimpsed a small cabin which, like a doll's house, had had one of its walls removed. Inside was a living room with an eager fire and hot food on the table – some kind of stew – and all that was missing were the life-sized dolls. A few moments later I saw a second cabin, almost identical to the first, except there were bookshelves all the way up to the ceiling. Then I was out of the trees, back in brightness, feeling once again the thrill of motion over whiteness beneath a sky so blue it shouted as we rose up to the summit. Already the air was thinning, getting colder, sharper, and this reduction in oxygen, the challenge to breathing, heightened the perception that I was floating over the snow. There were more cabins, all of them empty, except one in which I saw Edie and myself entwined on that languorous morning after our first night together when she kept asking for orgasms on toast. Further up, I saw myself outside another cabin, watching a mob of crows feeding from Min-seo's outstretched palm with an impressive calm, their beaks making such minimal contact with her skin that each seemed an expression of gratitude. Seeing myself in both those places, in two different times, started a fast vibration in my feet that quickly sprang up the hamstrings, pooled in the pelvis, set bells clanging in the gut, more in the chest, triggered an urgent fizzing in my throat that swiftly built in pressure, foamed over the tongue and made my lips feel as if a fat finger was flicking them to make a blubbery noise that sounded childish, stupid, and possibly just right. I felt drunk while still being lucid and coherent – on my skis I was steady – and when I looked at those cabins again and saw myself with Brendan, licking jam from his fingers on a spring morning two years ago, the feeling got stronger and stronger until my body was a shaken bottle of champagne on which the head was a cork wanting to surrender to the mounting pressure that would send it rocketing up, up, above the cabins, over the mountains, round the planet's curve. But this exhilaration did not make me forget that the cabins in which I saw myself were surrounded by vacant structures, which was certainly not what I would have chosen – who wouldn't prefer a bustling town or sprawling city? – and yet the solitary nature of those dwellings did not seem sad or insufficient: even a small settlement, of minor history, can leave eternal traces. During the final ascent I closed the distance with Tomasz, I could see him in profile, but instead of speaking I was captivated by details of the scene that were as vivid and distinct as the facets of a crystal slowly rotating to offer itself for inspection – the snow parting for our skis; sunlight reflecting from our poles; a boot buckle that needed tightening – and all these aspects were essential for me to register because I was certain that when we reached the top all this would be changed. Then we'd be going down – or further up – and in doing so creating a curve that mirrored our ascent as smoothly as a wave returns to the ocean, ceases to be singular, rolling, ascendant, becomes once again part of a collective without boundaries or will, a shifting set of intentions with no identifiable source. And as I came within half a ski's length of Tomasz I realised it was our last chance to talk, there were only a few moments before he reached the summit, and so I told him I was sorry about Agata, and everything else, that I loved him and was sorry, so fucking sorry, and then I shut up so he could say, *You killed us both*, or tell me to never speak to him again, but instead there was silence, and although this was not forgiveness, merely an absence of malice, the suspension of judgement was more than I deserved. When his skis touched the summit I saw a confusion of colours, a splitting of white, a kaleidoscope that offered the bright creations of a thousand phantom eyes. Then it was my turn, and when I acquired the peak a darkness dropped on the mountain as absolutely as if we were parrots in a cage for whom it was naptime... this darkness didn't frighten me, I'd swum so much in those waters... I believed I was still rising, moving against a soft breeze, yet there was also a heaviness to my body, a downward pull like sledging down an icy slope already polished by previous traffic to a state of maximum slipperiness so that instead of resistance there was encouragement, a gathering of mass and speed, an enlargement of presence... and Paris was lovely for that time of year, along the Seine there were blossoms, bookstalls, couples kissing French-style and not, old men playing chess in a fashion that seemed dialectical, binary pieces moving on binary squares, each argument advancing not just towards its opposition but sometimes into them as well, white queen and black bishop flickering on the same square, taking turns at occupation, inhabiting separate phases... I enjoyed my year lecturing at the Sorbonne... I got engaged to a girl from Marseilles... Brendan led me into the storeroom and put down a blanket... in Oaxaca we ate four meals a day and Edie instagrammed them all... Rustam played the drums in a syncopated style he said was a tribute to Gene Krupa... Dr Nilsson coughed... a cramp bothered my left buttock... Dejan's hand was steady as he shaved the side of Kim's head... I kept travelling, seeing new cities, loving those clean sheets... at the top of Bukhansan Min-seo insisted we eat teriyaki shrimp noodles while wearing cat masks... from up there Seoul was an expanse of cabins cleaned and ready for their next occupants... as Brendan and I walked round the meeting house it seemed a wheel of lights, turning as we turned, sending out its coloured shapes deep into the evening... 'Eat up,' said Edie, and passed me a taco... On our honeymoon we went to Scotland... When our hair was grey in a normal fashion we bought a cottage on an island where our nearest neighbours were deer... and when the doctor, after clearing his throat, asked how I was feeling, I replied to him, myself, all listeners:

There's time—

ACKNOWLEDGEMENTS

M ANY people helped this book find its present form. Neil Olson and Ryan Van Winkle offered valuable feedback on early drafts. Mark Richards at Swift allowed me to see where the novel needed to grow and where it should wither. I'm grateful to Creative Scotland for financial assistance, and to Martin MacInnes, Calum Barnes, Gëzim Krasniqi, Shannon Stephens, Dan Gorman, Yasmin Fedda, Peter Geoghegan and Serena Field for their friendship and support during these strange years.